Nasheema Lennon is a writer of Mauritian heritage based in Nottingham. She studied psychology and criminology at university before nine years working in the prison service, where she facilitated cognitive behavioural therapy programmes. She then changed paths to complete her PGCE, becoming a primary school teacher. Her first novel, *The Engagement*, was shortlisted for the Owned Voices Novel Award 2022.

THE ENGAGEMENT

NASHEEMA LENNON

HarperNorth
Windmill Green,
Mount Street,
Manchester, M2 3NX

A division of
HarperCollins*Publishers*
1 London Bridge Street
London SE1 9GF

www.harpercollins.co.uk

HarperCollins*Publishers*
1st Floor, Watermarque Building, Ringsend Road
Dublin 4, Ireland

First published by HarperNorth in 2022

1 3 5 7 9 10 8 6 4 2

A catalogue record for this book
is available from the British Library

ISBN: 978-000-856061-4

Printed and bound in Great Britain by
CPI Group (UK) Ltd, Croydon

This book is produced from independently certified FSC™ paper
to ensure responsible forest management.

For more information visit: www.harpercollins.co.uk/green

For my mum, Aissoo.

Chapter One

The Proposal

3 months until the wedding

With every pained word she utters, I feel my own past clawing me back to when *I* couldn't fight, couldn't scream, couldn't breathe. I shake my head free of the vivid imagery to refocus on Suzie, who has started tugging at her unwashed, overgrown fringe to cover her eyes. Her chewed fingernails barely visible under her tattered jumper. She is always so careful to make sure her sleeves are pulled down far enough to hide the scars on her arms and hands.

'I just feel so alone,' she mumbles.

I put my notepad down and pass her a tissue but instead of wiping her tear-filled eyes, she sits shredding each sheet to pieces.

'Suzie, do you remember the support group we discussed? Perhaps now would be a good time to think about it again?'

She's barely looking me in the eye, but I can sense her desperation. I wouldn't wish that feeling on anyone, let alone any of my clients. It's a feeling I know all too well.

'You're not alone, Suzie. At the group you'll get a chance to meet other likeminded people. People who know what it's like to start again.' I slide the leaflet across the coffee table. She shuffles awkwardly in her seat and just about manages a nod, taking the information before shoving it into her jacket pocket without a second look. At least she doesn't let it drop to the floor like last time.

'I am sorry though, Suzie.'

I tap my watch as our usual signal that it is time for our session to come to an end. She never looks like she wants to leave. She's survived so much, but still has far to go.

'Can I come back again this week? Monday's ages away.' Her eyes dart between the door and me.

I offer her a comforting smile. If she needs me I will be available to her but to keep moving forwards, she needs to surround herself with others who can share their own stories with her.

'Why don't we book in for Monday as usual but if you need to see me sooner, we can do that. I want you to really think about the group sessions in the interim though, OK? I really think it'll be helpful to you.'

She chews the end of her sleeve, like she always does when she is anxious, and gives a faint nod. I reach for the door handle to help her, but she hesitates in the doorway, seemingly stuck between stepping forward and going back to curl up on my sofa. My receptionist, Becky, seamlessly takes over making her next appointment as I say goodbye.

Closing the door, I'm relieved to be alone. Of all my clients' pain, Suzie's has a unique effect on me. I blink back the tears. I can't let Becky walk in and see me crying; to see I am struggling to maintain a professional distance from Suzie's issues. I know I should refer her to someone else, but I truly feel like I need to help her. That somehow helping her will help me finally put my past where it belongs, behind me. Still, I had hoped that the longer we worked together, the less painful it would be.

I slump back into my chair, slipping my shoes off and resting my aching feet on the coffee table. Maybe I just need to close my eyes for a few minutes. My head feels heavy against the wings of the armchair. Just as I begin to feel myself mould into the distressed leather creases, Becky knocks on the door.

'Suzie was your last appointment for the day. I'll just respond to some e-mails and then be heading off if that's all right?' Becky begins to turn but stops sharply, looking directly at me. 'Are you OK, Victoria?'

Her eyes zero in on mine, which are no doubt reddening. I muster a smile. 'Yes. Why?'

'Oh, erm… no reason, just checking.'

Her smile is half-hearted as she returns to her desk and busies herself, tapping on her keyboard. I'd like to be finishing up too but I have notes to write, so I move to my desk and start to flick through my binder. The phone ringing startles me, shaking me from being lost in rereading Suzie's notes. I want to leave it – I don't have the energy to talk to anyone else today – but someone might need me… It's no good, I just can't ignore it. As I pick up, the unmistakable frivolity of Gwen's voice booms down the line.

'Vic! What are you doing tonight? Fancy a drink?'

I carefully balance the phone on my shoulder so I can continue to organise my files.

'Vic? Vic?'

'Sorry Gwen, the phone slipped–'

I want to tell her I've planned to slide into a bath and ignore the world, to eat takeaway in my pyjamas and watch some reality TV but I know there is no point protesting. Gwen has an incredible ability to charm everyone around her, including me. She just makes me want to be part of the fun and excitement that always follows her.

'I have so much to tell you!' Her voice even more enthusiastic than usual. 'You'll never guess what's happened?'

'What? Have you sold another painting?'

'Nope, guess again! It's good, no great, news!'

I sigh, I hate these guessing games. 'I give up Gwen. I'm just so tired–'

'Oh spoil sport! Fine, I'll tell you. Tonight we're celebrating. Michael and I are engaged!' She lets out a girlish squeal. I do not. My mouth falls open.

'Vic… Vic are you still there?'

I hadn't realised I'd paused.

'Yeah… er… wow! That's amazing news,' I lie. 'Well? Do tell!'

I ready myself to hear the details. She relays every perfect moment of the perfect proposal, from the perfect man. It's not that I'm not happy for her – I adore her and only want what is best for her. I'm just not sure that what is best for her is Michael. There's something about him, something too good to be true, that reminds me uncomfortably of my ex – Dylan. Someone I'm trying hard to forget.

As I listen to Gwen natter on, regaling every minor detail of the proposal, I start to think back to when she and Michael first met. Not even a year ago! How can Gwen possibly feel she knows him well enough to want to marry him?

'So you'll be there… tonight? I really want to show you the ring. I'm not inviting anyone else unless you say yes!'

Obviously Gwen hasn't noticed how one sided the last few minutes of this conversation have been. She's always been the chatty one but this is next level excitement.

I wave Becky off as she leaves, wishing I could follow. But how can I say no?

'I can't miss celebrating your engagement!'

Can I? I desperately plead with my mind to concoct some fantastic excuse but no. Nothing. Not one plausible thought to get out of these drinks.

'I have some work to do first though, so won't have time to go home and change. Is that OK?'

I know how particular Gwen is about her appearance, although it's been some time since she gave up trying to convince me that anything could be done with *my* limp hair and out of date wardrobe.

'Oh Vic, I don't care what you're wearing! Just get there when you can, sweetie.'

With another squeal Gwen rushes off to call the others, eager to gather us all together for the big reveal. Amongst her many talents, making herself the centre of attention is certainly one of them, but everyone loves her for it. When I first moved to town all I wanted to do was hide. Yet from the very first minute of meeting Gwen, her genuine warmth and charm were irresistible, even if at first she was using her powers to sell me art from her gallery! As our friendship grew, she took me under her social butterfly wings, until I felt safe to come out of my cocoon too. I've never minded fading into the background when she is around, as somehow she always makes me feel like it matters that I'm with her.

My eyes are sore from the computer screen by the time I call a taxi to meet them all. It didn't even occur to me to check how I looked in the bathroom mirror before leaving. Not until I catch my reflection in the taxi's rear-view mirror do I see the dark circles under my eyes are getting worse and my hair is even more lifeless than usual. I ferret in my handbag for a hairband so I can at least attempt a neat ponytail. I'm not sure I actually look any more presentable – my oversized shirt and faded black trousers are hardly in vogue – but this is as good as it's going to get.

The taxi drops me outside the bar. I wander in to find the usual crowd already giggling at our table. I try not to interrupt as I slide into an empty seat, very aware of the effort everyone else has made to dress up for the occasion. Jessica looking as immaculate as always, in her figure-hugging black cocktail dress. Even Samira is looking particularly glamorous in a brightly patterned jumpsuit. Neither are even close to upstaging Gwen though, who is positively glowing in her vintage satin number. Emanating old Hollywood glamour in a way that only she can.

'Tell me all about it!'

Samira gushes as Gwen shows everyone the flawless jewel gracing her manicured hand. Her effortlessly curled blonde hair falls past her shoulders and her deep green eyes twinkle as she wiggles her fingers just enough so the large stone glistens in the light.

'Is that a pink diamond? Stunning,' Jessica oozes.

I can tell from the forced smile that she is already calculating the carats to make sure the ring isn't more expensive than hers. She and Gwen have been friends on and off for years longer than Gwen and I have known each other. Despite Gwen welcoming me into their friendship circle, Jessica and I have yet to find anything in common.

Shrieks of excitement spread across the table of women, as Gwen launches into the events of last night. I sigh inwardly. I've just heard this, but hearing it again still doesn't make me warm to the idea of this marriage. And judging from how the others hang on her every word about the *amazing* Michael, whilst pawing at the huge rock on her finger, it's obvious that I'm alone in having doubts.

They haven't seen the glimpses of Michael that I have. I remember when they first met at one of Gwen's gallery exhibitions last year. There was no denying they had instant chemistry, and at first I thought he was the perfect gentleman. However, it wasn't long before it went from an occasional appearance to him being everywhere, all of the time. Like she couldn't move without him being nearby.

I remember when he let his perfectly constructed mask drop just a little, when he snapped at me for the amount of time Gwen and I spend together. He seems to find it especially unnerving when he feels we are talking too much about their relationship; often deliberately interrupting our conversations when he senses Gwen is offering me too many details. I hate that Gwen laughs his behaviour off as a desire for privacy or attention. He's changing her. She's always shared everything with me, including talking to me openly about the men she's dated. Now there is a wall between us, one that Michael has built. The more I've thought about it the more uneasy I've felt, because that's exactly what Dylan did. In the similarly short time Michael has manoeuvred into Gwen's life, Dylan came between me and my friends. He made sure he was the centre of my world, and I can see Michael is doing the same thing to Gwen.

As Gwen continues reliving every romantic detail, I have an unsettling feeling that the Michael she has fallen in love with isn't who he really is. That eventually he will show what a controlling character he has hiding underneath. I dread what this will mean for Gwen.

Realising I have drifted off, I prick my ears up at the, '... and then, there were hundreds of red roses everywhere!' part of her story.

I join in the light applause as Gwen shows everyone the pictures on her phone. I must admit, the sea of deep red rose petals is impressive. But on seeing the selfie of her and Michael, I can't help but shudder. I know Gwen's type, and it's no mystery why he appeals to her. The tailored suits, the expensive cars, the way he can capture the attention of a room with some witty story – they are indeed a perfect couple on the outside.

I peer closer at the photo. Gwen's smile full and genuine, whilst Michael's lips are a little more tense – more reserved. I can't help but wonder if he is as happy as she is, or if he's a chameleon, presenting himself as whatever he thinks his audience want him to be.

Before I can dwell on it any further, Gwen grabs my hand. I can feel all eyes are on me. In that moment I wish I had been paying more attention to what was going on. My mouth feels dry as I try to read her face, my stomach sick at the thought that she knows what is really on my mind.

Chapter Two

A Toast To The Happy Couple

A hush has fallen over the table. My breathing becomes shallow as a wave of anxiety washes over me, with Gwen's serious expression focused on me.

'I know what you're thinking, Vic.'

I can feel the panic rise.

'And you're right… I can see from your face that you've figured it out.'

I try to speak but my voice is barely a croak.

'I *do* want you to be my maid of honour. Please say yes!'

Her eyes are suddenly round with hope, her exaggerated bottom lip out, her grip tightening on my hand just a little. I let out a huge sigh of relief. She hasn't noticed my distant stare or lack of enthusiasm at all. The last thing I want is to discuss my fears about her engagement right now, especially when she has been so reluctant to listen to my concerns about Michael before. And certainly not now when she is positively radiating happiness. I don't want to ruin this for her.

Everyone is still focused on me and I can feel my face flush at the attention. Samira nudges my shoulder and nods with a huge smile, reminding me that I still haven't answered.

'Well? Don't keep me waiting!' Gwen giggles, with an overly dramatic eye roll.

I reach over to hug her. Partly as I know this is a huge occasion for her, asking me to be her maid of honour is no small gesture after all, but I also want her to stop looking so intently at me. I've never been good at hiding my emotions and she'll see through my faux smiles soon.

'Of course I will be. I'm honoured.' I hug her even tighter. I really would do anything for her.

Gwen squeezes me back, mumbling how much she loves me. I can't help but notice Jessica's face behind her. She's known Gwen far longer than I have, although their friendship has been a little on again, off again, only reconnecting when they both drifted back to town after their university years. Her scowl tells me she must've expected to be asked.

Although I'm not particularly happy to be part of the nuptials, I am glad that Gwen sees me as her best friend – and a tad smug that it's not Jessica. It's nice to feel so special to someone. Plus, being Gwen's head bridesmaid will give me more time alone with her, so we can talk about whether this wedding is really a good idea.

When Gwen releases me Samira edges her chair even closer to mine until they touch, and reaches for my hand in support. She must have noticed Jessica's sour look too.

'You'll be a fab maid of honour, Vic. Better than my cousin was at my wedding, anyway,' she says, gulping at her drink. 'She got drunk and threw up on my auntie!'

As per usual Samira's stories are met with a mix of laughter and squeamish frowns – she always knows how to break the ice. My neighbour for the last couple of years is never one to shy away from speaking her mind. Her forthright nature is how we came to meet.

I tried to make a quiet entrance to the street, still in pieces after Dylan, but Samira routinely showed up to my door with meals and sweet treats to check on me. I think feeding people is how she shows her love. Being a mum of twins though, nights like this are rare. Yet every one of her outings are filled with mischief, devilish humour and stories that usually serve to lower the tone. I loved how quickly she and Gwen became friends when I introduced them, and there is no denying it, it's nice to have someone who can see Jessica for what she truly is: a bully with a Gucci bag and a little too much Botox.

Within a few seconds, a cheer erupts from the table as Samira and Jessica agree to be bridesmaids too.

'We'd love to darling,' Jessica enthuses with her cut glass accent. 'You'll need someone to help you choose your dress, hair, make-up, et cetera.' She looks me up and down in the unabashedly condescending way she always does when Gwen isn't looking.

'I'm sure Victoria won't mind. It's not her… well… passion, is it?'

Bitch, I think, whilst smiling and raising my glass to the newly appointed bridesmaids. Gwen, oblivious to the mounting tension, summons the waitress to bring more champagne. It's flowing easily, with clinking glasses and excited giggling as the conversation turns to the dress, flowers and, naturally, the hen night.

'There's something I should probably tell you all.' Gwen's words were beginning to slur. 'I want a winter wedding!'

'Perfect, that gives us a little over a year,' Jessica mutters, already scrolling through dates on her phone.

I notice Gwen bite her bottom lip before sipping at her drink. She's holding something back.

'Actually, I meant *this* winter. The beginning of December, so we can honeymoon over Christmas and New Year.'

The table quietens.

'But… but… that's only three months away!' I manage to whisper.

Chuckling, Gwen continues, 'I know it's a shock, but we've got the perfect venue and they had a cancellation, which happens to be around our first anniversary. The universe has decided!' She sways a little, her drink sloshing onto the table. 'You know I've always loved the idea of a winter wedding – can you imagine if it snows?'

I'm stunned at this little technicality Gwen left out in our earlier conversation. I had imagined that it would be at least a year until they would be married but three months? On their first anniversary? This is all just so fast. Too fast. Maybe that's why she didn't tell me in private. He moved in with her within a matter of weeks and now to be married a year after meeting?

I can feel my stomach drop at the realisation that the person I care for so deeply might be making a huge mistake. I need to talk to her – soon. Not now though. Now is the time for her to enjoy the moment and I need time to see if my fears are actually based on anything other than my instinct.

Gwen excitedly tells her keen listeners, in every expensive detail, why these grounds are *the* venue for her and Michael. The sprawling gardens surrounding the lake, and fountains lining the courtyard, would make for perfect photographs outside. Inside they will have full access to the marble floored music and dining rooms, selections from the highly sought-after wine cellar and the stately bedrooms… Money is no object – both Michael and Gwen's family are incredibly wealthy. The waitress brings yet another bottle of champagne to the table, clearly eager for the huge tip she'll be earning. I take a deep swig, trying to drown the very thought of helping to organise this wedding, or making Gwen understand why it maybe shouldn't happen, in such a short timeframe. Neither will be easy.

Then with immaculate timing, the door to the bar swings open and in saunters Michael. Is that his jaw clenching at the sight of the four drunken women before him? It's hard to tell as within seconds he has pasted on a flawless smile and is moving decisively towards us. His broad, muscular physique showing through his tailor-made suit. As he leans down to kiss his fiancée, he runs his hand through his impeccably coifed, dark hair, staring intently into Gwen's eyes. The whole table gushes again.

Jessica moves over so Michael can move a spare chair to be close to Gwen. He reaches his arm around her and pulls her closer to him. She beams as she nuzzles into him. The future bridesmaids start bestowing compliments about the romantic proposal and I refill everyone's glasses to avoid being dragged into the fanfare, but I cannot help watching.

Entwined together, the pair are looking at one another with such adoration. As if the rest of us aren't even here. I want to be thrilled that they're content, I genuinely do. Yet the more I look at his chiselled jaw, immaculately pressed suit and gleaming smile, I feel the same uneasiness I do every time I see him. What Gwen is accepting as affection, I see as him exhibiting possessiveness. But I have to try not to over analyse–

'You're spilling it!'

Samira grabs the bottle from me, breaking my chain of thought. I have been so transfixed on the happy couple that champagne is now spilling like a fizzy fountain over my fingers. Samira starts to organise a procession of serviettes down the table to help mop up the spreading puddle. Gwen and Michael don't even break their gaze from one another, him kissing her hands as she cuddles closer to him. Who am I kidding?

Maybe I am a little jealous. I miss the weekends when we would sit and watch scary movies and eat junk food together. Or the girls' nights where we would walk home barefoot, our feet sore from dancing. We have both worked so incredibly hard to have it all – the successful careers, the houses and cars – but we had never talked about what would happen if one of us got married. Never discussed the possibility that our quality time together would become limited and we would replace one another with someone else – like him.

I gulp more champagne at the realisation that our futures are going to be polite cocktail parties and talk of children and husbands. That I will likely be the only single person at said parties – everyone else will have given up the single life years ago. I've always known Gwen was dreaming of her 'happily ever after'. Now that she's found it – or thinks she has – what about me? What do I want?

Maybe Michael is not the issue here, maybe I am. There's every possibility that I am projecting my past anger and regrets onto him. I still hold so much frustration for not seeing Dylan for the controlling man he was, that I do wonder if I am seeing something in Michael that isn't actually there. Just because my relationship was toxic, doesn't mean Gwen and Michael's will be, I guess. He's not Dylan after all. Perhaps it's high time I stopped living in the past for good, and moved on with my own life.

Jessica gently taps her champagne flute, bringing the conversation around the table to an abrupt halt, and my attention back to the here and now.

'I think it's about time I made a toast to the happy couple.'

I kick myself. A toast, why didn't I think of that?

'We were children together, Gwen. Even though we lost touch at points, I'm thrilled that we found each other again in recent years.'

I'm not surprised Jessica is managing to get herself into a toast intended for the couple actually getting engaged.

'I cannot imagine you without Michael. You are so perfect together and I feel so blessed that myself, Samira and Victoria are going to be a part of your special day. So, can I ask that we all be upstanding for the future Mr and Mrs Jameson!'

As everyone stands and raises their glasses, Jessica stares at me smugly. Part of me resents her, the rest of me pities her need to continually create competition between us. Still, now is not the time to contemplate her superiority complex, especially when she has well and truly bested me with her confident, thoughtful words.

I want to stay standing, say something meaningful but I have lost the power of speech. My heartbeat echoes in my ears as I sit down dumbly and wring my hands under the table. I hate speaking in front of people.

I'm still mustering the courage to speak up when Michael stands, much to the pleasure of the table. He pauses to button his blazer, lifting his drink as if to say a few words of his own, before smiling and taking a sip, knowing full well the group had quietened to hang on his every word.

'Speech!' Samira impatiently demands, much to Michael's amusement.

'Yes speech!' Jessica joins in.

He holds his hand up to shush them before turning his attention to Gwen.

'Gwen, you are the person I am meant to be with. I am thankful every day that you came into my life. I cannot wait to share the rest of my days with you.'

Jessica and Samira start whooping at the happy couple sharing a kiss. I join in to avoid looking like I'm not equally blown away by his romantic words. I feel cold though – the hairs on the back of my neck bristling. Sharing? Gwen shares her most intimate secrets with *me*. Being a listening ear people can trust is my thing, and I'm sure it's one of the reasons Gwen values me so much as a friend. I'm her shoulder to cry on, the sounding board for her problems. As for Michael though… He's always so guarded. I still barely know him, not for a lack of trying. The way he often avoids conversations about himself or deliberately changes the subject is noticeable – to me anyway. I have to wonder if he truly does share himself with Gwen.

Thankfully, it's not long before Gwen and Michael decide to continue their celebrations alone, hugging and kissing everyone on their way out, after Michael pays the bill.

'Before we go,' Jessica commands, 'we should organise meeting up to sort a few things for the special day.' She catches my eye and smirks. 'Oh, Victoria, I don't mean to step on your toes.'

'Not at all, I agree. I'll need to delegate some tasks to you both, if that's OK?' I reply as nonchalantly as possible, making sure to hold Jessica's stare.

Samira snorts into her flute, sending bubbles flying up into her face. I love her. Jessica throws her a serviette, and a scowl.

'Anyway, I must be going. I look forward to your call Victoria.' Jessica lifts her chin just high enough that she has to look down at us to flash her practised polite smile and offer air kisses.

As soon as she leaves Samira and I shoot glances at one another like naughty school children, laughing and refilling our glasses. It would be wrong to leave the bottle unfinished, after all.

'It's about time you stood up for yourself, sweetie,' Samira muses.

All I can do is sigh.

'How are we going to pull off a wedding in three months?' I say, sipping my champagne. Samira pushes the bottom of the glass up until I am gulping, much to her delight.

'We're not like them, Vic. They have real money and connections. Whatever they want, they can afford to get it when they want it.' She sips from her own flute. 'Obviously I'll help as much as I can too.'

I watch as Samira drinks the last drops from her glass before finishing my own. Perhaps she's right – we're not like Gwen anymore.

Chapter Three

The Wedding Planner

2 months, 3 weeks to the wedding.

This week has been a blur of e-mails and phone calls. A rainbow of sticky squares surround my screen, covered in my scribbled notes of what needs doing for the wedding of the year. I really should file them into the colour-coded binder Gwen has provided but I've been back-to-back with clients this morning. I'm going to try and make time for Gwen this afternoon. According to my neon notes, I don't have time to waste.

I walk my last client of the day out. Becky takes over rebooking his next appointment after pointing to her watch, reminding me that I need to get to the train station. I just need a few minutes though.

Flopping onto my swivel chair, I turn to look at the piece of art hanging on my wall. An oil painting of the sun rising over the park by a local artist. It was the first decoration I bought for my new office when I moved here. Three years ago now, but the memory is still so vivid; Gwen introducing herself at her gallery, talking me through her collections. This piece felt symbolic at the time, a representation of a new beginning. That sale led to coffee and a tour of the town, and the start of an amazing friendship. I sometimes wonder how empty my life would be had I not stepped inside the gallery that day.

I stretch to relieve some of the tension in my neck and shoulders. I really need to find time for a massage. Before I can try and pinpoint the last time I've had a pamper session, my phone vibrates on the desk:

> Can't wait to shop, eat and gossip, just like the old days! xx

I smile and immediately respond to Gwen. I miss spending time with her. Even though Samira and Jessica will be joining us today, at least Michael won't be. Taking my cue to get my things together, I snatch at each note on my monitor and shove them into my bag – we can brief one another on all the progress made so far on the train ride. The weeks are ticking away until the big event and today is the day that we have to choose a dress. I'm glad I decided to think more positively about this wedding – today is going to be a great day.

I grab my coat and rush out, with just enough time to stop at a newsagent's and pick up some wedding magazines for the journey. I am the last to arrive, but Gwen is literally bouncing when she sees me, laden with armfuls of magazines too. The excitement is palpable. We quickly settle into our seats across a table from one another. All of us chatting and flicking through the bridal magazines, barely taking a breath between sharing ideas and pictures.

'What do you think to this one?' I ask, trying not to smile as I point at the most hideously feathered meringue creation I have ever seen.

'I love it!' Gwen shrieks. 'And you can all have this dress to match!' Pointing to what can only be described as a latex bin liner.

Tears roll down mine and Gwen's faces as Samira joins in, attempting to imitate the pouts of the cover models. It is times like this I miss. Jessica is far less enthusiastic about the frivolity, wanting to direct our attention to a more serious game plan for the day. Of course she does. Anything to try and take control.

'So do tell Victoria, where are we going first?'

I know she is trying to undermine me again but thankfully Samira had warned me that the finer boutiques all require appointments. I happily detail the numerous bookings I've made for the afternoon. Shocked into silence at the fine array I have chosen, Jessica finally reminds herself to smile.

'I looked at many of those for my wedding, I'm surprised *you'd* know about them.'

Samira shoots me a sideways smile and we both know Jessica is peeved that I might actually be the right choice as maid of honour. Not that she'll ever admit it.

The overhead tannoy signals that we will soon be pulling into London, so we quickly shuffle the magazines back into our bags, ready to depart. Just as we step onto the platform, Gwen's phone rings.

'It's my *fiancé*,' she says, dragging out each syllable as she turns away to take the call. She'll enjoy calling herself his wife even more. Their conversation is uncharacteristically brief though. I watch as she hangs up, her face no longer a picture of excitement as she stares at the now blank screen.

'What's up?' I know she won't mind the intrusion.

'Michael's working away again this weekend. He's doing that a lot lately.' She shakes her head as if to free herself of the negative thoughts she isn't sharing.

'Today isn't about Michael, it's about the dress, isn't it?'

She shrugs defiantly, clearly trying to convince herself of that. She laughs again but it is hollower than before. She avoids eye contact as she shuffles us along the platform to the exit.

Even though I want to discuss this further, she never reacts well when I ask too many questions about Michael, let alone when he's upset her. So I leave it. For now.

The next few hours are a daze of tube rides and dress shops. I think we may have tried nearly every shop in London. That's how my feet feel anyway. After an afternoon of learning so much about skirts and corsets, veils and tiaras we are all starting to get tired and hungry.

Gwen is looking deflated. Although we are clear on what she doesn't want, we haven't quite discovered what she actually likes. Not feeling great in everything she tries on is new territory for Gwen, and the fact she's resisted eating today, apart from a stick of celery and an odd green smoothie to preserve her svelte frame, isn't helping her mood at all. So when I catch her googling the nearest restaurant, it's a signal she is losing hope.

'Come on, there's one last appointment, we may as well go in now we're here.'

I move round to try and catch her eye. I can tell my growling stomach is undermining my bright tone, but as soon as she unfolds her arms, I know I've managed to convince her.

I link arms with Gwen, smiling intently at her until she sighs and smiles back. I pull her along the pavement, she can't help but roll her eyes and let me take the lead.

The others trail behind until we reach the last boutique in the chicest area of Knightsbridge. My face is numb from the cold and the balls of my feet are stinging. Gwen isn't the only one who's glad this is the last appointment of the day.

Striding into the pristine white store, I can see Gwen's spirits lift instantly. The warmth is a welcome respite from the autumn breeze, and we are greeted at the door by the most immaculate staff, dressed in matching black dresses and hair neatly wrapped into tight buns. They take our coats and encourage Gwen to step into somewhere called the *atelier*. I'm sure Jessica will explain what that means to me later.

With renewed energy, it doesn't take long before Gwen is reeling off all the dresses we've seen that she didn't like, what was wrong with each and how the perfect dress would have to have specific this and that. The staff hang on her every word, as if waiting for orders for a reconnaissance mission. Times like this remind me of the wealth Gwen comes from, how she is used to having things her way. Marrying someone with Michael's means is a natural choice – with him, she can certainly continue in the lifestyle she is accustomed to.

With a professionally uplifting smile, our helper leads the bride-to-be and me to one side of the store. Jessica and Samira separate to the other. We all know the drill by now, and the search through the expensively bare rails commences, with Gwen tilting her head every so often to take in the materials and designs in our hands. I can feel her anxiety when each isn't quite right, her shoulders drooping and her tone sharper with the assistants each time.

Then it happens. Gwen pulls a gown from the rack, her head tilts. But this time she pulls the gown closer, really studying the intricate flower organza overlay and the long train draping elegantly to the floor. A smile spreads across her face and with a deep intake of breath she announces, 'I *need* to try this one!'

I am so pleased to see her like this, bouncing on the spot and clapping her hands as the assistant carries the gown to the fitting area. Gwen follows closely behind, whilst I finally flump into a leather sofa. I'm relieved to be offered a complimentary drink. Jessica is continuing in her search of the rails just in case Gwen isn't happy with her choice, whilst Samira collapses next to me, resting her head on my shoulder as we wait to deliver our verdict.

The curtains open before us and Gwen emerges. Both Samira and I sit up abruptly, stunned into silence – Gwen looks magnificent. She twirls in the full A-line gown with a beaming smile. She doesn't need to say it: *this* is the dress.

Gwen runs her hands over the intricate embroidery and pearl beading, savouring the feel of it. The sweetheart neckline and corset accentuate her perfect hourglass shape. I watch as she examines every detail of her reflection in the large floor-to-ceiling mirrors around her.

'What do you think?' she asks, spinning to study each of our expressions in turn. Her eyes are sparkling with excitement.

Jessica rushes over to be first to reply, eager to make reference to the expensive material and beadwork. Yet all I notice is that she looks radiant.

Standing in front of her I gush, 'You should be on the cover of one of those magazines – simply stunning!'

I don't think her smile can shine any brighter. Choking back tears, Samira comes to stand beside me.

'You look incredible. Michael will fall in love with you all over again when he sees you in that!'

Something about her words pains Gwen and her glamorous smile fades. Just a little, just for a split second. Not enough for the others, or the assistants, to notice, but I do. She's never been able to keep anything from me. Before I can delve into what I have seen, Gwen regains her composure and stands on her tiptoes.

'I'll need to wear heels though, so Michael and I look perfect in the pictures.'

One of the assistants springs into action to bring her an array of heels to try, so they can measure the perfect length skirt. There is pinning, measuring, clipping, as the seamstress shows Gwen what the finished article will look like once they order her made-to-measure gown.

All of us are now fawning over the dress, with Jessica filling any silence with everything she knows about the designer and the latest trends. Samira does her best to include me in the conversation but it is clear Jessica doesn't want my input. She never does when it comes to discussing the finer things. It's not that I don't have the money to buy designer clothes, I've just never understood their importance.

'Would someone grab a veil for me to try?' Gwen asks.

'I'll go,' I offer, almost stepping over Jessica on my way to the veils section. Pulling one out after another, I don't really know what I'm looking for. They are all so pretty: lace and beads sparkling under the boutique lights.

Eventually, I find one with the same embroidery design as the bodice Gwen is still running her hands over. Her eyes light up when she sees me return with the cathedral-length veil encrusted with classic pearls, its hem gently curved. The assistant carefully fits it to Gwen's curls and as if in slow motion, when she releases it over Gwen's face, there is a hush in the room. We all know – this is it: this is the dress and veil she will wear on her wedding day. She slowly turns back to the full-length mirrors, and it is clear from her serene expression she feels it too.

'Mrs Gwen Jameson,' she whispers, before turning back to look at us. 'This is what I will be wearing when I finally become Mrs Jameson. Michael's wife.'

I busy myself taking photos of every inch of the dress and veil. Close-ups of patterns and stones so that we can make sure any accessories at the wedding tie together. Gwen is enjoying every second of attention, posing for each picture. We take a few bridal party selfies. Even Jessica manages to crack a smile for these.

Soaking up the last few minutes in the dress as the seamstress finishes measuring and pinning to her exacting standards, Gwen continues to whisper sweet nothings at Michael's imaginary reflection in the mirror. Yet, no matter how much we've enjoyed this day, I can't shake the feeling that all this love and excitement is for an unworthy man. I can only hope I'm wrong.

Chapter Four

Cold Feet

Later that day

We are all a little light-headed from the excitement and having not eaten all day, so we opt for a little bistro close by. Thankfully Jessica and Gwen are so famished that we are ignoring the wedding diet for now.

When Jessica and Samira excuse themselves to the ladies' room, I nervously swirl the straw around in my ice water. Now that I finally have Gwen alone, I should find a way to broach what I saw in her expression earlier, after her phone call with Michael, and again after Samira's compliment in the boutique.

'You're fiddling. What's wrong? It's the dress – you don't like it do you?' She hasn't breathed between her desperate spurt of questions.

'What? No, the dress is fine! Incredible actually.' My pulse quickens; Gwen is now focusing on me intently. 'It's just…' I stumble. 'Are you happy?'

I make sure to meet her eyes as soon as the words leave my mouth. Rather than instantly protesting her premarital bliss, Gwen sits back in shock at the question. My words hang in the air like a fog over what has been a lovely day.

'What? Of course I am!'

Had she not started playing with her napkin to avoid looking back at me, I might have believed her. And sure enough, noticing my persistent stare, she sighs and leans forwards. Her lips part, ready to spill whatever is weighing her down.

'He's been working away a lot, you know. One minute he seems to be so happy with me. The next… well, he's here but he's not here. He's just so distant sometimes.'

I'm not sure what I was expecting but this was not it – she does have doubts. Gwen has never said anything negative about Michael and yet now, mere minutes after buying her dream wedding dress, she is admitting; she isn't as content as she seems to be. With a sigh she sinks back into her chair. I can see she regrets saying it out loud, as if that just made it real.

One of the many things being a therapist has taught me is how important it is for people to be heard. Not judged. Not told how to feel or what to do, just listened to. So I do my best to not show any change in my expression. I *want* to tell her my fears; that I too think Michael is not all he appears to be, but I can wait.

'It doesn't matter,' she says, filling the silence. 'I'm being silly. Pre-wedding jitters.' With a nervous laugh, she straightens her serviette onto her lap. I stroke her arm and offer a sympathetic smile.

'It's just me here. Talk to me.'

She gazes thoughtfully at the engagement ring she is spinning around her finger, before looking at me, her eyes glassy with tears.

'I love him, I really do but…' Gwen swallows her words when she sees Jessica and Samira returning to the table.

'What have I missed?' Samira says, sensing the change in atmosphere. No one speaks – we only exchange awkward glances.

Thankfully, the arrival of our food is the distraction Gwen needs to regain her composure. The mix of risottos and pasta dishes fill the table, looking and smelling delicious, and the table is alive with chatter as we pore over photos of the dress.

I try my best to join in but my stomach is in knots as I puzzle over what else Gwen is hiding from me. I can see, between bouts of laughter and conversation, that same pained expression return to her face when she thinks no one is looking. I can't help but wonder why she would settle for someone who makes her have any misgivings. It's not as if she hasn't had a string of fantastic men pursue her. Curating art has given her access to many wealthy bachelors, including some who showed what kind and loyal partners they could be.

As she natters on about the trivial details of the big day: the tablecloths, the colour of the candles, the wedding favours, I know my conversation with her is far from over. While the main course dishes are being cleared, I excuse myself to the ladies' room, knowing Gwen will join me as she always does.

We walk up the corridor together, Gwen continuing to try to steer the conversation towards the banal. I think she knows what I'll say if she stops, even for a second, but I can't hold back any longer. The overwhelming urge to un-pause our previous conversation forces me to interrupt her.

'So, you and Michael. What was it you were going to say earlier?'

Her eyes drop to the floor. 'It's just he spends so much time away. I wonder…' Her voice begins to break.

'You wonder what?'

'What if he's seeing someone else?' Her face falls again.

Why would she agree to marry someone when she has such suspicions? I have so many questions, but she doesn't need questions right now. No, right now she needs a hug. Moving round to pull her close to me, I can feel her tears against my cheek. There's a pain in my chest, like my heart is being squeezed. She's confirming my fears – Michael is hiding something.

Hearing her sob throws me back to when I thought Dylan was cheating. Not thought. Knew. I didn't walk away either. Partly because I was convinced he would change and partly because I believed I would never find anyone else to love me. Once you're under the spell of someone that manipulative, it's hard to see a way out.

'I'm sorry, I'm being silly,' she says again, pulling away from me. 'I have no proof. Just, sometimes he feels withdrawn, like we're together but he's somewhere else.'

'So why say yes when he proposed?' I needed to ask.

'Because I love him. I love everything about him. I love how he makes me feel – most of the time. I know he's the one for me.'

Her eyes are pleading for me to reassure her – tell her it is all just pre-wedding nerves, but I see it too. Michael always falls short of fully divulging anything about his life to me. We will talk about films, the weather, work and Gwen, naturally; subjects of his choosing. Can this be why? He doesn't want me to discover some kind of secret. I lost so many friends because of Dylan, leaving no one to help me escape him. I have to be the friend I never had, for Gwen.

'How about I talk to him? See if I can dig a little?'

She recoils. 'No, no. It's fine. I don't want him to think I don't trust him. Please Vic, you won't say anything to him, will you?'

I promise I won't, but I'm not going to leave this alone. I need to clarify what is going on, one way or another. I'm just not sure how yet. I won't let her suffer the way I have.

We sit down for dessert, but I slide my cheesecake away, I don't have any appetite after my conversation with Gwen. Jessica is droning on about pre-wedding workouts, but I can't concentrate, not when Gwen's placid smile is clearly plastered on. I want to catch her eye, reassure her, but Jessica just won't stop. The most irritating part of Jessica's latest judgemental rant, other than her being completely oblivious to Gwen's demeanour, is that I know it wouldn't hurt for me to exercise more and eat a little healthier, but who has the time for all that? Ah yes, a socialite, whose very day centres around yoga and lunch dates. Listening to her prattling on about organic this and carbs that, I wonder if she has any understanding of what it feels like to have to work for a living.

'Victoria, are you not eating that?'

Jessica's eyes drift to my unwanted slice. I await some barbed comment but to my surprise she leans over the table with her fork, scooping at the creamy topping.

'One small mouthful won't hurt.'

I see Samira's jaw drop as Jessica savours the flavour.

'This is definitely the final simple carbs I have before the wedding,' she mutters, licking her fork.

Thankfully, with an eye roll, Samira jumps on the opportunity to change the subject to flowers and colour schemes. Gwen rejoins the conversation, the twinkle back in her eye. Naturally, she has ideas for nearly every detail. She's been planning this wedding in her mind for forever after all. It's a shame though, she would never have imagined that she would be more committed to her dream wedding than her future groom would be to her.

We are all exhausted by the end of the train journey home. I look out across the darkened landscapes trying to process everything that has happened today. I know I told Gwen I wouldn't get involved but I need to try and delve into Michael's life. If he *is* hiding something from her, then perhaps his friends would know something?

'A party!' I blurt out as we are about to separate into our taxis home. 'We should have an engagement party, don't you think?'

Gwen has repeatedly texted me saying we wouldn't have time to organise one with the wedding being so close, so I can see she is readying herself to say no.

'Come on Gwen, you've waited forever to get married, you can't miss out on something as important as an engagement party.'

She doesn't look convinced, clearly about to remind me of her strict pre-wedding schedule.

'I'll organise everything. We should really get the bridesmaids and groomsmen together before the wedding. To make sure we all know what we need to do for the big day, right?'

Samira claps excitedly at the idea, and Gwen's eyebrows furrow as she considers my offer. Then her face relaxes into a grin and she hugs me, holding on a little longer than usual.

'That's great – thank you. I love you Vic, you know that, don't you?'

Of course I do. Stepping back to look at her directly, I try my best to sound sincere as I lower my voice, 'Everything's going to be OK. Promise.'

She beams and hugs me once more. Inwardly I am sighing, I am even less supportive of this marriage now than I was when they announced it, but I don't want to upset her with my suspicions. I smile and wave as her taxi pulls away, my mind is already ticking over with plans for the event. One way or another, I need to know who Michael really is and what he is hiding from us.

Chapter Five

The Engagement Party

Two months, one week until the wedding.

I'm starting to get what I need. I've collected all the details for the party guests, which will come in very handy if I need to make contact with anyone in Michael's life after the event.

It's been no small task finding a date that suited all three bridesmaids, four groomsmen and enough of the couple's wider circles of friends at such short notice, but the RSVPs are in. With Jessica's help we've privately hired the most exquisite restaurant, owned by a *dear friend* of hers.

During a late-night crafting session I've made a bespoke game called, "How do you know the bride and groom?", to play during what promises to be a mouth-wateringly fancy dinner. The question cards will partly make sure the conversation keeps flowing but also ensure I can direct the topics to be about Michael. If I'm to try and unearth secrets about him, his friends, relaxing with good food and wine, will create the perfect opportunity. I've been careful to make sure that the questions are not so intrusive as to embarrass Gwen though; this is about discovering leads to his secrets – for me to follow up on discreetly after the party.

Michael paid for the evening, making it clear that Gwen should have whatever she desires, no expense spared. Not missing the opportunity to remind me that he is entirely self-made, having built his real estate empire from nothing. I can't help but wonder what else is self-made. How much of what he shows Gwen is the real him? Tonight I have to find out.

Adding one more coat of my blunt lipstick in the hallway mirror, I smooth down my faithful little black dress. The short-sleeved fit and flare is elegant without being too showy. I'm sure Jessica will have something to say about it but I feel nice in it. I'm not going to spoil my moment of confidence by focusing too much on the fine lines around my eyes, so with a final spritz of perfume I'm ready. Just in time too: the taxi driver's beeping outside.

The autumn showers are well and truly here, so I tuck the icebreaker game inside my long, single-breasted coat and lift the hood, before running through the drizzle to catch my ride. I have to be early to make sure everything is just so.

I needn't have worried about anything. When I walk in, I am in awe of what the restaurant staff have managed to create. I am welcomed by the soft ambient lighting; the air fragrant with elaborate fresh rose and jasmine bouquets running along the centre of the tables and the gentle sounds of classical music in the background. The long table is beautifully laid: the cutlery shining and glasses twinkling under the low-hanging chandeliers and perfectly spaced tealights. Waiters are busily straightening every element on the table, tying each place name to the stem of a single white rose with rustic brown string. I double-check they have followed my seating plan: a careful mixing of the groomsmen, bridesmaids and other close friends, ensuring everyone will mingle tonight. That will make it easier for me to flit between conversations.

Satisfied with the table arrangements, I move to the adjoining bar which is decorated in the same elegant manner. Nearly a dozen waiters and waitresses are there, some standing at the ready, others polishing glasses. I hide the icebreaker game at the far end of the bar, to keep it safe until I surprise everyone with it later. Then I stand back, genuinely pleased with myself for being part of such a sophisticated gathering. I know I wouldn't have managed it without Jessica's help, something she has continually reminded me of. I do wonder, if she came to see me professionally, if we could look into her need for such boastful behaviour but she is very far down a long list of priorities. There is certainly a part of me that is relieved she is so willing to help, even though I think she would happily see me fail in my role. She clearly wants what is best for Gwen – something we might actually be able to bond over.

Most of the bridesmaids and groomsmen have met in passing before, but tonight I want everyone to really get to know one another. So I can find out everything there is to know about Michael.

Who is he under that perfectly chiselled mask? Just enough alcohol might help loosen the groomsmen's tongues, although I will need to stay relatively sober to make mental notes of anything useful. No, tonight there will be no escaping my questions. Tonight, I am taking control. I have to – for Gwen's sake.

Straightening my shoulders as the first guests wander to the table, I take a few deep breaths. It's time to put on a show. Tonight I have to be chatty, smiley Victoria. Not the Victoria who wants to curl up with her duvet and a good book.

'Let's get this party started!' yells Isaac, the best man. His deep, confident voice booms above the calm chatter in the room as he helps himself to a bottle of champagne. He pops the cork, spilling a little on the table and the nearby guests, all of whom are too polite to complain. Or perhaps his warm, boyish grin is winning them over. His slight wobble and slurring words are not what I was expecting so early in the evening. I grimace as some of the groomsmen cheer, passing glasses forward to be overfilled.

I have worked hard to plan this evening but I had not taken into account the possibility of an unruly best man. My mistake. I certainly do not want the guests to be so drunk that they can't hold a conversation, but an alcohol-fuelled mess seems to be Isaac's aim. Mentally, I question how he and Michael are friends; Michael is so charming and refined, while Isaac is uncouth and irritating.

I notice Michael watching me intently. He often seems to, like he is trying to gauge my reactions, almost as if he's desperate to please his future wife's best friend. He smiles and looks away when I catch his eye. I know Gwen sees it as endearing, but this is what Dylan was like. Calculating.

Learning how to impress people around us so no one would suspect what he was really like behind closed doors. And if I'm right about Michael, Gwen is blind to him in much the same way I was blind to Dylan.

'Let's take it easy tonight gentlemen, there are ladies present.'

Michael speaks with such authority that Isaac settles almost instantly. As he shines his reassuring smile at Gwen, I see her light up in the way she should, his confidence and charm a match for hers, and all of a sudden I feel torn again. I truly want her to stay as happy as she looks with him now, and how can I be the one to ruin that for her? What if I find out Michael really is a cheat, as Gwen fears? I cannot picture how I would break that news to her. I smile weakly at Michael, raising my glass in thanks as the gentle hum of conversation returns to the table. His flawless smile radiates back.

As soon as the freshly baked bread arrives I can hear Isaac mumbling at the far end of the table about needing a real drink to liven up the atmosphere. I despise him already. However, tonight is not about reminding him of his manners, tonight is about something far more important. I straighten up and ready myself to make a toast. I cough to clear my throat and people's heads start turning towards me. Suddenly I'm horribly aware of how hot it is in the room, my palms sweating, my mouth dry. As if reading my mind once again, Michael taps his glass and the table quietens.

'Hello everyone. Firstly, I'd like to give my thanks to Victoria for arranging this evening to bring our friends together. Gwen and I are overwhelmed with the love and support in this room and treasure each one of you.'

Gwen beams at him, as everyone raises their glasses, clinking them together with a chorus of cheers. I look around the room at the adoring faces staring back at Michael, he has the entire room under his spell. I wonder if he knows that I'm not? Maybe that's why he's keeping such a close eye on me tonight, perhaps he knows it will take a special effort to manipulate me. I consciously smile just in case he happens to look my way. Is this how he captured Gwen's heart so quickly – by watching her every move and saying the right things at the right times? My hands clench into fists at the thought, but I cannot allow myself to be distracted from my purpose this evening. Standing, I take a deep breath in, put a smile on my face and tap my glass. I see Michael's eyes narrow at my clear attempt to divert the attention from him but he realises everyone is still watching us and raises his glass towards me before returning to his seat.

'Good evening everyone, I'm Victoria. The maid of honour.' I sip slowly at my water to try to unstick my tongue from the roof of my mouth. 'Thank you all for being here at such short notice to congratulate the most extraordinary couple Gwen and Michael, on their engagement–'

'Hear, hear! Cheers!' Isaac interrupts, swigging his drink.

Rolling my eyes, I broaden my fixed smile. Isaac sees my annoyance and puts his glass down.

'On the back of your name cards is a site I have set up for the happy couple. Please upload any photos or videos from tonight for them to treasure. Enjoy yourselves everyone. Cheers!'

As everyone sips at their drinks in response, I feel my cheeks burning, as they always do when I am centre of attention.

'Can we get a photo of the table, to get this site started?' Samira yells, and her husband Raheem passes his phone to an obliging waiter.

Several theatrically posed group shots and attempted selfies later, the giggling and chatting resumes, just in time for the starters to arrive. Gentle murmurs of pleasure fill the room as everyone tucks into their perfectly seared scallops with champagne sauce. There is an air of calm and genuine togetherness, with bridesmaids and groomsmen filling each other's glasses and laughing at one another's jokes. I observe the picture-perfect gathering before me. My instincts are telling me that this is the calm before the storm, that we should treasure this moment because it probably won't last for long.

We have the restaurant to ourselves, so between courses we break off into smaller clusters, with regular visits to the bar. Some guests wander outside, sheltering in the doorway for smoke breaks.

This is my opportunity. I move between the smaller crowds, topping up glasses so that there is just enough alcohol flowing to make inhibitions loose and the conversations easy. Mingling with the groomsmen, I had expected someone to reveal something unseemly to me – anything I can work with. Yet not one of them has a bad word to say about Michael. Each and every one of them seems to genuinely adore him: for his generosity, his hard-working attitude and the purity of his love for Gwen. I'm feeling tension leave my body that has been building since they announced their engagement. This is what I wanted to hear, surely? That his feelings for her are real? That there isn't some secret love affair? Perhaps there is a reasonable explanation for Gwen's suspicions after all.

Watching the happy couple slow dancing near the bar, to their song – Ed Sheeran's "Perfect" – is yet another reality check. Gwen's arms drape loosely around Michael's neck, whilst his hands are holding her waist, pulling her closer to him. Their lips close to touching as they stare deeply into one another's eyes. Right now, they are the only people in the room, perhaps the world. They are truly in love. Maybe all I need to do is tell Gwen that actually, there's nothing to worry about. That Michael is indeed the devoted man of her dreams. Now is not the time. Right now, it is time to just let everyone enjoy the party, including myself.

The camera flash from Jessica's phone jolts me back to earth.

'They really are beautiful together, aren't they?' she muses with a rare smile, before walking away.

I look at them again, Michael running his hands through Gwen's tousled hair, then lacing his fingers through hers. It feels awkward, just standing and watching. I need to leave them to enjoy this intimate moment alone.

There is laughter behind me. Looking around, I find Samira waving for me to join her group at the bar, a line of shots before them. Maybe it is time to get a little messy! I join her in downing a shot and slam the small glass back on the bar, as she cheers me on. This is the first time I think I've relaxed since the party started.

Posing for photos with Samira and some rather attractive groomsmen is perhaps a tiny bit better than being sat alone on my sofa at home. Just as we are perfecting our pouts, I notice Gwen come to the bar, alone.

'Where's Michael?'

'Oh, he had some important work call to take.' She shrugs.

'During your engagement party?'

Annoyance clouds her face. 'It's fine Vic, leave it.'

Over her shoulder I see Michael walking towards the kitchen area, presumably to find a quiet space to talk. Strange though, he isn't on his phone – it isn't even in his hand. Oblivious to his movements, Gwen grabs her drink and turns to watch the guests enjoying themselves.

'I'd better mingle.'

I, on the other hand, feel a magnetic pull to the kitchen. Before I can make a move, Gwen grabs my hand.

'Are you coming?'

My eyes flick between her and the sight of Michael disappearing into a distant corridor.

'I just want to thank the chef for tonight's meal,' I lie, deciding to eavesdrop on this urgent call of Michael's. What can be so important that he has to step away from his own engagement party?

'I'll come too–'

'No!' I interrupt a little too sharply. Then, more softly, as I notice the confusion on Gwen's face, 'I'll go, your guests are waiting for you!'

I pause, to make sure Gwen is locked in conversation before I pretend to walk casually towards the kitchen, checking over my shoulder to make sure she isn't watching. Then I slide around a corner, against the wall of the poorly lit corridor, concealing myself amongst the shadows. I can hear Michael's voice ahead. It sounds raised but then quickly drops to a whisper.

As I edge closer, I feel my stomach drop at what I hear next. A woman's voice.

Chapter Six

Party's Over

I hold my breath, leaping across the hallway to hide behind the cloakroom counter.

'You can't be here!' Michael hisses.

'I'm not leaving until you talk to me… does your bride-to-be know the truth? Does she know what you're capable of?'

My mouth falls open. Who is she? What is she talking about? I try to lean just a little over the wooden surface, to see this mysterious woman. I catch sight of her black wavy hair and flawless, dewy skin and can't help but notice she is breathtakingly beautiful. Does this secret meeting prove he isn't to be trusted?

I open my camera app and slowly raise my phone until it is just high enough to have her in the frame, then quickly hit the button to capture her image. Behind me, the sound of smashing glasses and cheering from the bar stops their conversation dead.

I drop to the floor as Michael begins pacing back in my direction. His footsteps erratic. I can't let him catch me like this, not before I find out what is really going on. I hold my breath and push myself deep into the rows of low draping, neatly hung coats, carefully letting those closest camouflage me. The heat under the layers is stifling, but I daren't move. His footsteps slow as the frivolity of the party continues to echo down the hall. He lets out a sigh and turns back towards her.

'Not here, please. We'll talk later. I'll meet you tomorrow, in the park by the town hall. Midday?'

His tone is somehow both commanding and pleading. This Michael is not the dominant character I know him to be. What power does this woman have over him? If she is a friend of his, surely I would have met her by now, even in passing? That, and she wouldn't be hiding like this, away from the party. My head is swirling with questions.

I move the coats, holding the edge of the counter to lift myself up high enough to peer again, I want to see her reaction to Michael's words. She seems less than impressed but nevertheless agrees to meet him before walking out, past me. I duck down once more, hearing her footsteps and then his not far behind. I hold my breath and stay as still as possible so the coats around me don't move.

After a few seconds I look through the gap in the cloakroom door and see her walk out through the main exit, the staff and guests too busy in the dining area to even notice.

Michael watches her leave before making his way back to the party. I slump back against the softness of the coats, filling my lungs as I plan how to get back into the party. I can't go straight away in case he notices I followed him.

When I judge he is far enough ahead, I tiptoe back to the party; I can see him making his way to Gwen, stopping as various guests want to talk to him. He looks flustered – his attempt at a smile barely visible.

I slip back into a group near the bar, still watching him but relieved he hasn't noticed me. Eventually he manages to reach Gwen, and slips an arm around her, kissing her cheek, as if nothing could be more natural. As if he hasn't just been having a covert conversation with another woman. These are all the warning signs I missed with Dylan. I won't miss them with Michael, though. I'll be there at noon tomorrow.

'What are these?' One of the groomsmen's voices, Connor I think his name is, booms at me over the chatter.

He has found the game I'd left at the end of the bar. I'd completely forgotten about it.

'Just an icebreaker. Doesn't seem any point now though, not to worry.'

I put my hand out to reach for the box, but maybe-Connor leans back just far back enough that I can't grab it. He unlatches the box to pull out the top card.

'Where did you first meet the bride or groom?' he reads loudly.

A group begins to reconvene excitedly at the dining table, and others follow – including Gwen and Michael.

'So, who's answering?' he continues.

Jessica puts her hand up. 'I will!' She is slurring and almost misses the chair she was aiming to sit on. The guests cannot hide their laughter. I laugh too, stopping when I realise drunk Jessica is *fun*! Who'd have thought it?

'Gwen and I were at boarding school together!'

Naturally the groomsmen manage to turn the conversation to sleepovers and pillow fights, their deep laughter bellowing across the room. More questions from the box follow, which to my relief, does indeed provide some light entertainment. For Gwen, there are embarrassing teenage haircut memories, school detention stories and even the occasional drunken misadventure shared. Michael's stories centre more around the squash club, work and the occasional boys' weekend. His younger years aren't mentioned at all.

'Boring!' Isaac yells, cutting through the jovial atmosphere. 'Let me do one.' He grabs at the box and starts flicking through the remaining cards.

'Oh, here's one, Michael and Gwen have to answer. Do you have any secrets from one another?'

What? I didn't write that, or any other question for Gwen and Michael, the cards were for the guests. I want to protest but the table ooohs and aaahs at the very idea, in mock scandalised tones. The giggling and calling out ridiculous suggestions as to what secrets there could be only adding to their light-hearted fun. I wonder if Isaac made up the question on the spot, but for what purpose?

The difference between Gwen and Michael's reactions are stark, both compared to the rest of the guests and to each other. Gwen looking to Michael for comfort. Michael's steely glare focused solely on Isaac, shooting his best man a frightening look. I watch as Gwen's eyes dart nervously from Michael to me, her gaze pleading for me to somehow stop this, but I don't know how. My body tenses with confusion. Maybe I want to hear the answer too. Either way I don't want to see her like this.

'I didn't write that!' I shout, attempting to grab the card from his hand but he moves too quickly for me, laughing as he wags his finger at me and tuts. There is now an awkward silence in the room. No, this isn't right. I had never intended for Gwen to be humiliated.

'We don't have any secrets!' Gwen blurts.

Her voice just a little too shaky and high-pitched to be convincing. I watch as she grabs Michael's hand to show their solidarity. There is a slight hesitation, on his part, before he manages to muster a smile.

'Of course we don't darling.'

Silence follows. Not just between them but all of us.

'Isn't it time to turn the music up and get dancing?' Samira sounds overly enthusiastic, even for her. A forced cheer goes around the room, and guests start shuffling towards the small dancefloor near the bar. It seems everyone is keen to abandon the game and leave a clearly sensitive situation.

Gwen is slowly drinking her wine, not making eye contact with anyone, whilst Michael is making an effort to comfort her. He reaches for her but she keeps deflecting his hands, her face worryingly unresponsive. I'm not sure what to do but I need to do something. I check to make sure the revellers have moved away, all of them now with Samira, who's busy asking the manager if she can change the music to something a little more upbeat to keep the party going. These slow tunes will clearly not do.

Out of the corner of my eye, I spot Gwen getting up and walking briskly to the ladies' bathroom. From the way her shoulders are gently rising and falling I can tell she is crying.

I try to catch up to her straight away but the music has already changed and the volume is so loud the guests cannot hear me when I ask them to move out of my way. They obviously didn't notice Gwen leaving or how upset she is. The sight of the bridesmaids and groomsmen doing the YMCA is not exactly in keeping with the type of night I had planned but they are clearly enjoying themselves. With no other option, I force my way through them to reach Gwen.

Gently pushing the bathroom door open, I spot Gwen leaning towards the ornate mirror, attempting to wipe the smeared mascara from around her eyes. She stops briefly when she notices me but quickly goes back to wiping her face.

'Here, let me,' I say as I take the tissue from her.

I dab at her ruined make-up in silence. It's not for me to begin the conversation about what just happened, that's Gwen's decision to make, but instead she is standing, staring at me blankly.

'He's keeping things from me, isn't he?' Her tone flat. 'I know he is, I just don't know *what* he's keeping from me. What if I'm right and it's another woman? What if he doesn't love me?'

She breaks down again and stumbles into my arms. I remain silent, rubbing her back as she sobs into my shoulder. She needs me to be the voice of reason, even though she has evidently picked up on Michael's awkwardness earlier. I know I am wondering if what he is hiding from her has something to do with the woman I saw him with earlier. I squeeze Gwen a little tighter as her tears continue to flow. I don't want to say anything that might hurt her, especially when there are heightened emotions and alcohol involved. Instead, I need to find out who that mystery woman of Michael's is, and what she is to him.

No amount of reapplying make-up can cover up her puffy eyes but we make our way back to the party anyway. With all the noise and merriment, it would appear the guests have continued to enjoy the evening without us. Bouncing on the dance floor, singing off key to whatever track is currently playing, their elated raucous behaviour is a sharp contrast to Gwen's solemn demeanour.

We manage to move through them easily, which makes me wonder if they were politely ignoring Gwen's clearly reddened eyes. For them at least, the awkwardness of the games seems long forgotten, thanks to Jessica, who in our absence has been an attentive host, and Samira is ever the entertainer.

Scouring each table, I catch sight of Michael, alone in a darkened corner massaging his temples, his eyes closed. Gwen sees him, too. She forces her shoulders back, and with her chin high, confidently stalks towards him as I trail behind. She is trying to put on a brave face, which I can only assume is to make sure her guests don't detect any tension between her and Michael. He barely manages to stand, let alone speak; his shoulders slumped and head low, it would seem he is also feeling the strain of this situation.

'Gwen…'

'I want to go home,' she interrupts bluntly, with so little emotion it feels robotic. Her eyes are glazed as if she isn't truly present. Michael simply nods his head. He knows this is a conversation Gwen wants to have in the privacy of their own home. He sighs and leaves to fetch her coat, probably realising that there is no avoiding her questions once they are in private. Part of me desperately wants to be part of that conversation, to see if he mentions the mysterious brunette, but I know Gwen will call me afterwards, when she feels up to it.

Gwen and Michael say their goodbyes to the remaining guests, who all wolf whistle and cat call, thinking the happy couple have recovered from the earlier hiccup and are sneaking away for a romantic end to the evening.

I know the truth, though. I sit back down at the table, rather deflated, wondering why Isaac asked the question he did. Was he just trying to create some drama, or is there some secret he was trying to spill? Who was the gorgeous woman in the kitchen? The melee of the dance floor holds no appeal for me now. I've tried my utmost to be happy about this engagement, but now I know that's impossible. My instincts were right all along.

There is little more I can do tonight. All I want is to get back to the bar, avoiding as many guests as I can on the way. As I weave through the dancers, I feel hands grab me around my waist. I spin around to see Isaac's smiling face. Well, more of a big and stupid grin really. He leans forward as if to whisper, but he ends up speaking very loudly into my ear to be heard over the music. I wince at the volume of his voice.

'Fancy a dance, beautiful?'

The very idea makes my eyes roll. 'No, I just need a drink.' Firmly pushing him away, I turn back towards the bar.

'Great, I'll join you.'

I'm not in the mood to argue any more than I'm in the mood to socialise with anyone who would call Michael a friend. That doesn't stop him from following me to the bar, swaying to the music as he walks, and ordering drinks for us both – whisky, neat.

'Oh sorry, is whisky OK? Or are you more of a white wine spritzer type of person?' The patronising soft giggle he adds does little to lift my mood. He's right, I'm not usually a big spirits drinker but I'm not going to admit that to him now, and the whisky is a means to an end.

'No, whisky is just fine, thank you.'

The bartender places the small glasses down in front of us.

'What shall we toast to?' Isaac asks in his annoyingly jovial manner.

I simply shrug and throw back my drink without a word. He raises his eyebrows with a smirk before following suit. The burning liquid forces me to start coughing. Isaac's laughter is instant and loud.

'That hit the spot. Shall I get the next round?' I offer defiantly.

'Please do!'

There's that stupid smirk of his again. Isaac beckons the bartender with a wave of his hand. I order the next round. And the one after that. The sooner this night blurs away the better.

Chapter Seven

A Night To Remember, A Morning To Forget

The light from my undrawn curtains hurts my eyes; even turning my head to check the time is painful and slow. 10 a.m. – time to get up, showered and to the park before Michael and that woman arrive.

My head is throbbing and my stomach gurgling, the taste of liquor now sour in my mouth. I try to reach for my phone on the bedside cabinet but my arm feels like it's pinned to the bed. Looking down, I see that it *is* pinned down – someone else's arm is laid across me. I hold my breath as I slowly turn my head, following the arm to its body. There, lying under the duvet next to me, is Isaac.

'Shit!' I yell, backing away from him, falling out of the bed in the process.

'Good morning to you too, beautiful.' He grins like a Cheshire cat. Still half asleep he lifts his head from the pillow, squinting down at me.

'What… what the hell are you doing in my bed?'

'Erm… the same thing you were doing in your bed.' He laughs, pushing himself up to lean on his elbow. I follow his gaze and realise I am laid on the floor in nothing more than my mismatched underwear. With a gasp I run for the en suite. I can still hear him shouting from the bed as I slam the door.

'You OK, gorgeous?'

I'm too busy wrapping a towel around myself to answer; stopping like a startled animal when he knocks on the door. In my confused, hungover mind I have no idea what my next move is. If I stay really quiet, will he go away?

He knocks again. I perch on the edge of the bath, my head in my hands, trying to figure out what to do.

'What are you doing here?' I yell.

'Just open the door, will you?'

I don't want to. He'll be there and this will be real. Yet clearly, ignoring him isn't having the desired effect either. I stand up too quickly, almost losing my balance. I'm dizzy, feeling sick and I think I may still be a little drunk. Taking a deep breath, ready to tell him to leave, I open the door.

I'm speechless. There he is, standing in only his boxers. My eyes move upwards, lingering perhaps a little too long on his perfect physique and flawless dark skin, until I eventually reach his eyes, sparkling with mischief. With a sharp intake of breath, I slam the door shut again, feeling flustered at the sight of him.

'Put some bloody clothes on!' I rest my head against the door, hearing him chuckle as he pads away.

Inching the door open again, I see Isaac buttoning up his shirt before digging around for his trousers. What *happened* last night? I can't remember the last time I had such a headache.

'I'm going to assume you aren't inviting me to stay for breakfast?' he mutters over his muscular shoulder at me. I open the door an inch more to give him my indignant response.

'I don't even know how we got here.'

I don't mean to sound so harsh, but I don't need this right now. I just need him gone. I need to get ready and get to the park as I'd planned. But first of all, I think I need to throw up or lie down, or both.

'I can stay, help you remember,' he smiles – that look again – reaching out for me as he steps closer.

He pauses when he notices my expression remains serious. 'Look, Victoria, you know nothing happened, right? Some kissing, a little cuddling but nothing more.'

I study his face, it's perhaps the most serious I've ever seen him. He has no reason to lie. I let out a sigh of relief.

'I can see you probably really do want me to go?' His voice a mix of hope and acceptance. 'I'll see myself out, shall I?'

He lingers, as if waiting for me to ask him to stay but all I can think to do is nod. I closely follow him down the stairs, holding the front door open for him.

'Look Victoria, if you want to meet up, for a drink or whatever, you have my number.'

With that he turns towards the street and I close the door behind him. I don't have time to think about Isaac right now, I need to get dressed.

Going back up to the bathroom, I catch sight of myself in the mirror. I'm still in last night's make-up, my hair tangled and matted to one side of my face. I can't tell if the dark circles under my eyes are from sheer exhaustion or mascara. What a sight. Unlike Isaac, who, other than a few stray hairs, still looked immaculate.

I close my eyes in the hope that when I open them it will have been a bad dream. Nope – Isaac definitely spent the night here. The smell of his aftershave is lingering in my room. I grab some paracetamol from the cabinet, swallowing them without water, before stepping into the shower. The hot water is sheer bliss. Yet as I close my eyes, snippets from last night start flooding back: the drinks, the dancing, the kissing in the taxi. I groan aloud with annoyance at my adolescent behaviour. This isn't me, I don't do things like this. I haven't even been vaguely intimate with anyone since Dylan, years ago.

After I've turned off the water I lean against the tiled walls, cool against my skin. If I didn't need to get to the park, I'd have happily spent my day off right here, followed by tea in my pyjamas. I know I can't though, I cannot risk being late. I grab a towel and search for my phone.

30 new messages. Quickly flicking through, I see there are a ton from Samira declaring her undying love for me – she always does when she's had a lot to drink – and a few from the other guests saying thank you, but nothing from Gwen. Nothing at all. I sit pondering what to do as water continues to drip from my hair down my back. I'll get moving as soon as I've texted her.

> Hey Gwen. Catch up later? Hangover is killing me. x

My only clean clothes are dark and plain – ideal for helping me blend into the crowd at the park. As I grab some less-than-fresh socks from the floor, I spot Isaac's tie lying, forgotten, next to them.

The memory of us stumbling through the bedroom door last night flashes through my mind, and I'm surprised to find myself smiling. The image is quickly replaced by one of Dylan, curling his lip when he saw that I'd left clothes lying around in our room. He couldn't tolerate mess. It would make him angry. I shake the thought from my mind – I need to focus on getting to the park.

The cold air hits me as soon as I walk outside. The streets are busy with the usual weekend dog walkers and people taking in the fresh air. I'm lucky to live in such a beautiful town. Filled with historic architecture and surrounded by stunning, wide-open spaces, yet somehow still small and comforting.

It's 11:45 by the time I make it to the park, with Michael and the beautiful brunette nowhere to be seen. I find the perfect spot to hide, to survey as much of the area as I can, under a rowan tree with low-hanging branches covered in scarlet foliage. If I wasn't so focused on Michael, I'd be enjoying the crunch of the fallen leaves beneath my feet. All I want to do is rest against the large tree trunk and close my eyes, so I'm glad for the strong coffee I picked up en route, sipping at it to stay alert.

She is the first to arrive. The sheer adrenaline rush of seeing her, confirming that this is real and not a figment of my drunken imagination, wakes me up far more than the caffeine. With no makeup, hair tied back in a simple ponytail and tailored jacket nipped tightly at her tiny waist, she is effortlessly chic. Far from the glamourous full hair and make-up Gwen usually sports.

Already this woman seems agitated, pacing back and forth nearby. It's only 12:05 but she's regularly checking her watch. I spot Michael striding confidently towards her, his face expressionless.

Their interaction is immediately strained. I can't hear what they mumble to one another, but her hands gesticulate her annoyance. His are held up in defence before his whole demeanour changes, stepping closer to her, his jaw clenched.

'You have to leave!' His voice is louder and domineering now, but she doesn't appear remotely fazed.

'Not until they all know about you – the real you!'

My ears prick up. What does she mean – the real him? Before I can try and read his expression, he pulls her close to him. I can't see his face, but I recognise what I see in hers – fear. Her arms tangled in front of her, she doesn't even try to struggle. Instead, her eyes widen as he whispers something into her ear.

My breathing become fast and shallow as I think back to when Dylan used to grab me in that same way. I rub my arms, almost feeling the bruises again. The sheer terror I would feel wondering what would happen when he finally let go.

Part of me wants to intervene, but then he'll know I'm here – I don't know what to do. Other people are starting to look at them too, and it won't be long before Michael realises and finds a way to make the situation look innocent. I need to get proof for Gwen, fast.

I'll film them! I'm annoyed I haven't thought to do that sooner. But by the time I have pulled one of my gloves off with my teeth and grabbed my phone from my pocket, I look up to see I've missed my chance. Michael and the mysterious woman are gone.

I step out from under the tree for a clearer view of the park, but they are nowhere to be seen. If I hadn't looked down for my phone, I'd know what prompted them to leave so quickly. Perhaps all the attention they were drawing from passers-by? Feeling my phone vibrate in my hand, I look at the screen and see a message from Gwen.

> Vic, everyone loved the party – fabulous job!
> Speak soon xx

I screw my face up as I read her message. Gwen sounds relaxed and happy, which is ridiculous considering how the night ended. Throwing my coffee cup in a recycling bin, I text her back, trying to avoid bumping into people as I type.

> I'd love a catch up. xx

I watch intently as the little dots appear on my screen and then disappear. I'm still staring at the screen, mulling over whether or not to call her, when I walk straight into someone. As I peer upwards, stepping back to apologise, I am met with Michael's fierce gaze.

'What are you doing here, Victoria?'

His stare is so intense, I lose all power of speech. He inches closer, repeating himself, slower, never breaking my gaze.

'I… er… have a hangover. I was just walking to clear my head.'

Even the way his eyes narrow as he tries to decipher if I am telling the truth reminds me of the way Dylan would question me if I was even a few minutes late home. My mind wanders briefly as I contemplate why Dylan has been so present in my thoughts lately, when I've worked so hard to leave him in the past. The answer seems obvious – Michael. The similarities are becoming more glaringly obvious. I can hear his breath, he is so close to me – trying to intimidate me.

I take a second to collect myself. He's not Dylan and I'm not scared. Well, at least I shouldn't be. I'm not the one doing anything wrong, and I need to remind him of that.

'What are *you* doing here, Michael?'

His face betrays a distinct note of surprise at my boldness, before he regains control.

'Same as you, we all had a lot to drink last night. It was quite the party. I should thank you for that.'

He's changing the subject. He must know he needs to explain himself more than I do.

'It's fine… anyway, I was just about to call Gwen. Shall I tell her you said hi?' I say sweetly, waving my phone so he can see my finger poised over her name.

'No need, I'm on my way home. Just need to grab some coffees. I'll see you later, Victoria.'

The speed at which he turns and leaves is telling, and just what I expected to happen. He definitely doesn't want Gwen to know he was here. Even so, I am still left with far more questions than answers. That needs to change.

Chapter Eight

Smile For The Camera

Before I can contemplate my next steps my phone rings. It's Becky. Odd she should call today; though I sometimes take clients on a Saturday, no one is booked in.

'Victoria, I'm sorry to call you on your day off.'

'That's fine Becky, are you OK?'

'Yeah, kind of. I'm at the office, just finishing off typing up some notes. Suzie came by.'

My office is a safe space, but Suzie knows she can't just turn up without an appointment.

'I told her you weren't in today but she's distraught.'

I feel a pang of sympathy, I know how lonely she feels.

'You did the right thing calling me. Is there any aggressive behaviour? Are you safe?'

'Oh, I'm fine, she's no harm. I've followed protocol, made her an appointment for tomorrow and given her the crisis line number but…'

'But she's still there?'

'Not exactly. She left and I've locked the door, but she's still sat on the steps crying. I thought you'd want to know.'

The last thing I need is to be thinking about anything other than going back to bed, but she's right. I certainly won't leave Suzie there upset, or Becky worried inside.

'I'm on my way.'

Becky's sigh of relief is a clear indication I need to get there quickly. Even her tone of voice as she says goodbye speaks louder than her words.

It's not long before I turn into Willow Street, its namesake trees dotted along the wide road. Their bare branches concealing some of the familiar triple storey white buildings lining the pavements – a hive of doctors, dentists and other private practices like mine.

My heart sinks when I see Suzie. Her shrouded silhouette is easy to see against my block steps, gently rocking as she bites at her fingernails. She looks so small, so vulnerable. She doesn't even notice me approaching.

'Suzie, is that you?'

Raising her head, she blinks slowly through the tears.

'Victoria? She said you weren't here today.' Her voice raspy and cracking as she throws a bitter look at the door.

'Becky's right Suzie, it's my day off today but I left my laptop here by accident. That's the only reason I've come in.'

I explain carefully why Suzie being here without an appointment is not appropriate, but ultimately offer her ten minutes inside, just to get a tissue and collect her thoughts. After all, I know all too well that sometimes even a few minutes of kindness can mean the world to someone whose trust has been destroyed by the person they love most.

Even as I'm guiding Suzie inside, pretending not to notice the perplexed look on Becky's face, I know the decision to let her in isn't the correct one. Most therapists' rulebooks would say as much. This won't help Suzie to set healthy boundaries, and perhaps more worryingly, it says I have a problem setting them myself. Since this drama with Gwen's engagement began, I've been thinking about Dylan more and more. From noticing similarities between Dylan and Michael, together with hearing Suzie's pain, the progress I had been making in my personal life is slipping into reverse. Now it seems, so is my professional life. I can feel my determination to uncover Michael's misdeeds – real or imagined – is fast escalating into a fixation, and I know it's not good for me. Especially now I am experiencing flashbacks about Dylan – I dread to think how far this could set me back if I'm not careful.

When Suzie leaves, I feel a sense of panic. I've always taken comfort from knowing whatever life has thrown at me, my therapeutic work has given me the tools to cope. But right now, I can help others, if I'm no longer able to help myself?

As soon as I get home that afternoon, I toss my discarded clothes in the overflowing laundry basket before slipping into my pyjamas. Isaac's tie is still lying where he left it, on the floor next to my bed. Was it really only this morning he was here? I flop back onto my pillow. Visions of he and I eagerly kissing flood my mind. The feel of his lips on my neck as I ran my hands down his back bring a smile to my face.

The image quickly disperses as I recall barely speaking to him as I escorted him out of my house this morning. I pull a pillow over my face in embarrassment, a wave of guilt rushing through me for treating him so poorly. I'll have to text him and apologise soon, but first I'll ring Gwen, now I finally have the chance. It goes straight through to voicemail. Picturing the aggressive way in which Michael grabbed that woman, I feel nauseous. Who's to say he hasn't done something similar to Gwen? I'm at the point of dashing outside to drive around to her house, still in my pyjamas, when I remind myself – for the umpteenth time – that Michael isn't Dylan.

At last my phone lights up, and the sense of relief is huge.

Just in the middle of something - will call soon. Xx

That isn't the response I wanted but at least it's a response. What follows next is hours of uncomfortable silence. The next couple of calls I make are sent straight to voicemail again.

She only replies with:

I'll call soon. xx

It's getting late and she still hasn't. Resigning myself to an evening waiting by the phone, I decide to keep myself busy. Until she tells me otherwise, or I find out who the pretty brunette is, I owe it to Gwen to go on helping her to plan this wedding, which is only a couple of months away now – maybe. So I sit down in my study and open up Ourweddingpix.co.uk to see what pictures everyone has uploaded from last night.

The first photo is a group shot of the groomsmen before they started drinking, with Isaac in the middle. I groan – why did the first picture have to include him? I can't keep avoiding it, I need to at least text him. I fire off a message before I can change my mind.

Sorry about this morning - hell of a hangover.

I throw my phone onto my desk face down, to stop myself watching for his reply. My stomach is beginning to rumble, so I wander off to the kitchen. On opening the fridge I am met with the familiar sight of mostly bare shelves. The bag of salad on the bottom has started to expand, its contents browning and slightly watery. The fruit doesn't look much better. The pizza gives me some hope but on checking the label, it's past it's sell-by date by more than just a few days. Takeaway it is, I guess – again.

I chomp on a bag of crisps whilst I order, occasionally wiping the salt from my fingers on my pyjama bottoms, to stop my phone screen from blurring. Happily, the Chef's Kitchen has saved my usual order, so I don't have to waste time flicking through the menu. Delivery in forty-five minutes – that might leave me enough time to finish looking through the photos. Part of me is comforted by the thought they might prove there were some good parts to that evening. Perhaps there will be some happy memories to share with the rowdy guests, no matter how it ended.

The group photos are actually pretty good, although some of the selfies are of foreheads and chins – those are comically awful. There are close-ups of the food, and a beautiful picture of Gwen and Michael holding each other on the dance floor. This must be the one Jessica took. I feel at odds looking at it: I was there, I saw this moment and it felt so real. So intimate. I wish Gwen would call me, just to let me know she's alright. I pick up my phone to text her again, as I crunch on another crisp. This time, to my surprise she calls me back straight away.

'I'm sorry…' she says.

Over the next few minutes Gwen pours her heart out about how *completely fine* everything is. Michael has *tiny* nerves about the wedding because he didn't feel good enough for her, but now they have talked and cried together, they've sorted *everything* out.

'We're truly made for each other Vic!'

I'm not sure who she is trying to reassure, me or herself. *Nerves*? So that's how he played down his awkwardness at Isaac's question about secrets. I guess this means I'm meant to find him endearing? Someone overwhelmed by his own insecurities? I want to believe it almost as much as Gwen does. Yet I know where he was today. I know his mystery woman was there at the party too. I know how he reacted to her both times, and to seeing me at the park. None of that can be explained truthfully as pre-wedding jitters. No, sad as I am to admit it, I'm almost certain he is having an affair.

Maybe this other woman wants to tell Gwen, spoil the wedding? Or maybe she wants him to leave Gwen.

It is far too soon for me to tell Gwen about this though; there were too many questions left unanswered. I need proof if I want her to truly believe me when Michael tries to weasel his way out of a confession – clearly he has a way with words. I've no doubt he could explain away the little I've already seen.

The doorbell ringing with my food delivery is the perfect excuse to end my call with Gwen – I don't want to hear any more about Michael's lies.

I grab a plate and fork from the dishwasher and traipse back to the study to flick through the photos as I pick at my chicken chow mein, almost spitting out my noodles laughing when I get to the "Gangnam Style" pictures. The look of pure joy on the guests' faces is brilliant, and Samira is clearly throwing herself around in the opposite direction to everyone else, which is just so her!

Picture after picture of smiley faces, some posed but some natural, capturing the happy occasion. Then I flick back to the picture Jessica took of Gwen and Michael dancing, and my heart sinks. She looks so confident wrapped in his arms, and he looks at her like there is no one else in the room. I know the fears she had about him before the party even began, let alone the doubts she had by the end of the party, but now she expects me to believe that all of her worries were unfounded. That they really are the joyful couple in this photo?

I reach for my phone, scrolling to my stolen snapshot of Michael and the mystery brunette, and upload the image to the computer so I can see it on the bigger screen. I fixate on her dark features and how intensely she is glaring at him. Yet no matter how long I stare at it, the picture offers me no clues as to how I can find her.

Frustrated, I minimise the picture and start sorting the others into folders, occasionally selecting one to be printed and displayed at the wedding, as Gwen has asked. Click, click, click – going at such a pace I nearly miss it. There, just at the right-hand side of one of photos. I put down my fork and move closer to the screen. It must have been early in the evening, before the end of the meal.

The picture shows the groomsmen, maybe-Connor, and the taller blond one who was quite shy, outside the restaurant, having a smoke. That's not what caught my eye though. Behind them, just visible through the window, there is a figure – a woman – seemingly holding a card from my icebreaker game, and a pen. At first I struggle to understand what I'm looking at – who is she and what is she doing? The more I try to zoom in, the blurrier the image gets.

Then it dawns on me. I scramble once again for that picture on my phone and hold it up next to the screen. The face may have been pixelated on the computer but there is no doubt it is her – same clothes, same hair. Michael's mystery woman was at the party longer than I had realised. She was snooping in my question box long before anyone else opened it. It must have been her who changed the question, not Isaac. *Do you have any secrets from one another*?

It all seems clear now – the secret she wants Michael to admit to is about her. That certainly links to what she was saying in the hallway. *Does your bride-to-be know the truth?*

She must have been planning to announce their relationship at the party. I flop back into my chair, trying to take it all in. I click through the rest of the photos, looking for more proof, and find her in a handful more. In each she is watching, waiting, on the periphery. Dressed so plainly she could have blended in with the staff without drawing any attention, which she evidently managed – the rest of the party appears clueless to her presence, myself included. I wonder if Gwen knows her. If Michael has already manipulated her into thinking this woman was a legitimate guest. Or if Gwen, like the others, never realised she was there at all.

The loud ring of the doorbell interrupts my whirring thoughts, and I'm relieved to get out of the study. I need a break from these pictures. Lack of sleep, combined with last night's alcohol intake, hasn't helped with the growing pain behind my eyes. Failing to look through the glass panels as I open the door, I almost fall backwards at the sight that greets me.

'Surprise!' Michael says cheerfully, holding an expensively tied bunch of lilies. 'Can I come in?'

I'm lost for words. He's never been to my home without Gwen before, let alone uninvited. Why is he here – alone, with me?

Chapter Nine

Picture-perfect

His presence shocks me into silence, but I'm immediately annoyed with myself for letting him in. His chatter is overflowing with enthusiasm, in complete contrast to his demeanour in the park earlier. I wonder if this unpredictability in his behaviour is deliberate, a ploy to stop me getting too close to understanding his true nature, whatever that is. As he follows me to the kitchen, I'm suddenly conscious I am wearing my pyjamas.

'Help yourself to tea or coffee. I'll just go and get dressed,' I say, taking the flowers from him and resting them on the counter.

He doesn't stop talking as I dash upstairs, his deep voice reverberating effortlessly through the house.

'I just wanted to thank you for the party. Sorry I was so miserable at the park, that hangover was a killer.'

There is a clatter as he turns on the kettle, and opens and closes several cupboards, probably looking for a mug. As he goes on making small talk, I try my best to oblige, shouting back downstairs as I squeeze into a pair of jeans, nearly losing my balance when I'm jumping on the spot to slide into them, before dragging a brush through my knotted, windblown hair.

Rushing back down the stairs in my jeans and hoodie, I nearly miss a tread in my haste, but he isn't in the kitchen. I spin round to see if he's made his way to the living room, but with a jolt I hear where his voice is coming from – my study. I rush in and see he's making himself at home at my desk, in front of my computer.

My eyes dart across my screen and desk, trying to recall if I'd closed or minimised the pictures of the brunette. Were they still zoomed in on her?

'I hope you don't mind, I noticed these are from the party?'

He doesn't take his eyes off the screen, casually clicking the mouse. What can I say? That I don't want him poking around my desk as I'm busy trying to find proof of his infidelity? I slyly retrieve my phone before he can look down at it and follow his gaze, still staring at the monitor. That's when I notice the tiny tab at the bottom. The tab, that if he clicks, will show him the picture of the mystery brunette. The one I took in secret. I can't let him open it. Unless of course he already has?

'Yes,' I mutter, 'some of them are great. I'll sort through them and send you the link to the completed album.'

I try to casually take the mouse from him, but he relaxes back into the chair, apparently enjoying himself. I examine his face, my heart racing. Is his pleasure sincere, or is he playing with me? There's that tightness in my chest again. I can hear my blood pulsating in my ears.

'Oh come on, some of the bad ones are the best!' he says with a low chuckle, tilting the screen to show me a photo of the groomsmen baring their behinds.

My heartbeat returns to a slightly more normal rhythm, but all the while I keep one eye trained on that little tab. He sighs proudly as he looks up from one of the many photos of him and Gwen together.

'She'll love this one.'

His smile is broad and genuine – isn't it? I sit on the edge of the desk, watching his every reaction. Is he here to prove to me that he loves Gwen? I watch one smile after another, with the occasional laugh. Then he stops. His face falls just a little, and he casually tilts the screen out of my view – but by the time I've leaned forward to get a clear view again, he's clicked away from whatever he was looking at. Shit. What did he see?

'It's a shame the night ended as it did.' His eyes are now firmly on me, his smile vanished.

'I never wrote that question.'

I don't know why I felt the need to say it. To show him I'm not responsible for ruining the evening? Or maybe to see if he knows who really was behind it? Not that he would let on if he did.

'It doesn't matter about that silly game now – we just need to remember the fantastic job you did with the party, and all you are doing for the wedding. Nothing else matters.'

I can feel the anxiety rising in my throat. I want to say something, tell him I know about his secret meetings, ask him about that woman. Maybe tell him I'll go to Gwen, but the words won't come out. Standing up, he towers over me.

The image of how he grabbed that woman in the park flashes through my mind and a shudder rips through me.

'Please, Vic. I want us to be on the same page. I had a minor case of cold feet. It's ok though, Gwen and I have talked and we're stronger than ever.'

I wonder what he's trying to prove by saying all of this to me. Is he testing me, to gauge my reaction? Surely he knows Gwen will have told me about his alleged anxieties herself. My heart is thudding again and it dawns on me how vulnerable I am right now, alone in the house with a man I do not trust at all.

As if reading my mind, he purrs, 'Gwen trusts you. She values your opinion. I know she will come to you for advice and support, and I really hope that we can still rely on you, with the wedding and… everything. Can we?'

'Rely on me for what?'

Michael closes in on me. His body is now inches from mine and still moving nearer. Just a little too slowly, staring at me a little too intensely. I slide off the desk and back away from him until I'm up against the bookshelf.

Leaning close to my ear, in almost a whisper, he says, 'Can you support us with this wedding? She means everything to me, Vic. I won't let anyone interfere with that.'

I don't know how to respond. I can barely breathe. My whole body is tense, anticipating his next move. That's when I see it, the tiniest flicker of a smile in his eyes. He's enjoying seeing me afraid. Panicking, I push past him and out of the study, telling him through the doorway.

'It's getting late, you should be going now.'

I can hear the tremble in my voice and judging from his smirk, so can he.

'Look Vic, Gwen's told me all about your ex. How sometimes you get confused between me and him. But you can't hate me just because I remind you of your own poor taste.'

My jaw clenches. The fact Gwen told him about Dylan stings. Those conversations were between us. More disturbing, though, is how quickly Michael has flitted from warm and friendly, to casual cruelty. Dylan had me utterly convinced he was a decent guy too – until he wasn't.

Michael doesn't wait for a response. Striding straight up to me again, he kisses me on the cheek, and walks out of the front door. Pausing, it seems, to enjoy the emotion welling in my eyes.

Hours later, as I lie awake in bed, I roll onto my side and, in the darkness, I can just about make out the picture of me and Gwen on my dressing table. We're posing during some random night out, holding our cocktails towards the camera. I remember us laughing as the picture was taken, thanks to Gwen spilling her drink. We were happy.

I flick on the bedside lamp so I can look at the framed memory a little better. We've been friends for three years and in that time, Gwen has rebuilt me from the person I was when I first moved here, fragile from a painful breakup. There were times back then I felt like never getting out of bed, let alone building a successful client base and social circle. Will she let me return the favour when she finds out about Michael? Michael's not who she believes him to be, and she needs to know. Tears prick my eyes at the thought of the pain that's in store for her. I squeeze them shut to try and rid myself of the images of her crying in the bathroom last night, and Michael sneering at me earlier. It's a relief when the ping of my phone forces me to open them again.

It's OK. Talk soon?

Isaac. I'm hardly in the right mind-set to have a conversation right now but I have been less than kind to him so far and that's simply not fair. I shouldn't make him wait for a response.

Talk tomorrow? Going to catch up on some sleep tonight.

I look forward to it. Nite. x

I slide my phone back on the bedside cabinet and without even turning off the light, I let the exhaustion take over.

Chapter Ten

Bridezilla

The next day, 2 months to the wedding

I have so much to do today but I can't bring myself to get up. I want to just lie star-shaped in bed. All I can think about is Michael's visit yesterday – his jokes, his threats – and I don't know what to make of it all. The creak of my gate shakes me to my senses, followed closely by the clatter of heels on my path and the doorbell. I trudge downstairs and see Gwen's silhouette in the misted glass panels. I'm still too tired to think straight. What am I going to say to her?

'Come on Vic, I'm going to drop all this stuff!' she yells through the door.

Patience has never been her strong suit, and she presses the doorbell repeatedly until I finally open the door. She is already halfway down the hallway to the living room before I can even utter a greeting.

'I've brought breakfast!'

She has a cup holder with two takeout coffees in one hand, a bulging paper carrier bag in her other hand, and that dreaded wedding folder tucked under her arm. Every time that thing makes an appearance, my to-do list gets longer.

I follow Gwen meekly into the living room and swipe the leftover snack packets and mail from the coffee table so she can set our breakfast down. Gwen daintily picks up a jumper I'd left splayed across an armchair, folds it and places it neatly over the arm before sitting down.

'I really wish you'd get a cleaner Vic. This house is too big for you to keep on top of by yourself.'

I know she's right, even if there never seems to be the time to find a housekeeper, let alone do the housework myself. I look at her, sipping at her coffee in blissful ignorance to what Michael has been doing. I know if I don't talk to her about it straight away I'm going to lose the courage.

'Gwen, can we talk?'

'Yes! I have lots to talk to you about! Here, grab your coffee.'

I take the bag too, hoping for some kind of baked goods but no, it's fruit salad. The disappointment on my face must be clear because she recites Jessica's mantra.

'Don't forget the wedding diet!'

I roll my eyes and slide back into my seat on the sofa, savouring the first burning sip of coffee, whilst Gwen nibbles on some blueberries before opening that bloody folder on her lap.

'So, I've had some more thoughts about–'

'Gwen – stop…'

I can't listen to her talk about the wedding. Not after what I saw and felt yesterday. But at the thought of talking to her about that woman and Michael, that familiar squeeze across my chest comes back, and that's even worse. She looks up from her notes, her expression puzzled.

'What? I haven't even started yet.'

'I saw Michael yesterday, at the park.'

'OK?' Her eyes narrow, as she waits for me to get to the point.

'He was talking to someone, a–'

'Oh, that must have been his former client. Apparently she's a bit of a nightmare. He said it was so awkward seeing her on his walk.' She giggles.

My mouth falls open. Michael has already told her? He must've known I was going to say something and got to Gwen first with this ridiculous story. A dull ache spreads across my temples. No, there is no way what I saw was a professional interaction and it certainly doesn't explain her presence at the party.

'Anyway, I'd really like for the bridesmaids to wear one of these style dresses,' Gwen continues, holding a ripped page from a magazine out to me. I lean forward half-heartedly to take it, as I try to work out my next move. I watch her lips moving and her hands gesticulating towards the folder, but her words sound far away.

'He came here yesterday, Gwen, he–'

'Did he remember the flowers? I told him I'd bring them today, but he really wanted to thank you himself, for the party. Actually, that reminds me, I loved those rose place names, can you–'

I should have guessed that he told her he'd come here. Her absolute willingness to not see through his façade is either naivety or, something I'm all too familiar with, a defence mechanism. Her tunnel vision on herself and this wedding a do-or-die attempt to paper over the cracks in their relationship.

'He was so intense Gwen, like–'

'He really can be, can't he? I love that about him, he's such a passionate person.' She wiggles her eyebrows and winks at me. 'You know what I mean? Anyway…'

There are those wide eyes again. Glistening with romantic hope that he is her happily ever after. Michael has really pulled out all the stops to manipulate her, and outmanoeuvre me. She seems oblivious both to the pained expression on my face, and my desperation to talk about yesterday. It's odd, when we first met her unfailing ability to understand her worth was one of the things I found so inspiring about her. Now that very same trait seems to be stopping her from really reading either Michael or me.

I lift my feet up to hug my knees. This man has my usually astute, intelligent friend wrapped around his little finger. It would be so easy to show Gwen the picture I took at the party, just to sow a seed of doubt in her mind – make her ask questions. Yet as I look at her, eyes sparkling as she imagines the smaller details of the future nuptials, I'm not sure she will see the photo the same way I do. Just like the ones on my computer, it doesn't actually prove anything. I need more evidence for Gwen to really hear me over whatever story he concocts.

'So what do you think, the cream or the ivory napkins?'

She holds up one of each to show me. They're just napkins. Who cares? I fake a smile and point at one of them, meeting her approval.

'Oh and we've decided on the wedding registry. Would you mind sending this site out to everyone?' She hands me a small business card with gold lettering for one of the high end stores in town. 'They have some exquisite crockery and you just have to see the crystal glasses in there. Perfect for when we host our first dinner party as a married couple.'

She claps her hands excitedly at the image. Bloody wedding gift. I hadn't even thought about that. I put the card on the arm of my seat. I'll send this out and do whatever it takes to help Gwen, even if right now that means working through this ridiculously long to-do list. I can appear supportive, whilst I look into Michael and his mystery woman without raising his suspicions.

Gwen's ramblings are starting to sound like a broken record as she sits pointing to a variety of pictures on her phone. I, on the other hand, can't help but replay last night's confrontation.

'Sorry Vic, I know this is a lot. It's just I've got this exhibition coming up at work, and there's so much on my plate – you're such a superstar for helping.'

Exhibition? Gwen's exhibits are the talk of the art world – according to Jessica. Whenever she has a new show opening, she pours all of her energy into making sure they go perfectly, obsessing over every little detail. I can already see she will be torn with having this big event *and* wedding to plan – no doubt my responsibilities will multiply. I'd hate for her business to suffer because I couldn't find the time to help source canapés and candles, but I do wonder if she realises that I have a career too.

'That reminds me, I'd love the hen do to be more of a spa day than anything tacky…'

The bloody hen do. How am I going to get this all done? I keep nodding along, planning to call Samira and Jessica for support as soon as Gwen's released me from this increasingly stressful conversation.

'No problem. Don't worry about the hen do, I'll add looking into spas to my to-do list.'

She heaves a loud sigh of relief, beams at me, then slams her folder shut. 'Right, now that's done with, I think it's about time you tell me what happened at the party.'

I pause, confused. She can't know about the brunette, can she?

'Er… what do you mean?'

'Come now, don't be shy! I hear you didn't leave the party alone.'

It takes me a second longer to understand what she's talking about. *Isaac*.

'What happened?' she persists, leaning forward on the edge of her seat like an excited school girl. I let out a nervous giggle, not really knowing what to say.

'Nothing! Well, nothing much. We drank a lot...'

'And?'

'And what?'

'Did he stay over?' Gwen's eyes are popping with expectation.

'Erm…' I can feel myself blush at the question before Gwen launches a cushion at me.

'Aren't you a dark horse! You're going to see each other again, aren't you? I know he acted the idiot at the party but he's a good guy Vic. Just what you need.' She winks at me with another snicker.

With a start, she looks at her watch and jumps out of her chair to say goodbye. 'Must dash. I don't want to be late for my dress fitting.'

With Gwen gone, I clear the plates and cups from the messy living room, halting at the sight of Michael's flowers, wilting, still on the kitchen counter. I hadn't really looked at them when he came by and I definitely don't want to look at them now either. I open the bin and slide them in, before texting Samira and Jessica to invite them to a video chat, to divvy up our tasks.

I'm glad when they answer the call at the same time. After some quick greetings, I launch straight into the massive to do list. I love that Samira sits clapping when she volunteers to take over choosing the bridesmaid dresses. I'm equally impressed when Jessica volunteers to take on the entire hen party.

'I have just the spa in mind – naturally we'll have to have private hire,' Jessica offers.

I want to roll my eyes, God forbid we mix with the actual public, but Gwen will love it and I'm just appreciative that Jessica has taken on the job. I feel like a weight is lifted when the call finishes.

With the larger wedding tasks sorted, I can get on with the most important task, finding out what Michael is hiding. I have so little to go on but the mystery brunette's words still ring in my ears, *...until they know about you – the real you.*

With no other options I turn to Google to see if I can find out anything about Michael that could be of help. Typing in

'Michael Jameson', the search returns over 100,000 results. What did I expect?

Flicking through the images of random strangers, at last I spot the Michael I am looking for. A professional headshot, wearing his characteristic shirt and tie, which, when I click, takes me to his company page. No matter how far I scroll to find other photos or information about him, there's nothing. I know he dislikes social media, but this is just odd.

Gwen, by contrast, is well documented online: there are articles about her gallery, some photos she must have left public from her Facebook and Instagram accounts, and even details of a charity event she attended out of town last year. So why is it so hard to find something – anything, relating to Michael?

Accepting that I've hit a brick wall, I sink back into my chair. Then I have an idea. There is one person I can talk to who knows him well, Isaac – but I know this will potentially open a can of worms. I did tell him we'd speak today but right now I don't have the time or energy to want to get into what happened that night. I take my time to compile a message that won't come across as romantic, despite the very pleasant memories I have of us kissing. I just want information.

> Can we meet? We need to talk about the wedding.

Chapter Eleven

Popping The Question

1 month, 3 weeks to the wedding.

I've found nothing on Michael so far so I'm glad to be busy right now. Any distraction from thinking about him is welcome – even the barrage of e-mails and texts I've been getting from Gwen's mother. Gwen is her only daughter after all. She's determined that no expense or tradition will be spared – and certainly none of the maid of honour's time.

I can't help but roll my eyes when my phone buzzes beside me on the desk. I look, half expecting another random request from a guest about vegan menu options, or specific rooms for their overnight stay. I had hoped to gather my thoughts between appointments, but these messages cannot be ignored. I am pleasantly surprised to see it's actually a text from Isaac. I've been waiting for his reply all day but now it's here, I'm not sure what to do.

Sorry I took so long to reply. Work's been crazy. Fancy dinner? X

I sit up, alert, in my chair. Why dinner? Dinner is long and intimate, for people who can relax in each other's company – I can't imagine how awkward that would be. No, a drink, somewhere busy and casual is a much better idea. This isn't a date. I want, no, I *need* information from him. If we're only going for a drink, if I'm not getting anything useful from him, I can just leave at any time.

Let's start with a drink?

Isaac could be the person to shed some light on the mystery woman issue. As the best man, he must know Michael pretty well. Having said that there's no denying that at some point we will need to clear the air over what happened between us too – I shudder at the thought. I can't remember the last time I was that drunk, let alone woke up next to a man I barely know. Or woke up with anyone for that matter. I look down and see those three dots, appearing and disappearing – he clearly cannot decide what to say, which strangely makes me a little nervous. Dare I say excited? Eventually he responds.

I'd prefer to buy you dinner but a drink would be great for now. x

Before I can reply my office line rings. As I swiftly take notes from a call with a new client, I keep looking over at Isaac's text. Hanging up the line, I reply.

Same place as the party. 7 p.m?

I contemplate what questions I should ask. I'll start carefully, with a subtle approach – see what information Isaac will give me when he doesn't know what my motives are. I can't imagine he'll be too forthcoming in providing me with any potentially damning information about his best friend. I lean back in my chair, enjoying the tea Becky has just brought in. His confirmation is almost immediate. He must be keen. I just have to make sure that he realises that tonight I will be going home alone.

The afternoon flies by in a blur of calls, client meetings and wedding related messages. By the time my last appointment ends I am absolutely exhausted. If I wasn't so desperate to find something out about Michael, I'd cancel my drinks with Isaac. I stare at the mirror in the ladies' room and my tired reflection looks back. I look as lifeless as I feel. I throw some water on my face to try to refresh my drained complexion, to no avail. What does it matter anyway?

It's raining outside, and I'm soaked by the time I slide into the taxi. I arrive at the bar at 7 p.m. on the dot. The atmosphere as I walk in could not be more different from the party. The restaurant is strewn with small, intimate tables – mostly occupied by couples – and the delicate jazz music playing in the background a far cry from the party tunes Samira had orchestrated. I move through to the bar, unravelling my scarf, and catch sight of Isaac already perched on a stool at the counter. He hasn't seen me yet, and I'm hit with a sense of deja vu – is that the exact same place he was sitting the last time we were here together? My palms are already sweaty as the memories flash through my mind, of us laughing and drinking and... How badly he behaved during the meal. What a mess of a night.

As I move closer, I take in the way he's swirling the ice cubes around his empty glass – he must have got here early – which almost makes him look nervous. He politely nods and smiles at the barmen as he places a fresh drink in front of him. Whisky? Not again! There is no way I'll be drinking that tonight.

As I notice the way the light touches his tightly curled hair and deep brown skin, more fragments of memory come back to me. How his hair felt between my fingers and the warmth of his breath. When he turns and sees me, as if in slow motion, his face lights up with a welcoming smile. Broad and genuine. I don't know how long I've been stood here staring but as he stands to greet me, I'm spurred on towards him. I can feel myself flush at being caught watching him. I try to use my fingers to comb my straggly, wet hair, tucking it behind my ears, anything to try and look a little more attractive. I wish I'd worn heels and maybe put on a little lipstick, suddenly aware of how sloppy I look in comparison to the effort he has made. I can't help but gawk at his crisp blue shirt, complementing his deep, dark eyes.

What follows can only be described as the most awkward hug, handshake, single cheek kiss I have ever experienced. Isaac taking a few moments too long to release me from his grasp, even though he's trapped what was my outstretched hand against his chest. A very firm chest at that. I'll admit, I also took a little too long to step back away from him. Yet as we both giggle in embarrassment, I feel more at ease with him.

'First I want to apologise,' he puts simply. 'The other night, my behaviour at the meal.'

I'm taken aback by his candour. I had not expected him to be the one apologising. Not after the way I treated him the last time we met. I've been so focused on gearing up to ask him about Michael and that woman, that I'm not at all prepared for this disarming warmth of his. I shake my head and stare at the bar instead of into his gaze. I can't allow myself to waste this opportunity. I have to stay on track and ask my questions.

'Maybe we should grab a seat?' I suggest.

He pulls out the stool next to his for me, still radiating charm. This must have been the side to him that I saw when we were sat drinking together at the party. Catching me staring at him again, he chuckles bashfully and shifts in his seat. It's endearing, and not at all arrogant – is this the real him? Was the party animal I met at the party just an act? He waits for the bartender to bring my drink, before clearing his throat.

'So, shall I start then?' he asks and then does, without allowing me time to actually answer. 'I really enjoyed myself with you. You know, after I made a fool of myself during the meal.'

'Yes, you certainly were… a character.'

'Yeah, I'm sorry about that. A terrible mix of an open bar and a particularly pretty woman I was trying to impress.'

I feel butterflies with the intensity of his gaze, averting my own so he hopefully won't notice me blushing. Taking a deep breath, I feel I have to explain my own behaviour too.

'I'm sorry too, for you know, what happened in the morning. It's just I wasn't expecting you to be there and at first I couldn't remember–'

'You don't have to apologise at all,' he interrupts, letting his hand casually stroke mine on the bar. The warmth of his skin lingers on mine but this isn't why I asked him for a drink so I slip my hand away from his. 'But you do remember everything now?'

'Pretty much. Kind of.' I shrug, sipping my drink, trying not to show any shakiness in my voice as I recall us being all over each other in the taxi to my place.

'As I told you, there was kissing. A lot of kissing.' He chuckles. 'But do you remember me saying that I could wait until we were sober to take things further?'

I shake my head.

'You said I could stay anyway as the taxi had gone and it was late. Then we fell asleep. That's it. I would never take advantage of you – ever.' He lowers his voice further, leaning towards me. 'Not unless you want me to!' He sniggers, clearly amusing himself.

I laugh too. It's been a long time since I've been attracted to someone – but why the best man, of all people – why a friend of Michael's? I try to reorganise my thoughts, remind myself what I need from Isaac tonight but why does he have to smell so good? The fragrance the same as the one that lingered on my sheets.

'So how about a fresh start tonight?' he offers, the corners of his mouth lifting into a devilish grin.

I start to wonder what tonight could be the start of. What it would mean to let someone into my life again, but the thought of becoming romantically entangled with anyone fills me with dread. After everything I went through with Dylan, I just don't feel ready. I can see though, I will have to be careful and work hard to resist Isaac's charms.

As the evening flies by, the conversation flows almost as freely as the drinks and bar snacks. Through our conversations, I have learned very little about Isaac and Michael: they have only been friends for a couple of years, since Isaac became his accounts manager. Every time I try to dig deeper, casually trying to steer the conversation towards Michael's ex-girlfriends or other topics that might offer me some insight as to who the mystery woman is, Isaac swerves the conversation back to me. It unnerves me a little. How he can so effortlessly control the conversation? How is it the information he shares seems plentiful, but is still very much on his own terms? I wonder whether this deliberate evasion of my questions is modesty, or if he's hiding something. I watch him, looking for any sign that he is uncomfortable, but he seems relaxed in my company. Now and then he's gently touching my arm or hand, laughing deeply. It feels like we are crossing the boundary to more than a little flirting. Do I pull back, collect myself?

'You ask a lot of questions you know, about me and about Michael,' he smirks.

I look down at the glass in my hand, suddenly aware that I have been staring at him a little too intently. 'Sorry, occupational hazard.'

'Ah yes, the therapist. Tell me, what deep insights have you made about me tonight?'

I can tell he is playing with me, fishing for compliments. Leaning close enough to me that even his smile feels intimate.

Before I can respond, his eyes narrow. 'Hmm… your silence begs the question… which of us are you more interested in? Me, I hope? Surely not Michael?' He laughs, but all I can do is stutter in response. Inside I am kicking myself for being taken by surprise. 'If I were the suspicious kind, I'd think this whole meeting was a ploy for you to find out more about him, and not about me at all.'

How can I respond to that and sound genuine?

'Isaac, I–'

'Relax! I'm joking,' he laughs.

There is, perhaps, a few seconds' delay before I laugh nervously with him. I can't tell if he really is joking. Maybe I haven't been as subtle as I should have been. Should I be bothered by this? Surely, I shouldn't care that he might think I'm not interested in him? There is a small part of me that doesn't want to ruin this though – someone I find interesting and attractive wants to get to know me. Surely there can't be any harm with enjoying the attention?

Chapter Twelve

The Best Man

I let him keep steering the conversation away from Michael and the wedding. My suspicions as to his motives for doing so start to fade. He has such warmth in his eyes when he speaks, I know I should be careful, but I feel… something. A feeling I haven't felt in a long time. When he holds my gaze for a second too long, it's exciting. The questions I have about Michael are still scratching at the back of my mind though – if I could just find the right time to ask them, between the many questions Isaac is asking me.

'Anyway, there's something else I need to know,' he says, resting his elbow on the bar so he's facing me directly, even closer than before. 'How is it someone like you is single?'

Someone like me? What does he mean – plain, boring? I scrunch my face up, which from his smile, clearly entertains him. He responds for me, as if reading my mind.

'Attractive, intelligent, completely unaware of how interesting you are, it seems.'

I shuffle in my seat. His smile softens.

'Sorry, that was a little forward, wasn't it? You are though…'

I am lost for words, embarrassed and flustered. This barrage of compliments begins to ring alarm bells. Once upon a time I fell for these kinds of sweet nothings. I was younger and more naïve then. I'd hadn't heard of 'love-bombing' until it was too late. Having survived it, I now realise such affections are just words, and words can hide a person's true nature.

'An enigma,' he continued. 'You're nervous and confident, gorgeous but modest. So, no boyfriend?'

I look down at my drink. 'No, not for a while. Bad break up,' is all I want to offer.

Something shifts in Isaac's gaze. Is that sympathy, or pity?

'I'm a good listener if you want to talk about it?'

I really don't, but I have to say something to stop him persevering. 'Not much to tell. We were in love until we weren't.'

'Is he still around?'

I gulp my drink before shaking my head. There's an uncomfortable silence now.

'Well, he's a fool for letting someone like you go.'

His words pain me. If only he knew. Thankfully the clatter of the bartender clearing our empty glasses gives me the distraction I need to compose myself. Isaac cracks a joke, then another joke, and another, and before I know it, the bar is starting to empty. We must have been here for hours.

'It looks like it's nearly closing time… shall we move on somewhere else?' he asks.

I look at him and the wry smile on his face. He reaches forward, pushing the loose strands of hair from my face, and I find myself hypnotised by it. As he brings his face closer to mine, it dawns on me that I have completely lost sight of why I came tonight. I can't get carried away like this. I have to dig a little deeper about Michael. I lean away from him, forcing him to recoil uncomfortably. I try to sound calm and unassuming but clearly I've had too much to drink to be subtle.

'So, what was that secret Michael didn't want to spill at the party? Do you know?' I blurt.

Isaac eyes me suspiciously, clearly unsure whether to laugh or frown so does a mix of both. 'I don't know what you… wait, you mean the game, that card I read out?'

I nod. 'His reaction to that question was a little odd, don't you think? Why wouldn't he just say "no"? Why did he pause like that?'

He sits back, taking in every inch of my now strained facial expression. I guess he cannot see how we've gone from almost kissing to this, but there's no taking my question back now.

'You know I met you here tonight because I wanted to get to know *you*. That's not why you're here though is it? Was I right earlier? Has this all been about Michael?'

He's upset with me, and I deserve it. I avoid his intense gaze – I cannot lose sight of my aim to protect Gwen.

'Ouch… I guess I shouldn't ask questions I don't want the answers to, eh?'

Isaac summons the bartender, throwing down cash to pay off the tab. I want to speak, to say something, but I can't deny any of it.

'I'm sorry, I just need to know–'

'If I answer you, will you even believe me?' His tone is serious now, his voice quiet.

I lean towards him, waiting for him to tell me some dark details.

'There's no big secret. Michael is just flustered with the wedding plans. Didn't help that I think I'd annoyed him by drinking too much. He probably thought I was ruining your meal.'

I look at Isaac intently. Everything about his body language shows him to be as open as he has been all night, but there has to be more to this, surely?

'Why did you even write that question?' he asks.

'What? I didn't!' I protest.

His furrowed brow is genuine too.

'I did write most of them but not that one.'

Another awkward silence.

'Please tell me that you haven't been waiting all evening to ask me about this?' he says.

I can see he is hurt, and my silence speaks volumes as he becomes fixated on swirling the remnants of his drink.

'I'm just looking out for Gwen, if there's something she needs to know–'

He rests his hand on mine and looks deep into my eyes. 'If you believe nothing else, believe he loves Gwen. Believe he wants to spend the rest of his life with her... even if they've only known each other for five minutes.'

'What?' Do I sense a change in tone?

'I know she's your best friend – although you two are a weird mix. It's just…' He pauses to sip his drink. 'They've been dating for such a short period of time, don't you think it's too soon for them to be getting married?'

He is having doubts about Gwen? She isn't the one hiding things, the one with the strange, menacing vibe. And what does a 'weird mix' mean? Before I can articulate a reply, the last orders' bell rings loudly next to us.

Isaac sighs and sets down his glass. 'Look, I don't mean to offend, but he just seems to throw money at her and–'

'Are you implying she's a gold digger?'

'Shit, no–'

'She has her own money, she has her own business, and at least *she's* not sneaking around with anyone else.'

Well that's the final nail in this evening's coffin.

Isaac's wide-eyed, open-mouthed expression is a clear indication that I should've kept that last comment to myself.

'What? He wouldn't.' He is instantly defensive.

'I know what I've seen. As for Michael, who even is he? He just appears in Gwen's life out of nowhere, no past, nothing.'

I can feel both our hackles rising. I'm not sure he could be leaning any further away from me. Part of me wants to stop, go back to when he was moving the hair from my face, his warm hand against my skin… That moment has passed. There is no going back.

'I'm not sure what you want to hear Victoria, but I have nothing else to tell you. If you feel there is more to this, maybe you should speak to Michael yourself.'

I tense up at that suggestion. He is right, but I don't have the courage to do that just yet. I simply nod.

He sighs again and gulps the last of his drink. Standing, he reaches for my coat to help me put it on, no longer looking me in the eye. As soon as we are outside he hails me a cab, which arrives frustratingly quickly. We stand facing one another but I don't know what to say, unsure of what I even want from him – do I want him to *like* me? Am I ready for this? My conflicted emotions must show, because Isaac exhales loudly, then steps closer. Stroking my face gently, he leans in to kiss me delicately on the lips.

'For what it's worth,' he says, 'I'd like to see you again. *If* that's what you want too?'

My pulse quickens at his words: he'd like to see me again. The way his eyes hold mine is electrifying.

He moves back and opens the taxi door for me, and as I climb in, he pauses. 'You've clearly got doubts, but Michael's a good guy, Victoria. Are you sure Gwen is right for him?' He slams the door, and waves me off.

As soon as I get home, I kick off my shoes and undress, throwing my clothes onto my bedroom floor. I can't help but cringe at how the night has ended. Part of me hopes Isaac will call or text straight away, invite me out again, but I know I'm not ready to pursue anything with anyone, let alone Michael's best friend. Besides, what he said about Gwen threw me. It has never dawned on me that anyone would question her motives for marrying Michael. I must have really annoyed him to prompt an accusation like that.

Catching my reflection in the bedroom mirror, I cringe again. How can someone who looks like Isaac find such a plain mess, attractive? I flop onto the bed, and sigh into my pillow at how badly I handled the situation. Even worse than my appalling manners and total lack of charm, is the fact that I still have no idea who the mystery woman is.

At least there's one thing I am sure of. Isaac isn't any more supportive of this wedding than I am. That may be useful.

Chapter Thirteen

It's a Date

6 weeks until the wedding

As I mindlessly scroll through my social media feeds at work, waiting for my next appointment, I can't help but groan. More photos of perfect abs and hundreds of ways to prepare cauliflower. Who decided cauliflower is a thing now anyway? I poke at my less than toned stomach, hearing Jessica's judgemental harping about pre-wedding diet this and workouts that. It's a relief when Becky knocks on the door, warning me Suzie has arrived.

I am expecting Suzie to come in shoulders slumped, eyes down, chewing on her sleeve, as usual. So when she makes eye contact as she greets me, her hair brushed and her clothes tidy, I'm a little taken aback. As she slides into her usual spot on the sofa, she even manages a smile. It's small, barely there, but it's a sign of confidence worth celebrating. This is huge for her.

'You're looking well, Suzie!'

'Yeah, I'm feeling… good.'

Interesting that 'good' is the word she chooses. It's perhaps the only positive affirmation I'd ever heard her say. She still sits quietly to begin with, which allows me time to take in how her differently she's presenting herself. Even her skin is cleaner, her eyes a little brighter. Small but significant changes. I want to make a note of them right away, so I excuse myself briefly to grab my notebook from where I left it earlier, on Becky's desk.

'Sorry Suzie, I won't be a sec…'

She nods, with another smile as she relaxes into the seat. By the time I return to the room she is stood up, looking out of the window.

'So, what's been happening since I saw you last, Suzie?'

Her eyes meet mine, and there's joy behind them. 'I made a friend.'

Ushering her to sit down again, I think back to how her ex had left her feeling. So isolated and unworthy of friendship that to connect with someone has been an important goal of hers.

'Would you like to talk to me about them?'

She shifts a little in the chair. 'There's not a lot to tell you yet, but it's been nice to have someone to text and meet for coffee, you know?'

Even her shrug makes her seem calmer, more relaxed.

'Did you meet at one of the groups we discussed?'

'No, just in passing…'

She is being deliberately vague, but that's not uncommon for Suzie. I know not to push too much when she is like this; I want to model what respecting her boundaries should look like. So, we spend some time affirming the importance of building on this positive step she's made in her recovery. That she shouldn't attach too much importance to one particular person, and should see this as proof that she is able to forge new connections – that she is worthy of friendship.

Eventually she opens up enough to tell me about a trip she made with her new friend to a local coffee shop. As she speaks, she is animated, her hands gesticulating rather than folded across herself. I sit back and listen intently, taking in the light in her eyes that has been painfully absent, until our time runs out.

'I look forward to seeing you again next week, same time OK for you?'

She nods before opening the door for herself and making her own way to confirm her next appointment. Even Becky's eyebrows arch at the change to our usual routine of almost prying Suzie away from me. It is astounding the difference a friend can make in someone's life. The impact loneliness has on us isn't one that should be underestimated. Gwen was my breath of fresh air, giving me hope that I mattered when we first met. Perhaps this new friend is that same new lease of life for Suzie. I certainly look forward to hearing more about it in our next session.

I have some time before my next client, and feel the need to get out of the office. The cold breeze wraps around me as soon as I step out onto the street, taking my breath away. I button up my coat, to help stop my teeth chattering as I make my way to the café to grab my usual coffee. I don't have a croissant though – that's progress on the wedding diet at least.

I continue my walk into the park and the gentle breeze whisks up the golden leaves around me and the sun breaks through the clouds, warming my face. It's almost deserted, and the peace and quiet is just what I need. I look up and see a figure in the distance, a morning jogger no doubt. The figure isn't moving though, how strange. There is something unnerving about the unmoving silhouette. I shrug it off – I need to get back to work, my next client will be there soon.

I start to walk back but an uneasy feeling makes me turn around, and the figure is still there – are they watching me? I check to make sure there are other people in the park, but by the time I look back round, the dark shape is gone. I pull my coat a little tighter around me, fear sending a chill across my skin. I remember the days of Dylan watching my every move all too well. I shake my head, reminding myself of the advice I gave Suzie about positive affirmations. It must be the lack of sleep and too much caffeine making me paranoid.

When I get back to the office, I am met with a giddy grin from Becky.

'Gwen stopped by. She left some wedding stuff on your desk, and I put a special delivery in the office for you!'

It isn't unusual for her to accept my deliveries, but the strange way she said it makes my brow furrow. Walking in, I pause. Standing there, running his hands along my book collection, is Isaac. I gently cough, and he spins to look at me with his disarming smile.

'Hi,' is all I can think to say, taken completely by surprise by his visit.

'Are you OK? Am I disturbing you? Your receptionist said you had a little time before your next client.'

'Er… Yes and no. Internally I am kicking myself for my complete inability to form full sentences. He chuckles as he perches himself on my desk in front of me. He knows he is making me nervous. Yes I'm OK, and no, you're not disturbing me.'

I turn to close the door and see Becky, who is still hovering with the same grin.

'Erm… so were you just passing?' I notice that I'm wringing my hands, so I tuck them into my pockets.

'I'd like to say yes, keep it casual, but I can't stop thinking about you.'

I laugh nervously, wishing he wasn't this attractive. His eyes focus on me and I can feel myself blushing. He stands and walks towards me, putting his hands on my waist and I let him pull me gently towards him. I hold my breath as he leans in to kiss me without any hesitation on his part – or mine. I give in, letting myself melt into his embrace. When we part, he makes sure to keep his arms wrapped loosely around me.

'I really am sorry you know. I know what I said about Gwen upset you. I have a habit of talking too much.'

The way he tilts his head slightly to meet my eye gives me goose bumps, but the mention of Gwen brings me crashing back to reality.

'Please, don't apologise… It's alright.'

'In that case, how about we make some plans–'

I have to interrupt. 'Listen, Isaac. Michael really is hiding something. Even if you don't believe it.' It's a little more direct than I had planned, but I've said it now. I feel his grip loosen as he takes a step back from me, sighing. I must admit, that makes my heart sink a little.

'Please. Must we start this again?' He moves to look out of the window onto the street below.

'Yes, I'm sorry but we do. I just need you to listen to me, because you might be the only person who can help me work out what's going on.'

He spins back around to look at me but keeps his distance. Folding his arms. 'Well? Go on then.'

The knock on the door and Becky couldn't have come at a worse time.

'Sorry to interrupt Victoria, but your next client is waiting.'

Isaac politely smiles at Becky then walks back over to me, taking my hand. 'How about we try that dinner? Sit down and clear the air?'

Standing close, he smells so good. He looks so good, but I know his version of clearing the air is probably different from mine. I'm also very aware that Becky is still standing in the doorway wide-eyed, every bit as eager for my response as he is.

'Sure,' I say, as breezily, as I can. 'Dinner would be great.'

'Perfect, how about Friday?'

I find myself nodding before thinking.

'No! Sorry. That's the night of Gwen's exhibition opening.'

'Saturday then?'

I nod – somewhat relieved that he can barely hide the huge smile on his face.

'I'll let you get back to it. I'll call you to sort the details.'

Before I can respond, Isaac kisses me lightly on the cheek and walks past Becky to leave.

Her jaw drops and she mouths, 'He's gorgeous!'

I shush her as I make my way back to my armchair, awaiting my client. I can't help smiling, but I'm full of nerves. I need to figure out what I want from Isaac. What I want for myself. The warmth of his lips as he kissed my face was enticing, but tempered with fear: how will he react to what I have to say about Michael?

I just know I can't waste the opportunity to talk to him about those photos.

Chapter Fourteen

Girls' Night

I'm looking forward to meeting the girls in town tonight, even putting on my faithful little black dress for the occasion. My phone rings while I'm slipping on some heels.

> All booked. Pick you up Saturday at 8. Looking forward to it. x

I smile at Isaac's message, feeling nervous admitting to myself how much I'm looking forward to seeing him already. I need to get moving, there's no time to dwell on it.

By the time I arrive at the restaurant they're already seated, shouting my name and beckoning me over to the table. I look for my usual cocktail but a disappointing ice water is waiting for me.

'We've ordered salads for everyone, you included,' Jessica explains, looking me up and down.

Wow, she's starting early tonight.

'I can't wait to be married,' Gwen grumbles, 'then I can eat cake all day.'

We clink glasses and launch straight into the purpose of tonight's meal – to finalise a few of the plans for the wedding. Between us we have already chosen: the flowers, the table décor and the food, and confirmed the most beautiful spa in the dales for the hen do, miles from any interruptions. With the wedding being so close, this has been a real group effort.

'Oh, we still need to decide on the music, you'll need something romantic to walk down the aisle to,' Samira announces, scrolling through her own to-do list on her phone.

'I think Vic is becoming a bit of an expert in romance, aren't you Vic?' Gwen shoots me a look which entices Samira to quiz me.

'Oh, do tell!'

I can only have paused for a second before Gwen dives in.

'Isaac… he and young Vic here have been seeing each other!'

And with that, all the wedding pictures and notes are set down as all the group's attention turns to me. Gulping at my water, I try not to choke on the ice shards I accidentally swallow.

'Isaac? The best man? Really? But he's gorgeous!' Jessica has such a talent for somehow turning a compliment into a dig. Whatever makes her feel better about herself, I guess.

'I don't mean to be rude Vic, but do you dress like this when you go out with him?'

'Jessica!' Gwen retorts, scandalised. Her sudden realisation that Jessica is a miserable cow is of little comfort, if not out of character.

'Stop being such a bitch!' That's my Samira – far more to the point!

'Anyway, *music*. I have actually sorted it – the venue has your selections,' I report, ignoring Jessica's comment – and the topic of Isaac – entirely.

There is a pause, it looks like I'm not going to get out of their interrogation so easily, but thankfully Gwen's mobile rings before they can push any further.

'Vic, will you talk everyone through the venue please? The future husband's calling,' she says, waving her phone at us.

As the others start blowing kisses at Michael's photo on the screen, Gwen quickly picks up and takes her conversation outside. I watch her through the window, twirling her hair around her finger as she smiles at whatever he's saying. She is positively glowing as she talks to him. I can't help feeling a knot in the pit of my stomach, at the thought of him and what I'm keeping from her.

As instructed though, I talk the ladies through the venue arrangements, and then the chatter turns to bridesmaid outfits and hairstyles, the last piece of the actual wedding day to complete. Samira starts showing us pictures of some dresses she has found which match the colours Gwen had asked for. This leads to much laughter at some of the more revealing choices. She always likes to flaunt her assets, much to Jessica's disgust.

By the time Gwen returns, looking a little flustered, we have narrowed down our favourites. We have agreed on a variety of styles in the same deep claret colour, so we will match but with an elegant twist, and Gwen loves the idea.

As the conversation turns to the hen night, excitement ripples around the table and when Jessica updates us on the arrangements she's made for an ultra-exclusive spa day, even I have to admit she has outdone herself. Naturally Jessica spends just a little too much time detailing the event, never one to shy away from celebrating herself. However, a day of luxurious pampering is going to be exactly what we all need, after the pace we're keeping to get this wedding happening.

Looking around, it's striking to see Gwen surrounded by such loyalty and adoration. In a matter of weeks we have accomplished so much because we all love her. When the truth about Michael comes out, whatever it is, she will need this solidarity even more. The realisation is jarring, that what I find out could take all of this away from her. I feel the prick of tears and excuse myself to the ladies' room.

When I come out of the cubicle, Jessica is leaning against the sink, reapplying her lipstick in the mirror.

'That's a pretty colour,' I say as I join her to wash my hands.

She turns to face me, stern as always. 'Look, Victoria. I know we haven't always been the best of friends –' the best of friends? how about friends at all! '–but when I make comments about how you look, I don't mean to offend you. It's more… tough love.'

Her superiority complex is astounding. I am lost for words, turning my attention to drying my hands to avoid her laser-like stare.

'I'd like us to go shopping. Just you and me. You could be so… presentable, with a little help.'

Without invitation she moves behind me, coaxing me to stand straight in front of the mirror, a handful of the back of my dress in her grip.

'See? You can wear more fitted clothing to show off your figure… and as for your hair–'

'Stop!'

I yank myself free from her claws. It's one thing for her to make digs at my appearance, but this is way too full on. I'm tired of putting up with the glaringly obvious, inflated opinion she has of herself. Tired of her jibes, which often seem to stem from little more than a need to entertain herself.

She simply sighs in response, going back to applying her lipstick, turning her face this way and that to check her flawless skin.

'I want you to look good at the events leading up to the wedding – we're all there to represent Gwen you know. It's not like you can't afford it. And now there's Isaac to think about. Let me know when you've come to your senses and are ready to accept my help.'

She turns on her heel and leaves, whilst I'm stood looking at my plain reflection in the mirror. Bitchiness aside, she is right – all of Gwen's other friends are so glamorous, I'm always the odd one out. As for Isaac? Maybe he is out of my league, but he seems to like how I look. Although I guess there would be no harm in making a little more effort, would there?

A pair of bubbly, slightly inebriated ladies burst through the door, giggling as they struggle to steady themselves – a sign for me to go.

When I return to the table, everyone is pretty much done pushing their unwanted salads around their plates.

'Sorry to abandon you all,' I say, 'but I have clients early tomorrow…'

Samira looks accusingly at Jessica for my early departure and protests that I should stay a little longer, share a cab home with her, but Gwen knows I've made my mind up.

'Thank you so much Vic,' she says.

Before I can make my escape though, Jessica pipes up. 'I've offered to give Victoria a bit of a makeover. What do you think, ladies?'

I wince, as do the others. 'Actually, I'm not sure I–'

'It will be a chance for us to get to know each other better, won't it Victoria,' she ploughs on, clearly not reading the room.

Samira spits out her drink. 'Wow… just wow!'

'Have you two ever spent time alone together?' Gwen asks, eyebrows raised.

The answer, obviously, is no.

'I for one,' Jessica persists, 'think it's a fabulous idea. After all, look at what my advice did for you, Gwen.'

All eyes are now on Gwen. What had Jessica done for her? Gwen's laugh is uncomfortable – it's not like her to shy away from attention. It dawns on me that I've never actually seen any pictures of her as a teenager. I wonder what Gwen looked like before this alleged makeover. If it was as dramatic a change as her mortified expression suggests, she must have really hated her previous image.

'That's true, you're certainly a talented shopper Jessica,' Gwen says quietly, not meeting any of our eyes.

'It's settled then,' Jessica's tone is positively triumphant. 'Send me some dates and times when you're free, Victoria.'

'Good luck!' Samira whispers to me when it's her turn to say goodbye, barely stifling her laughter. I'm going to need more than luck.

When I get home I wander into the kitchen, kicking off my heels as I go. The coldness of the tiles soothes my feet. My whole body is aching; how can a simple meal feel so exhausting?

I'm so hungry. I've never understood people who go all the way to a restaurant just to order a salad. Slinging my bag onto the counter, I open the fridge, but it's pretty empty, as always. I drink some orange juice straight from the box, and resolve to stock up on groceries tomorrow. Right now I just want my bed.

I leave the juice on the counter and make my way to my room. I barely have the energy to undress before collapsing onto the bed. One more night of sleeping in my make-up won't hurt either – I'm far too comfortable to move now.

Thankfully sleep finds me quickly, but my nightmares are vivid. Michael and Gwen are at the end of the aisle, and I'm being pulled back, further and further away from them, before a door slams shut between us.

I wake gasping for air and sit bolt upright, my mouth dry. I've only been asleep for three or four hours, which is frustrating. I need to sleep before work tomorrow and my head is throbbing. Maybe a hot drink would help.

I make my way down the stairs in the dark, to the kitchen. The sudden brightness as I switch on the light makes me dizzy, but I stumble on towards the kettle. I can feel in the air that something is off, but I can't quite put my finger on it. I flick the kettle on and rest against the island. Where is the orange juice I'd left out earlier? It isn't here. Maybe I put it in the fridge without realising?

I pull the fridge door open. I'm not sure if I'm still dreaming. Shelf upon shelf of fresh produce stands in front of me. I step back and hear a gentle whirring. My eyes dart left and right to find the source of the sound – the washing machine is on. My chest tightens, I don't know what is happening.

I slowly turn around, taking in more things I hadn't noticed at first. The worktops are clear, the sink empty. Even my shoes, which I'm sure I kicked off, are no longer in the middle of the floor where I discarded them. I close my eyes tightly to concentrate – I have to be sleeping still. The last thing I can remember is falling into bed. I try to focus. Steady my breathing: in through my nose, out through my mouth. In, out.

That's when I feel it; my eyes still squeezed shut.

A draught. As if a window or door is suddenly ajar. My eyes flick open. I try desperately to rationalise what I just felt. Is it my imagination? It could be my imagination – I've been so tired lately, and under stress too. I hold my breath and listen, too scared to even move. Are those… footsteps? They are so muffled I can't tell exactly where they're coming from. But the sound is unmistakable.

There is someone in my house.

Chapter Fifteen

The Uninvited Guest

The house has gone silent again. I stay completely still, holding my breath to keep as quiet as I can, listening again for any source of movement. Nothing.

The hall light switches off. Fear surges through me.

I summon all the courage I can, grabbing a knife from the block and making a dash for the stairs. I daren't look back, focusing solely on making it back to my phone, which I left in the bedroom. I turn on all of the lights as I run, to scare the darkness away.

As soon as I get into my room, I slam the door shut and lock it behind me. Diving towards my mobile, I pin myself against the headboard. One trembling hand trying to unlock my phone, the other outstretched pointing the knife at the door. Watching the light from the crack underneath, I pray I will not see any movement. I jump when the phone rings in my hand. I answer it but can't find the words to speak.

'Sorry Vic,' Gwen's voice shatters the silence. 'I know you've probably been at home a while, but you never texted to say you got in safely. I was worried… I tried texting but…'

'Gwen, I need help. I don't think I'm alone in the house,' I whisper. 'There's someone here!'

She says nothing. Then I hear her breath hitch, her tone quicken. 'What? Can you get out of the house?'

'No, I've locked myself in the bedroom.'

That's when I see it, a shadow moving under the door. I stare at the door handle, willing it not to turn. The knife begins to shake uncontrollably in my still-outstretched hand.

'Have you called the police?' Gwen is asking.

'Yes I've called the police, they're on their way!' I shout, desperately hoping the tremor in my voice isn't obvious to the intruder. The shadow skitters away.

'Fuck, Vic. You haven't, have you. Stay on the phone, I'll use Samira's phone to call them.'

I shake my head to try to clear my it, but I'm too frightened to respond. All I can do is wait for help to arrive. The sound of my heartbeat is so loud in my ears, I can only just about hear Gwen rushing around on the other end of the line, offering me words of comfort, telling me she is on her way.

It seems to take an age until I see the flashing of blue lights from under the curtains, but I'm rigid with fear, unable to move.

'Vic, I'm outside with the police, they say the door isn't locked. They're coming in.' Gwen is clearly trying to remain calm.

I can hear the door open and the sound of heavy booted feet in the hallway, before they separate and move in different directions around the house. They ascend the stairs and at last I feel that I'm going to be saved.

There's a knock on my bedroom door. Shaking, I'm still holding the knife ahead of me as I rise from my seated position, my hand throbbing from gripping it so tightly.

'Miss Summers? I'm PC Jim Kerr, and I'm with PC Jane Larson,' says a gruff male voice on the other side. 'We've checked the house, you're safe to come out.'

I drop the knife so I can reach for my robe – I'm still in my underwear – and walk unsteadily to the door. By now Gwen has hung up the phone.

On the landing, both officers are looking at me with unreadable expressions. PC Kerr, a huge figure of a man, stands back to let me walk past him. The much slighter PC Larson offers a kind smile as she escorts me to Gwen and Samira, who are waiting in the hallway. They rush over and wrap me in their arms. I have never been so happy to see them.

'It doesn't look like any doors or windows are open, and there's nothing to suggest anyone has attempted to break in,' Officer Kerr reports in a very matter of fact tone. 'We'll continue to patrol the area, but it seems like *if* there was anyone here, they aren't any more.'

The way he stresses the *if* is infuriating. I wouldn't just make this up, would I? I mean, I *think* I'm sure that I heard those footsteps, saw that shadow. I definitely didn't do all that stuff in my kitchen.

'What do you mean *if*? Someone turned off the light!'

The officers turn to one another before PC Larson steps into the hallway and flicks the switch back and forth. Nothing. No light.

'Looks like the bulb has gone.'

I see them look at each other again. They don't believe me.

'Would it be possible for you to have a quick look around, see if there is anything that you feel has been taken or disturbed?' Officer Kerr says.

It feels like they are going through the motions. Gwen reaches for my hand.

'I'm coming too and then she's coming straight to my house, alright?'

The officers nod and follow closely behind us, notebooks in hand. Gwen leads me through the downstairs rooms as Samira trails nearby.

'Did you finally get a cleaner Vic?' Gwen asks. 'The place is spotless.'

My chest tightens again when I see what has been done. Each room we walk through looks immaculate. Organised and dusted, with nothing out of place.

'No, this isn't what it looked like when I went to bed. Someone's been here.'

'Sorry Miss Summers, are you saying someone broke in and tidied your house?' The way the Officer Kerr scoffs infuriates me, even though I understand his disbelief. It does sound ridiculous.

'Don't be stupid. Of course she's not saying that, are you Vic?' Gwen is nodding at me hopefully, and when I stay silent, the officers shoot a less than subtle look at one another.

Moving from room to room, each one cleaner and tidier than the last, I can barely stand to look at my own house until we finally make it to the kitchen. Samira edges past us to make tea with the fresh milk that's just appeared in the fridge – keeping unusually quiet for her.

The police continue to question me once we are sat down.

'Look Miss Summers. Is it possible that you forgot you had done this housework? Or someone you know has come in to help?'

'Why on earth would anyone do that in the middle of the night?' Samira asks, handing me a steaming mug.

I sit and listen as Gwen and Samira protest on my behalf, but the officers seem unimpressed to say the least.

'You say you had returned from a night out. How much alcohol have you consumed tonight Miss Summers?'

I don't need to speak. Samira is completely enraged now.

'What are you implying? None of us have been drinking tonight.'

I remain silent, trying to take everything in. Who has ever heard of a break-in where the perpetrator popped in for a bit of light housework? Although I'm thankful that Gwen and Samira are being so supportive, even *I* don't believe me.

Finally, PC Larson breaks her silence, the softness in her voice at least attempting a level of sympathy.

'I'll leave you my card. If you can think of anyone who may have entered your home or if you notice anything missing, please call me.'

Gwen sees them to the door whilst Samira sits with me, holding my hands. As soon as Gwen returns, I bury my face into her shoulder, tears streaming, my voice muffled.

'I'm sorry, I just don't understand...'

Smoothing my hair, she hugs me. 'You're tired and I don't know what's happened here, but you're coming to my house.'

'Good idea. Let's go and pack some things together,' Samira orders.

What would I do without these two? Dazed and confused, I do as I'm told, but as I grab the banister I feel a terrible nausea rising, and I rush to throw up in the bathroom. Gwen and Samira are only a few steps behind me, quick to hold my hair and rub my back.

All I can do is sob on the floor. I don't want to stay here, but the thought of going to Gwen's house isn't much better. I don't want to be anywhere near Michael.

'Let's get you up and dressed.' Gwen strains to lift me back up.

'Actually Gwen, it's fine, honestly. I don't want to disturb Michael, I'll stay here. I'll be OK. Or I can stay at Samira's.'

Samira is nodding, but Gwen is quick to interject.

'Don't be silly, you're not staying here. Anyway, he's at some work thing tonight. Samira will be rushing around with the children in the morning. You can get some proper rest at mine. Come on, we'll deal with all of this tomorrow.'

'I guess that makes sense. My two will make a right racket. I'll come round and see you in the morning at Gwen's, Vic.'

I am struggling to think clearly enough to argue with either of them, but I feel a little relief at not having to face Michael tonight.

Sitting on the bed as they pull items from my dresser, the true horror of the situation hits me. There are no clothes on the floor, no dirty glasses on the bedside cabinet, and the drawers are full of neatly folded clothes. Someone has been in my room, while I was sleeping. Moving around me. Touching my things. The realisation makes me rush back to the bathroom, but I have nothing left to throw up.

Gwen doesn't try to offer any more comforting words – instead she and Samira help me dress in silence, then call a taxi. Their haste betrays the fact they don't want to be in this house any longer than I do. As we hurry out of the house, I grab my handbag and keys. The police have already checked the doors and windows, so we aren't going to hang around any longer than we need to.

'Just get us out of here,' Gwen commands the taxi driver as I slide into my seat.

We don't speak in the car, dropping Samira off a few seconds down the road.

Gwen's house is quiet and dark when we enter. I feel so numb that she has to help me up the stairs to the spare room. She hovers a little too long, sitting on the edge of the bed.

'Are you OK, Vic? I mean, I know you're not OK but the tidying and cleaning…?'

She doesn't believe me either, I can feel it. She's wringing her hands.

'I just want to go to sleep.'

Reluctantly, Gwen stands to leave. I feel guilty for snapping.

'Thank you, Gwen, really. I don't know what I'd have done without you two tonight.' I can feel the tears trying to escape again.

'Get some sleep,' she says over her shoulder, as she reaches for the door handle. 'We'll figure this all out in the morning.'

The room feels so much bigger and darker when she's closed the door. I struggle to drop off, tossing and turning, watching every shadow, waiting to see if any of them move. Then I hear the front door open and close, followed by footsteps. Michael.

'Shh, you'll wake Vic,' I hear Gwen say in a low voice, apparently blocking him from climbing the stairs.

'What's happening? I got your message about the police.' His last few words are more muffled as he understands her request to be quiet.

I want to try to get to sleep, but I also want to know what Gwen's thoughts really are on what happened tonight. Edging to the door, I slowly open it just enough to hear their conversation travelling up the stairwell.

'They said that there was no indication that anyone had tried to break in.'

My stomach sinks. If she doesn't believe me, no one else will. I don't want to hear her say it, so I close the door again and crawl back into bed, staring up at the ceiling. I'm not afraid anymore.

All I can feel is anger welling inside of me. I'm angry at whoever came into my home and touched my things. I'm angry at the police for implying whatever it was they were implying but actually, I think I'm more angry at Gwen. I would never doubt anything she said to me if she were in that situation.

I pull a pillow over my face to drown out the sound of my sobbing – hot and bitter tears running down the sides of my face, soaking my hair. As I try to steady my breathing, I force myself to think rationally. In the morning I'll call the office and leave a message for Becky. There's no way I'll be fit for work, and I know she'll handle it. I just need the world to stop turning for a little while until I can get my head together. Maybe then, I can really think through what happened tonight.

Chapter Sixteen

Over The Threshold

The next morning

I awake next to my buzzing phone on my pillow. I trying to sit up, but my headache has other ideas. I lie back down and reach out blindly to make the noise stop.

'Hi, it's Becky. Are you OK?'

She sounds her usual cheery self, tinged with concern. I rub the sleep from my eyes and pull myself up to concentrate on her voice. What time is it?

'Er… yeah… yes I'm fine. Sorry Becky, I meant to call earlier. I think I've caught a bug.'

I'd hoped it had been a nightmare but no, here I am in Gwen's spare room.

'Oh no, is there anything I can get for you?'

'No, it's fine thank you, I just need to rest.'

'If you're sure? I'll rearrange your appointments for today. Is there anything else I can do for you?'

'No, that's great Becky. I'll call you a little later to let you know how I'm feeling. We can decide what to do about the rest of the week's appointments then. Ok?'

'Absolutely.' She pauses. 'Are you sure you're alright? It's just, you've never had a sick day before.'

Even sitting me up is sending waves of nausea through me – I just need this call to end. 'I'm sure. It's nothing serious but I just can't face work. I'll call later. Thank you, Becky.'

I hang up before she can ask me any more questions.

I drop my phone on the bedside table and pull back the duvet to go and find Gwen. My first attempt to stand up doesn't go well and I stumble back onto the bed. As I steady myself against the bedside table, my head is spinning. I have to lean on the furniture and walls as I walk to stop me losing my balance.

Making my way downstairs, gripping the banister as I go, I'm surprised to see Gwen sitting in the kitchen reading a magazine, sipping coffee. I had half expected her to be either working or busy on the phone, as she always is. She notices me hovering by the door.

'Morning Vic.' She rushes to stand. 'Let's get you some coffee.'

Silently I sit down and wait for her to pour me a cup from her cafetière. Without needing to ask, she adds the cream and sugar, just the way I like it, totally avoiding eye contact. She is trying not to say or ask me something, probably about last night. I wait for her to slide the mug in front of me, then close my eyes to just enjoy the comfort and safety in this moment, absorbing my drink's warmth and inhaling the rich aroma. When I open my eyes, Gwen is looking at me, her brow furrowed and the edges of her lips down turned.

'Do you want to talk about it?' she asks tentatively, reaching for my hand.

I sink back in the chair, holding her hand tightly with one hand and setting my mug down with the other. What more does she want me to say?

'No matter what the police said, I know what I heard and saw. Someone was in my house.' I can feel my voice cracking but I don't want to cry, I'm tired of crying. 'Gwen?'

'Yes Vic?'

'You do believe that someone was in my home, don't you?'

I watch her try and hide any reaction on her face, in her usual controlled manner.

'Oh Vic. I believe you think you heard someone.'

I pull my hand free. 'What do you mean?'

Her eyes widen as she sees that my hands are clenched on the table.

'I'm sorry, I didn't mean…' Gwen moves round to the chair closest to me, grabbing my hand again.

'It's just… about the cleaning and the fridge…'

'Look, I know how ridiculous it sounds, but the fact is I didn't do any of that.'

She sighs, pursing her lips. 'But why would…'

She's never made me feel belittled before. Why now? She stops, noticing I'm not able to hold back the tears any longer, and squeezes me tightly in a hug. I can't bring myself to hug her back. These are tears of anger. How can she question me like this?

'I'm sorry, Vic. Don't cry. I do believe you – really stay here for a few days, please?'

I want to, even if it's obvious she doesn't actually believe me. The thought of going back to my house, alone, fills me with dread. Yet looking at the many photos hanging on Gwen's walls, it is hard not to be reminded that it's not just her I'd be staying with.

'Where's Michael?'

'He's still in bed, he didn't get home until late. Let me make you some breakfast. You'll think more clearly after some food.'

'I'm thinking clearly now,' I snap.

I'm not sure I am though. My head hurts, I feel sick and I'm tired. What happened last night can't be all in my head. Can it?

'I know, but… look, you're exhausted. With the wedding, work… tiredness can do funny things to the mind.'

'What are you trying to say Gwen, that I imagined it all?'

She flinches at the harshness of my tone. My headache is worsening the more I clench my jaw. The fact she is taking so long to answer doesn't help either. I wish she'd say something, anything. Watching her get up to make toast rather than respond is infuriating. With her back still turned to me she finally breaks her silence.

'Vic, I believe you but…'

'But what?'

'You don't need to be so angry.'

I recoil. I know she can be precious but how am I the one at fault here? She takes a deep breath, then returns to my side with a more sympathetic smile.

'Look Vic, I know you. I know you're stressed, and I can only imagine what feelings dating Isaac is bringing up about… you know… your past. I remember you saying that Dylan used to be a neat freak. All of that must be playing havoc with your mind. You're the therapist – what do you think could be going on?'

I'm taken aback, blindsided by her bringing up Dylan. That is not what this is about. Before I can respond, she goes on.

'Vic, please be honest. Is all of this, the wedding and Isaac… is it all too much for you?'

This could've been the perfect opportunity to come clean about how I really feel about the wedding, tell her exactly why it's taking up so much of my time and energy, but it could come across as an attack. She'd never listen. I slam the chair back to stand at her eye level.

'My house was broken into! So yes, that is a bit much for me to deal with right now. Your wedding isn't the be all and end all of everything!'

Gwen retreats from the sheer volume of my voice. I can feel my chest heaving. She doesn't speak. Probably shocked that, for once, I've pointed out that the world does not revolve around her. I don't know how to end this conversation calmly – right now I just want to leave. I need to be by myself.

I storm back to the spare room to get changed, Gwen follows closely behind me, apologising profusely. I know she wants me to stop and talk. I wish I wanted to. But I need to be out of here before Michael gets up. I yank my pyjamas off, throwing them down carelessly on the floor, only just missing Gwen. I grow even more frustrated with my top tangling around my arms as I try to dress quickly.

'I just need some air. I'm going to the park.'

Gwen doesn't try to stop me anymore. Out of the corner of my eye I can see her eyes well up as she folds my pyjamas

'I'll give you a minute to finish getting dressed.'

When she's gone I sit on the bed, head in my hands. My breathing still feels erratic so I close my eyes to centre myself. Whether Gwen believes it or not, I'm certain there was someone in my house. Wasn't there?

I pull out some clothes from the bag Samira packed for me. Even though I'm in desperate need of a shower, I have to keep moving. When I reach the top of the stairs, Gwen is sat on the bottom step, clearly upset. A surge of guilt rushes through me. After all, she is the person who came to my aid in the middle of the night. I shouldn't be making her feel like this.

I stop – she's talking to someone just out of sight. Is it Michael? I desperately don't want to see him, but as I cautiously descend I see I had nothing to worry about – it's Samira.

I don't even manage to say hello before she rushes towards me; her arms wrap around me so tightly she squeezes the breath from me. Finally releasing me she stands, looking at me sympathetically. Gwen hovers beside us, looking uncomfortable.

'I'm sorry Gwen,' I say, 'I didn't mean to snap just now.'

'No, I'm sorry, I really don't want you to go. Especially alone.'

'Erm, where are you going alone?' Samira asks.

'Vic wants to leave, get some fresh air.'

'Not without me you're not.' Samira links arms with me. 'Are we going to the park?'

I know there's no point arguing with her. If she's decided she's coming with me, then she's coming with me. She lets me go for long enough to put my shoes and coat on.

Before we leave, Gwen grabs my arm. 'Call me later, let me know you're OK?'

I'm glad to be going before anything more hurtful is said by either of us.

We're barely out of Gwen's drive before I can feel Samira's sideways glance at me.

'So, where do we start?'

'What do you mean?' I say, confused.

'Something's happened between you and Gwen, hasn't it?'

I relay the argument as we walk to the park, admitting my lack of control as well as Gwen's. We sit on a bench and again, she's unusually quiet, listening without comment.

'Why aren't you saying anything?' I ask, hoping Samira isn't too hard on me for the way I treated Gwen.

'I think the only person you have to worry about right now is you. Your home was broken into and you're taking on too much with this wedding.'

She is so matter of fact. I've always loved that about her, but I can feel she's holding something back.

'And…?'

'At some point you're going to have to go back to your house, and I'm coming with you. That's all we need to think about.'

She's right, we can't sit here too much longer, I'm already starting to lose feeling in my toes and the clouds are threatening rain. There are so many better ways I could've responded to Gwen though – I'll have to apologise properly when she calls later.

'You can stop that right now!' Samira elbows me.

'Stop what?'

'That thoughtful expression, the glazed eyes. You're worrying about someone other than yourself. Stop it.' There's a teasing twinkle in her eye and I can't help but laugh at her.

She pulls me up from the bench and starts to drag me by the hand, towards home.

'Let's rip the plaster off. We need to check your house. Now it's daylight you might spot something else important for the police.'

Having Samira with me, my courage is restored, until we reach my driveway. My house looks exactly as I imagine it would, as it always does, but it is so different at the same time. This time yesterday this building was my sanctuary, now… I don't know how to feel.

Taking a deep breath I move up the path to the door, my hands shaking as I try to unlock it. Samira has to take over, and she makes a point of stepping into the house first. I notice how fresh it smells when I walk in. No more day-old takeaway smell, but clean and airy. The floor is too shiny for my sore eyes and I flinch, sending more shooting pains through my temples. Samira squeezes my hand in reassurance, but I pull away to keep moving through the house.

There doesn't seem to be an inch that hasn't been cleaned and organised. My heart is racing at the thought that someone was able to do all of this whilst I slept. How did they even get in?

A memory flashes through my mind, when I was on the phone to Gwen and she said the front door was unlocked when the police arrived. Did I leave it unlocked? Did someone just walk in? I shake my head. Opportunist intruders take things, they don't randomly clean.

I keep going, making my way to the kitchen, and grab a glass to fill with water so I can take some headache tablets. Yet as I reach for the polished cupboard door and see row upon row of clean glassware, the dizziness worsens. My eyesight is blurry and I'm starting to panic, struggling to catch my breath, struggling to even stand, my legs wanting to buckle underneath me. I manage to grab the island to support myself before I feel Samira's arm wrap around my waist to steady me.

'Vic, you need to rest.'

The stairs seem like a mountain to climb, so she guides me to the sofa instead. As soon as I lie down, I can see into my study through the open door. I hadn't gone in there with the police last night. I could see the computer was still there, and there wasn't anything else of any value to check on. Now, from the sofa, I see something I didn't notice last night: the screen is on, flicking between various photos I have as screen savers. I feel that same shiver as last night – I never leave my computer on.

Samira has already left the room to make me some sweet tea, so I lean on various pieces of furniture as I make my way to my desk, my eyes fixated on the screen. I reach for the mouse to wake the computer and gasp, falling into my chair. On the screen is a website: an information page about intimate partner violence. I never searched for this page, why would I when I have enough experience of my own? Then at the base of my screen, I notice another tab. It's a Word document. Clicking on it, a one-page file, with a single sentence typed on it.

> You cannot run away from your pain. Take care of yourself.

I let out an audible gasp, my eyes widening as I read the message over and over again. Who? Why? How? Was this even here when we left last night?

I can't breathe. Every time I try, my lungs just won't fill. I can feel the burning taste of vomit welling in my mouth. Without hesitation I rush to the downstairs loo, my stomach churning as I retch. I feel hot, sweat beading on my forehead before the dizziness washes over me once more. This time I see the floor rushing up towards me. Then, darkness.

Chapter Seventeen

Unwanted Gifts

4 weeks until the wedding

The smell of vomit and bile filling my nostrils stirs me. Opening my eyes, I see Samira knelt over me, her voice a mere echo. I protest when I hear her mention a hospital. Even though she clearly disapproves, she helps me sit, propping me against the wall.

'How many fingers am I holding up?' Samira waves her hand in front of my eyes.

Thankfully I must've managed to answer correctly as she drops mention of the paramedics. My legs are too weak for me to stand. Everything is hurting. Everything is spinning but I don't want to waste a busy doctor's time. I probably just need to eat. I sit as Samira attempts to clean my face and clothes with a wet towel. I flinch as she wipes at my cheek – I must've hit the floor face first.

'I'll get you an ice-pack when I'm done,' she says.

She continues to clean the vomit as best as she can from my hair – her motherly instincts have well and truly taken hold. I sip at the now lukewarm sweet tea, which Samira brought to me, which does actually help.

We both listen as my phone rings on and off in the distance somewhere. There's no point trying to get to it, I'm not even sure how I'm going to stand up. Thankfully, with Samira's help I use the little strength I have to reach for the sink, pulling myself up to my feet. When I am upright I catch sight of my reflection in the mirror. Samira had cleaned the worst of the vomit away but there were still remnants of it in my hair, and there's redness spreading across my left cheek.

All I want to do is lie down again – but I need to wake up properly. First, I will shower. I know getting up the stairs will be no easy task, so I grip the banister hard as I take each step slowly, Samira one step behind with her hands ready to catch me. I'm not sure if she thinks she actually could but I love her for being here with me nonetheless. When we eventually make it to the bathroom, clean towels are hanging on the rails, the toiletries neatly lined up on the glass shelves. Nothing has been left untouched.

'Do you want me to help you undress?' Samira says.

'No, I'll be fine.'

She eyes me closely.

'Fine but don't lock the door, and I'll stay within shouting distance. OK?'

I can't find the words to thank her right now, so I turn my attention to the crisp water, and find the energy to climb under it. Enveloped in its warmth, my legs tremble but I don't want to get out again, so I slide down to sit in the base, letting the shower rain down on me from a height, massaging my tense shoulders. Bringing my knees up to my chest, I rest my head on top of them. I want to cry but it's like there just aren't any tears left. Instead, I count my breaths, trying to keep calm.

Last night plays over in my mind. After everything that happened, I'm glad Michael wasn't at Gwen's when we arrived. Seeing him was the last thing I could've coped with on top of everything else. He probably wouldn't have wanted to see me either.

I gasp and my eyes shoot open. Where was Michael last night? I know Gwen said he had a work thing, but does she really know where he is half the time? Probably not seeing as he's seeing that mystery brunette on the side. As far as I'm concerned, he was unaccounted for when someone was in my home.

Sitting upright, I try to work it out. He didn't get home until well after I got there. I stop myself, recognising I'm making huge assumptions. Although it's clear from our last encounter that he is not scared to toy with me, do I really think he would have broken into my home and *tidied* it? No, it does not strike me as his style at all. He and Gwen don't even clean their own house, choosing a maid to avoid even the smallest of tasks. There's no way this was him. It wouldn't hurt to find out where he was last night though.

I stay in the shower until the water starts to run cold. I do feel a tiny bit better and incredibly hungry. When I go into my room to grab something to wear, Samira is sat on my bed, waiting for me, next to the knife I abandoned last night. I put on my bravest face, ignoring it, but I know she sees through me. I try not to let the neat rows of clothes hanging in my wardrobe and folded in my drawers bother me. Not even the socks, so neatly paired. I actually can't even remember the last time I have worn matching socks, as I run my hand over the little folded mounds. My jaw clenches again as I pull some underwear out. The thought that someone has touched everything… no, I can't think about that right now. I don't want Samira to worry more about me than she already is. I choose a loose jumper and leggings, something comfortable and warm. I try to nonchalantly pick up the knife to put it away, but Samira reaches for my hand.

'Do you want to talk about it yet? Last night?'

All I can do is shake my head. If I tell her about the note on my computer, she'll never leave and I'll have to explain the website, which I just don't have the strength to do right now. I want to spend some time alone so I can think about who would leave such a cruelly triggering web page like that open for me to find.

I take the knife downstairs with me. When I slide it back into the wooden block the image of me rushing to arm myself with it, scared and alone, floods my thoughts. My heart starts racing again, but I can feel Samira standing behind me holding an ice pack. If she sees me panicking, she'll definitely stay. So I put the pack to my face, flinching at the sudden cold, and concentrate on the sound of my stomach rumbling, which seems to echo in the empty room. Out of instinct I reach for the fridge door, regretting it instantly. The bright array of colours of the various foodstuffs is overwhelming. Every shelf stacked perfectly with fresh fruit, vegetables and meat. I slam the door shut and turn to Samira.

'I don't know what I'd do without you Samira – thank you for coming here with me.'

'Don't be silly, you don't need to thank me.'

Releasing her, I take a step back. 'If it's OK though, I think I need some time alone. To think about all of this.'

I can see from her furrowed brow that she doesn't want to go, but I walk to the cupboard, pulling out a packet of biscuits to snack on. My stomach needs the sugar but Samira looks alarmed.

'I really think I should stay, make you something proper to eat, you're not well.'

'Some of your cooking would be amazing – later maybe? Please, I just need time to put things back to how I want them to be, so I can be comfortable again, you know?'

I can see she is torn. She wants to argue with me but now isn't the time.

'Fine. But I will call and text you all the time and if you don't respond immediately, like I mean within half a second, I am coming back round.'

Grabbing the half-eaten biscuit from my hand and shoving it in her own mouth, she smiles at me, crumbs falling down her top.

At the front door, she pauses and turns to me. 'Make sure you lock the door.'

I nod and see her out. I turn the key and listen as the lock clicks. I'm almost sure I did this last night. I return to the kitchen to open the fridge again, and a surge of anger courses through me. Who the fuck breaks into someone's house to put things in? How dare they?

I grab at item after item, aiming at the bin but not caring if I miss. Eggs smash on the floor, salad leaves hang out of the top of the bin and tomatoes slide down the wall, but I don't stop. I want it all gone.

Hot angry tears stream down my face, the saltiness dripping between my gritted teeth. When every shelf is empty, my chest is heaving from the exertion, a pool of spilt fruit and vegetables sits at my feet. Stepping back away from the mess, I need to get out of here. Now.

I sling on some trainers and a jacket – stopping only for my bag and phone before rushing into the cool air outside.

My still wet hair whips my face as I stride down the pavement, heading for the high street and the comfort of my coffee house. I notice Samira's curtain twitching as I pass her house; her door opens and she shouts over to me.

'What's wrong? Where are you going?'

'Nothing's wrong, just fancied a croissant. Can I get you one?'

She eyes me suspiciously, holding up her phone. 'Just remember, I'm going to keep checking on you!'

Samira comically points two fingers at her own eyes then at mine before relenting and closing the door. The streets are busier now than before, with couples walking hand in hand and dog walkers stopping to talk in the middle of the pavement. I hadn't even realised it was raining until I noticed other people's umbrellas. I avoid all eye contact, wanting to just disappear amongst them.

The warmth of the café is a welcome respite from the bitter cold outside. I place my order before huddling away at a corner table. I don't care if anyone is watching how hastily I wolf down my first pastry, only slowing down when I'm halfway through the second.

Relaxing back into the chair, I watch the world go by outside the window. It strikes me as odd that I can sit here in turmoil, yet the world keeps on going as normal, or so it seems. Such are the lives we lead I guess, we never really know what other people are going through around us.

'Would you like a top up?' asks the perky waitress, standing next to me with a steaming teapot in her hand. With a nod from me, she refills my cup – just the invite I need to sit here a little longer to think of my next steps.

I pause to look at my phone. I have a huge number of missed calls and texts – mainly from Gwen and Samira. I text Samira first of course. Even a few moments' delay to my return home could see her sending all of the emergency services looking for me. I send her a picture of what's left of my croissant, which seems to appease her. Gwen on the other hand can wait. She isn't my priority right now.

I begin scrolling through a variety of pages until I find what I need: an emergency locksmith. The one I pick sounds pleasant enough on the phone. *I'll be there in an hour, love.* Perfect. That's the best news I've heard all day.

An hour leaves me enough time to make a couple of calls before the walk home. Becky first. I let her know she can start to rebook appointments from tomorrow lunchtime.

She sounded relieved I was going to be back. I ponder if my next call should be to Gwen, yet as my finger hovers over her number, I decide against it.

I sip more of my sweet tea and my phone lights up – she's calling me. I watch it until the missed call message appears. Before I can decide when to call her back, she rings again. I guess she'll just keep trying until I pick up.

'Thank god Vic, I've been so worried!' She breathes dramatically when I answer.

I try and listen to her apologies but I am still so tired, I am struggling to concentrate.

'Vic? Are you OK?'

'To be honest Gwen, the house feels weird. I couldn't stand to look at it all that stuff in the fridge – I lost my temper and emptied it…'

'Oh Vic… I'm coming over.'

'No, it's fine, I'm at the café on the high street,' I say. 'I have a locksmith coming soon – I'll feel better once he's been.'

I'm glad I have a good excuse to stop her visiting, I'm not in the mood for her – neither her need for attention nor her judgements about my recollections of last night.

'Alright, but… Look, I know you don't want to stay at mine… how about I pack a bag and come and stay at yours for a couple of days?'

I'm torn. I need some time alone in the house, to study what was left on my computer, but no matter what happened between us earlier, I would prefer not to be by myself overnight.

'Actually, I'd love that. Maybe pop round a little bit later though, if that's OK?'

'Great, I've got a couple of meetings at the gallery and then I'll be over early this evening. I'll bring dinner.'

Hanging up, I feel a little more in control. My house will be safer by this evening and so will I.

The locksmith's large red van, with a huge lock picture emblazoned on the side, is obvious to see as soon as I turn into my street. I make my way to the heavy-set man taking tools from the back of the van.

'Hi, I'm Victoria.'

'Perfect timing – Kev,' he says cheerfully, holding his large hand out for me to shake.

He sets to work on changing both the front and back door locks. As I go inside to make him a tea with three sugars as requested, I remember with a jolt of embarrassment that I need to clean up the mess I left in the kitchen. I'm not sure how I will explain it to Kev if he sees it, and I can only thank god that the milk was spared from my outburst.

I close the kitchen door behind me, ready to grab the broom, but what I see stops me dead, anxiety hitting me like a train all over again. There is no mess. No food spilling out of the bin. Nothing but a perfectly mopped floor.

In the middle of the island sits a large traditional hamper, piled high with what looks like luxury beauty products. All elegantly held together with a large, red satin bow.

What the actual fuck is going on?

Edging towards the wicker basket I see it's packed with a wide variety of moisturisers, face masks, hair masks…

and a note. I don't recognise the handwriting on the envelope. Sliding the small card out I clasp my hand over my mouth to stop from screaming.

> Don't be angry – You need to relax and take better care of yourself.

Every muscle in my body tightens painfully, my hands start to shake violently.

'Excuse me, luv, did you say you want a chain adding on the door?' Kev asks as he bursts into the kitchen unannounced. His eyes darting straight to the hamper.

'Wow! Get a load of that, looks expensive. From a secret admirer, is it?'

I've lost the power of speech.

'Are you alright luv? You look like you've seen a ghost!'

'I'm – I'm fine,' I lie and force a smile on my face. My mind is swirling with questions. Who did this? When? Why? How? I can tell from the perplexed expression on his face that Kev isn't sure what to make of me.

'Kev, after you've changed the locks on the doors, can you check all the windows please. Make sure the locks are OK on them too?'

By now his brow is completely furrowed. 'That's going to take a few hours, and you know you're paying me on an emergency rate? It would be cheaper if you booked me to come back tomorrow.'

'No!' Damn, that came out more shrill than I intended. I take a deep breath to regain my composure. 'Please, I'm not worried about the rate – I just want it all done today.'

Shrugging, he nods and goes back to the front door. Filling the kettle, I keep my back to the hamper. I can't cope with thinking about it right now but as I open the fridge to grab the milk, I can see the shelves have been neatly restocked. I feel so numb that all I can do is ignore it, closing the fridge door as quickly as I opened it. I pick up my phone to text Samira but she's beat me to it.

> Saw the van outside. Good idea to get the locks changed. xx

I just send her a thumbs up. If I mention the hamper she will rush around and I would prefer her not to just now.

Kev is thankful for his tea and biscuits, although he seems oblivious to the cold flooding through the front door.

'I might go and have a little lie down on the sofa, Kev. If you need me, shout me. OK?'

It's weird but right now, I feel safer napping in the knowledge that this stranger is in my house than being alone. I shut myself in the living room and launch the neatly puffed up cushions onto the floor, where they are usually kept. I lie down listening to soothing sounds of Kev's drill-ing and hammering. He'll make this house safe again.

Chapter Eighteen

The Clean Up

'There's a couple of ladies at the door for you, luv!' Kev's brisk voice wakes me from my nap.

I pull myself up to sitting, just in time to see Gwen and Samira push past him with a pizza box in their hands.

'Vic, will you tell him you know us…'

It takes me a second to understand what's happening. I wipe the sleep from my eyes.

'Kev, sorry, these are my friends.'

'No worries – I've done both doors and checked the upstairs windows. I'll get on with the downstairs ones now, alright?'

'That's great, thanks. I'll get you another drink.'

Gwen eyes him suspiciously as he makes his way through my house. Lowering her voice, her face close to mine, she says, 'Why's he checking the windows?'

I ignore what feels like a painfully obvious question and move unsteadily to the kitchen to put the kettle on, averting my gaze when I catch sight of the hamper.

'Ooh what's this? A gift from Isaac?' Gwen coos, putting the pizza box down next to it.

Without needing an invitation to, Samira starts pawing at its contents, missing the note – I'd already tucked that underneath everything so I didn't have to look at it.

Isaac? For a split second I hope it's a harmless – if oddly generous – gift from him, but I know different. The note – the way it was smuggled into my house uninvited.

'What's the matter? Did I say something?'

Gwen still hasn't looked up at me, instead sniffing at the perfume Samira is busy spraying on her wrists.

'He has great taste, this is so expensive!' Samira gushes.

I don't know what to say, so avoid responding, hypnotising myself with the gentle swirls of the water darkening in the cups I'm stirring. By now Gwen is stood by me, spritzing her wrist with their new find too. I ignore her as she holds her arm close for me to smell the fragrance.

'Can you get the milk please?' I ask.

She huffs, but walks over to the fridge and opens the door to pass me the milk, as she would usually. As she hands it to me, her jaw drops open and she goes back to staring at the fridge. Slowly she turns to me, then Samira, then back to me.

'Where has all this come from? I thought you said you threw it all out?' There's a pause, then her eyes widen at the realisation of what this means.

'Where did all this come from, Vic?' she says, sliding the perfume from her hands back onto the counter. We stare at each other, finally on the same page. She finally believes me.

'Wait, what have I missed?' Samira says, feeling the tension between us.

Gwen's lips part, ready to say something.

'I'm just going to give the kitchen windows a quick once over,' Kev announces, whistling as he walks into the middle of our conversation. 'Oh is that for me? Lovely, thanks,' he adds, grabbing his mug on the way by.

'We'll talk when he's gone,' I mouth at them both.

We all stand dumbly watching Kev at work, sipping our tea until he says, 'All of your window locks are secure; locks are changed on the front and back door, and I've added a deadbolt to both doors too.'

Placing different piles of keys onto the counter, he starts to fill in various forms.

'These are the front door keys.' He places a set of three keys in front of him. 'And the back door.' Another three keys. 'If you can just sign here,' he says, holding out his pen for me.

I sign, and he slides the keys over. I push a key to Samira – she always has one just in case of emergencies – and throw the spare into the drawer under the island.

'I really do appreciate this Kev, thank you.'

As I walk him to the door, he gives me instructions on how to use all the new locks. His detailed descriptions of metal types and mechanisms are hardly fascinating, but make me feel safer with every word. By the time I make my way back to the girls, Samira is already well into her first slice of pizza.

'Diet's going well I see.' I shoot her a half smile.

Without dropping the pizza Samira taps on the seat next to her, ushering me to sit. Gwen sits on the other side.

'Talk to us.'

I drag the hamper towards me and pull out the note, nestled under the eye masks and nail files. Gwen clenches the note as she reads it before passing it across me to Samira.

'What the hell does it mean? Who would send this? Why?'

All I can do is shrug at her questions, I have the same ones after all.

'It sounds like a threat. What did the police say when you called them?' Samira cuts in, stopping for a second when she sees my gaze drop. 'You have called them, haven't you?'

I shrug again. 'Why? So they can look at me like I'm delusional drunk again? No.'

'But–'

'But nothing, Gwen. I've changed the locks. I don't know who was getting in or how, but that should stop them doing it again.'

She looks horrified. There's no way I can tell them about the other note or the webpage left open or the fact that I think Michael is somehow behind it all.

'I'll understand if you don't want to stay tonight though.'

I wouldn't understand. I need her to stay.

'Of course I'm staying,' her hand reaches for mine, 'unless… you don't have wine? Then I'm leaving!' She laughs at her own joke.

Samira and I can't help but laugh too, like we all feel the need to lighten the atmosphere.

'Look,' says Samira, 'I'll see if my mum can come round and help look after the kids tonight. I'll stay too.'

'Really, don't go to all that trouble. You're only a few doors away if we need you.'

She begins to pick at her pizza topping. I can tell she is building the confidence to say something to me. Eventually she comes out with it.

'I would prefer you told the police about this though.'

There is no way I want to do that. Not only because I don't want them to patronise me again, but whoever left that webpage open seems to know about my past – about Dylan. I don't want that can of worms opened by the police or anyone else. I've spent too long starting a new life here to be dragged back into all that.

'I'll think about it, OK?'

That seems enough to placate her. She nods and leaps from her seat.

'But for now, let's empty the bloody fridge and get rid of this hamper. It's creepy!'

Together we fill a bin liner before Gwen carries it outside for me. It's a relief to see my fridge its usual empty self. I sneak the note into my pocket before they get rid of the hamper though – my gut feeling is that I need to keep hold of it.

The next few hours are like old times: we camp out on the sofa, eating snacks, drinking wine and watching old movies. Having them both here for company is soothing, though it doesn't stop me checking the locks every time I go to the bathroom or kitchen.

When Samira goes home for bath time, I walk her out and take the pizza box out with me. Once she's turned into her drive and out of sight, I crush the box into the wheelie bin. Something makes me look up with a start.

I feel an odd sensation, like I am being watched. I usually love living on such a quiet street but looking at the bare trees, no cars, no people, it feels eerie. I hurry back inside, the click of the locks and the smooth sliding of the bolts just the sense of security I need.

I head back to the living room but I can hear Gwen on the phone, to Michael it sounds like, so I go upstairs and get changed into my pyjamas to give her some privacy. That, and every part of me is still convinced that even if Michael didn't break into my house, he must be somehow behind these weird notes. I'm just not sure how he's doing it, or why. One thing I feel sure of is that when he was last here, he must have seen those photos I was looking at. Maybe this is some cruel attempt to distract me from looking into him any further? I do question if I am being rational in my thinking here, but either way, I take long enough getting changed that I don't have to listen to Gwen saying sweet nothings to Michael – it's more than I can handle right now.

By the time I come downstairs Gwen is clearing away the empty glasses.

'Is everything alright?' I ask.

'Yeah, just Michael checking in with us to make sure we're OK.'

I know it is a long shot but I have to ask, just so I know for sure. 'So, did he have a good night last night?'

Gwen looks confused at the question, I guess because it is unusual for me to ask after him.

'Yes, he's really hungover today. Spent most of the morning in bed. He couldn't even face the short drive to work, so worked from home with me in the afternoon. Why do you ask?'

'Oh, just wondering where he was at breakfast this morning,' I lie.

So he's been at home all day with Gwen. That's settled, he can't be the one who delivered the hamper. But what about last night?

'I hope me being there last night didn't bother him. Where did you say he'd been?'

'I didn't say.' Her eyes narrow. 'Why are you being so weird? Of course it didn't bother him. He was at some investors' meal, with Isaac actually.' A sly smile creeps onto her face. 'Maybe you should call him, Isaac I mean, if you're so interested in what they got up to.'

'That's not what I was getting at!' I force a laugh, launching a cushion at her.

Michael has an alibi for both the break-in and the hamper. How is that possible?

'All I mean is, I know you've got a lot going on here Vic, but maybe Isaac can be the ridiculously good-looking, smartly dressed, well-mannered distraction you need?'

I cannot think of anything less of a priority than my love life right now. It has been nice texting Isaac on and off, but mainly, he is still my best route to finding out more about the mystery brunette.

I try to stifle a yawn but Gwen spots me.

'Anyway,' she says, 'it's getting late. We should get some sleep.'

When she takes herself off to the spare room, I check the locks again then go back to my computer. Moving the mouse to wake it up, the note lights up the screen instantly. I sit, taking in every word.

It dawns on me. What else could my visitor have accessed on here? I open my browser history. Before they accessed the domestic abuse information page, the only other page they seem to have visited was the wedding photos site. I rush to click on it myself, to see if any of the pictures showing the mystery woman have been deleted, but they are still there. I begin to clear my history, removing all pre-filled passwords. I have plenty more I want to look into and I can't risk Michael knowing what I'm doing, if he is somehow involved in these break-ins.

When I'm sure the computer is securely logged out, I make my way to bed, recapping the notes over and over in my head. It's been a long day. I don't know how Michael is doing this, but he is the only suspect in my mind. And it is his face I fall asleep thinking of.

Chapter Nineteen

The Exhibition

As I walk through the foyer, Becky hands me the usual stack of messages, this time with a huge smile on her face.

'It's good to see you're feeling better.'

'Thank you, it's good to be back – and thank you for holding the fort whilst I've been gone.'

'There's a special message on your desk,' she reports, holding the door open for me.

I see it as soon as I walk in. A huge box of chocolates and bottle of champagne. I feel sick at the sight of them, the hamper flashing through my mind. I tentatively put my messages down on my desk before edging towards the card on the bottle. I turn the envelope over, no writing on the outside. I'm both desperate to read the note within it and dreading it.

Looking forward to dinner this weekend. Xx.

I exhale with relief, falling slightly against the desk for support – Isaac.

'He seems keen!' Becky giggles before quickly scurrying away back to her desk.

I move the chocolates to a nearby shelf and the champagne to my desk drawer. I don't think a large bottle of alcohol on display is what clients should see when they walk in. With everything that's been going on lately, I must admit the dinner had slipped my mind, but I don't want to cancel. I message Isaac.

> Gifts look delicious. Thank you. See you tomorrow. Xx

The day flies by and I'm on my way home to get ready for Gwen's exhibition before I know it. This is where she excels – Jessica tells me that Gwen's talent for curation has drawn acclaim from across the fine arts community – and tickets were sold months in advance. In fact, the tickets were sold well before she decided to get married. Not the best timing, Gwen.

With everything that has happened to me lately, Jessica hasn't pursued her idea of going shopping together – thank the heavens for small mercies! – but it didn't stop her forcing one of her older dresses on me for tonight and one for the rehearsal dinner. Well, not old, worn once maybe. She made it clear they're last season's, so she wouldn't be caught dead in them anymore. She was very specific that tonight the silver one was most appropriate. It's far tighter and shorter than anything I would normally wear, but she's right that I should make an effort for Gwen's big night, so here I am wearing it.

Climbing out of the taxi, I can't help but fiddle with my hem, pulling it down as far as I can before I walk up the pathway to the venue.

Gwen has really outdone herself this time, hiring a former church in the middle of town to provide a dramatic backdrop to this year's theme: Desire. She's becoming well known for finding these unconventional spaces to showcase her collections; artists vye for her attention and critics look to discover the next must-see pieces of art among those she chooses to feature.

Every inch of the incredible gothic architecture has been illuminated to perfection, casting the finely balanced light and shadow around the paintings and sculptures placed carefully throughout. Even for someone like me, who in all honesty does not understand art in the same way as Gwen, it's awe inspiring.

I've arrived early in case she needs any help, but other than minor checks on the drinks and music, she is completely organised, as always. This is her domain and she's glowing with excitement, whilst making it all look deceptively effortless at the same time.

I wander past the easels, admiring the workmanship of those as much as the art they hold. Gwen had them custom made, each handcrafted in wood to match the gothic structural features surrounding us.

People are starting to arrive and I join in with their polite conversations. I have learned enough about the art Gwen likes that I can just about manage to sound intelligent discussing it, but it has been a long-running joke between us that I do not always understand what I'm saying! If I'd had a normal amount of time and headspace, I would've looked into the show beforehand to prepare myself better, but tonight improvisation will have to do.

The venue quickly fills and the more I hear about points of view and brush strokes, the more out of place I feel. I keep reminding myself that I am not here to impress anyone, I am here to support Gwen – not that she needs it. She looks radiant working her way through her audience, accepting praise and answering questions with exceptional ease.

I try to avoid eye contact with any more attendees, leafing through the programme to try and gain some understanding of the work we are all looking at. I pause at one piece and find myself tilting my head this way and that, squinting to even comprehend what I am looking at. To me it resembles my living room wall when I had used one too many tester pots trying to find the perfect shade of green.

My thoughts are broken as the couple next to me start talking about the depth of emotion portrayed by the young, local artist and his clear hostility towards the establishment and passion for freedom. What? I wonder if we are looking at the same thing. I roll my eyes and move on.

I must admit though, I am in two minds about the theme of her event tonight. On the one hand, it's innovative and interesting – typical Gwen. On the other hand, it reminds me that she was inspired by her then new relationship with Michael. That seems such a long time ago now. I turn a corner, stopping to study a piece that catches my eye. An oil painting from some classic Italian artist – a rendition of Samson and Delilah; even I can tell what it portrays. Art like this I can appreciate. The colours and detail are really quite impressive. Every line of Samson's pained physique painted in incredible detail with vibrant colours, as he lies helpless and exhausted in his lover's arms. The woman he entrusted with his secret looks down at his cut mane. Every strand of hair and fold of fabric is exquisite. The chatter of other guests nearing spurs me to move on though.

Stepping a little further, my eyes glue to the next piece. A woman strewn unconscious across a chaise longue, with what looks like a demon sitting on her chest. Her delicate gown hugs her feminine curves, whilst the wide-eyed beast sits crushing her, its face made bold by the shadows cast upon it. Its darkness contrasting her light. I find myself hypnotised by the beast's glaring eyes, edging closer and closer to the print to take in every tiny detail.

'It's called *The Nightmare*,' a familiar voice whispers behind me.

I'd been so lost in the demon's eyes that the sudden disruption makes me jump. I turn to see who is speaking. Jessica. Her red lipstick perfect, and every hair in place. Anyone would have thought that she was the woman of the hour tonight. Yet, instead of the usual scowl, she looks quite serene.

'It's a Fuseli. There have been many debates amongst scholars as to what he meant by it,' she continues, facing the painting.

Her hands point excitedly as she speaks – far removed from the cold demeanour she usually displays. Jessica is genuinely passionate about something important to Gwen, and I have spent so many of these events avoiding her that I missed it completely.

'Some feel that the ogre is her nightmare, whilst others interpret her pose as suggestive and inviting. She *wants* the ogre to visit her. Indeed, her fear and desire are difficult to distinguish in this work of art, don't you agree?'

I pause, open-mouthed. I am so lost in some, well, all of what she just said. Both due to her unfamiliar friendly manner but also the in-depth analysis she has just offered. I clearly wait a little too long to reply.

'Sorry, I get carried away talking about the Romantics. It really is a beautiful piece though, isn't it?'

She's really unnerving me now. It's not just me who avoids her at these events, the feeling is mutual. She's never managed more than a polite nod when we've seen each other before, and now this?

'That dress looks divine on you by the way.'

I follow her gaze to the borrowed garment. 'Oh yes, thank you.'

Then there it is, the usual awkward silence I've become used to when Gwen isn't around us.

'Anyway, I'll leave you to look at this in peace,' I say, but before I can walk away, Jessica lightly grasps my arm.

'Look, Victoria. I know we're not… close or whatever. But are you OK?'

I study her face. Her expression is mostly relaxed but her eyes are fixed on mine. Is that genuine concern I see in them?

'Yeah, I'm good, thank you for asking.'

'It's quite alright Victoria, but please, if I can help with anything, taking on more tasks for the wedding, please let me know.' She turns and moves on to some other guests.

I want to believe her words are as sincere as they sound, not that she is still trying to take my place as Gwen's maid of honour, but before I can dwell, I hear Gwen calling to me.

'Vic! Vic! I'm so glad you're still here.' I turn to see her rushing towards. 'I thought you would've snuck off by now!'

By the time she releases me, Jessica is enjoying an in-depth discussion elsewhere, whilst Gwen drags me to meet some of her regular clientele. Great, I am now in the points of view and brushstrokes brigade, except they've moved onto texture and depth. It is beautiful to see Gwen in her world though, hands gesticulating enthusiastically as she speaks about each artist with incredible confidence. Her smile radiates warmth and the little clique swarms around her like moths to a flame. After a short time, Gwen shoots me a smile, our signal that I'm free to leave the conversation if I want to – she knows this isn't really for me.

As I allow my gaze to wander from her to see where I might go next, I notice Isaac, helping himself to a drink from a passing waiter. He is the last person I expected to see here – this evening is certainly full of surprises.

Chapter Twenty

Drink Up

As if he can feel me staring at him, his deep brown eyes suddenly look up to meet mine. There's that fluttery feeling in my stomach again. I return his smile and he responds by beckoning me over. There is something about the way he looks at me – the intensity of it – that makes me feel a little uneasy but flattered at the same time. I straighten myself and try to stroll across to him with the most confidence I can muster, knowing he is watching my every move. Inwardly I'm just praying I don't trip up in these heels.

'Please tell me you hate being here as much as I do?' he whispers to me as he kisses my cheek. No awkwardness this time. He hovers next to me just long enough that I can inhale the enticing smell of his cologne and feel the softness of his freshly shaven his face. I hesitate, not wanting to sound disloyal to Gwen, so he wraps his arm around my waist and whispers again. 'Blink twice if you're being held hostage here!'

'Actually,' I reply with a sly smile, 'I quite enjoy the ambience, and I love exploring the themes and motivations of each artist.'

Isaac sees straight through my thinly veiled attempt to sound like I belong in Gwen's clique, laughing gently. His gaze is making me nervous, so I turn to look at the closest painting, well aware of the colour rushing to my face.

'Well, I'd rather appreciate the ambience of the bar around the corner,' he says. 'Shall we?' He nods towards the door with a smile that makes me catch my breath. I must admit I'm tempted. Noticing me looking guiltily over at Gwen, Isaac persists. 'She won't mind. Come on, you owe me a drink!'

'For what?' I say, arching my eyebrows.

'For not inviting me to share the chocolates and champagne I sent you!'

'What… I literally got it today!'

His brow furrows. 'That's odd, I sent them a couple of days ago?'

He doesn't know I've missed a couple of days at work. I move away from him, trying to think how to respond. For just a split second I'd forgotten about the break-in but here it is, in the forefront of my mind again. Isaac moves closer, sweeping the hair from across my eyes.

'Is everything OK?' His eyes search mine, and it feels as if everyone else has faded away.

'What are you two up to?' Gwen enquires with a glint in her eye, appearing from nowhere.

She must have noticed that she's startled me, I can see her stifling a giggle.

'Victoria and I were just saying that it would be good to take a few minutes to talk through our speeches for the wedding,' Isaac lies, winking at me as he does.

'Let me guess, that means you'll have to leave? Together?' I'm not sure Gwen could smile any wider or arch her brows any higher. Subtlety has never been her strong point.

'Not *together* together,' I fluster, my face now positively crimson.

'It's quite alright Vic, I'm only kidding! I appreciate you coming but this really isn't your scene, is it? Don't worry, Michael will be here soon. Go, enjoy yourselves!'

As she air kisses me goodbye I am glad she doesn't mind, and even more relieved to be going before Michael gets here

Isaac puts his arm around my waist again to lead me outside, grabbing our coats from the cloakroom on the way. Even with the extra layer, I shiver as soon as I step outside, but Isaac steps up close behind me, rubbing my arms to warm me.

'We should get moving, you'll freeze if we stand here for too long.'

We walk through the shadows the church is casting across the courtyard. A few stragglers arriving late or smoking outside are the only other people in the otherwise empty grounds. Making our way around the corner and up the steep, cobbled hill to the winery, I nearly trip, but Isaac tightens his grasp to help steady me. There is no hesitancy in the way he touches me, and I'm amazed by how natural it feels. The gentle music from the gallery is now far behind us and the street ahead is empty. The clicking of my heels on the pavement, together with our giggling conversation about our great escape, are the only sounds I can hear. As soon as we're inside the bar, the warmth from the fireplaces at either end of the intimate room wrap around us.

'You grab a table near the fire, I'll get us drinks,' he says.

I do as he suggests and sit looking over at him, reminding myself how easily I had been swayed by his charms the last time we met for a drink – how I had wished I had got to my questions sooner, when I was more sober. I can't get lost in his flattery this time, I have to show him those photos on my phone at the first opportunity. I stare into the fire, using the time I have to try and plan what I'm going to say. The flames crackle as the logs crumble within their heat. It doesn't take long for Isaac to join me, sliding effortlessly into the chair opposite.

'This is it. Good fire, good wine and a good woman – what more could I want?' he sighs, with just enough of a teasing laugh that his comment is charming as opposed to presumptuous. The reflection of the fire flickers so brightly in his eyes, that I have to shake my head to remind myself not to get distracted.

'Oh come on, it's ok to admit you find me adorably charming,' he continues. 'It can be our secret!'

We both laugh. I know he probably uses the same lines with other women, he's far too smooth to be a hopeless romantic, but I enjoy his care-free vibe. In a way, he is exactly what I need in my life. His obvious flirting is a huge confidence boost for me. On the other hand, I do still wonder what he sees in me. Compared to the likes of Gwen, I know I'm just ordinary, and I'm definitely not the life and soul of the party like Samira.

'Penny for them?'

'What?' I say, confused.

'You look deep in thought. Care to share?'

'To be honest, I was thinking how much my opinion of you has changed since the beginning of that engagement meal.'

He laughs, running his hands through his hair and sipping at his drink almost nervously. 'I didn't make the best impression on you, did I?'

Now it's my turn to laugh nervously.

'For what it's worth, my opinion of you hasn't changed at all.'

Remembering the array of compliments from our last meeting I cannot help but smile. I feel like such a teenager, taken in by his flattery, but it feels sincere.

'Although, as we're being honest, even though I like you, I'm not always sure where I stand with you.'

My smile tenses a little. I've spent so long questioning his sincerity that it never occurred to me that Isaac was asking the same questions about me. He has been the one contacting me, sending me gifts, making his feelings clear. I on the other hand have been blowing hot and cold – but how can I not, when even *I* don't know where he stands with me?

'Sorry,' I mumble. 'I'm not great at this stuff.'

I shift uncomfortably in my seat and find myself peering into the fire to avoid his eyes again. Perhaps I should be a little more honest and open with him, I have no reason not to be. I deserve to surround myself with people who care about me. That's the advice I've given countless times to clients like Suzie, who are working through similar traumas to my own.

'Look,' I venture, 'without wanting to kill the mood, I had some issues with an ex. He… he didn't treat me well and it's made me a little wary.'

Isaac reaches over to softly wrap his hand around mine, offering a warm smile. 'I'm sorry. I didn't mean to pry.'

'No, it's OK. I want to be honest. You've been nothing but lovely but it's just, it took me a long time to get my life together after him – Dylan. I just don't want to rush into anything new.'

Raising his glass, Isaac says solemnly, 'To taking things slowly and enjoying our time together.'

My heart warms to his reaction, he didn't try to snoop or dismiss my fears. I lift my glass and clink it lightly against his. 'Cheers to that.'

If I could bottle this moment – the ease of it, and dare I say the thrill? – I would.

What follows are some awful jokes from him, and genuine laughter from me. We did, as promised, begin to discuss the wedding but as per usual he moves the topic of conversation quickly back to me. He is interested in everything about me: where I'm from, my work, what I've been up to this week... That last one stalled the conversation a little.

'Are you OK? You've gone pale.'

'Fine, yeah. This week's just been super busy.'

I gulp at my drink. I don't want to relive the tale of the incredible burglar-cum-fairy-godmother who broke in, to clean and leave me gifts. This however, is my reminder to steer this conversation to Michael.

'So, what have you been up to? Seen Michael much?'

Isaac sinks back from the table, physically distancing himself from my question. 'Not much, except for an investors' dinner,' he says. 'He's so busy with the wedding and work.'

I know I have to say something now or I'll never find the courage to.

'I sorted through some of the photos from the party.'

His eyes narrow as he waits for me to make my point. I can feel my chest tightening – god, I hate confrontation – but if there is something he knows about Michael and this mysterious woman, I need to know too.

'There are some brilliant ones from the dance floor and of you groomsmen doing shots at the bar,' I continue looking him straight in the eye. 'There was one though… well a couple... They kind of solve the mystery of who wrote that question you read out.'

He leans forwards, hanging on my every word now. I reach into my bag for my phone, scrolling through the photos until I find the zoomed in picture of the mystery brunette placing the card into the box. I take a deep breath before holding it out for Isaac to look at. He peers down at the screen, squinting, then his eyes flick back to me.

'What am I looking at exactly?'

His voice is full of suspicion and annoyance in equal measures. I lean forwards, enlarging the picture more.

'Do you recognise her?'

He looks again. 'No, who is she?'

I scroll to the photo I'd snuck of her and Michael. 'OK, how about in this picture? This one's a much clearer picture of her face.'

'Nope, never seen her before.'

He is so matter of fact, but he seems sincere, analysing my face as much I am his. I believe he doesn't know her.

'What's this all about, Vic?'

'This is who Michael's having an affair with.'

There, I said it. I watch every part of Isaac's face, waiting for a reaction. He sighs, taking a huge swig of his drink. No doubt buying himself some time to think about what he is going to say.

'If – and it's a big *if*, Vic – he's having an affair, I don't know anything about it.'

The last time spoke about this, he was adamant that Michael would never do such a thing. What has changed? Now he's the one rubbing the back of his neck, letting his gaze drift to the fire to avoid looking at me.

'What aren't you telling me, Isaac?'

Before I can ask any further questions, out of the corner of my eye I see Michael walking through the door to the bar, making a beeline for us. I can't understand why he's here and not at the gallery, especially as he was running late anyway, but one thing is crystal clear. The look in his eyes is one of pure fury.

Chapter Twenty-One

Something Old, Something New

Three and half weeks until the wedding

'You should both be at the exhibit!'

Michael charges over to us, his voice deep with simmering anger. The sheer audacity of his tone shocks me into silence – what an odd overreaction. Isaac however stands up calmly to face him.

'Hang on mate, we've been to the exhibition. Now we're just having a drink. What's the problem?' Isaac holds his hands up submissively.

Michael edges closer to him, his eyes no less enraged as he tries to lower his voice through gritted teeth. 'Nothing you do is harmless. What have you said to her?'

His demeanour is not like I've ever seen him before, even going beyond how he was when he came to my house. Long gone is his sophisticated, unflappable veneer. What does he think Isaac has shared with me? His breathing is laboured, his nostrils flaring. It feels like the longest pause as both men refuse to break their laser-like stare from one another. Summoning what tiny courage I have, I stand up.

'What's this about? What do you think Isaac has said to me?'

They look at me, then at each other. Isaac's gentle shrug of his shoulders implies he isn't sure either, which only appears to anger Michael further. His face contorts into a snarl.

'Outside!' Michael commands, poking Isaac hard in the chest.

'Come on, Michael. Why don't we stay here where it's warm and have a little chat?' Isaac responds, smiling and winking at me. He's trying to defuse whatever this situation is but I can see Michael is about to explode at Isaac's nonchalance. His fists tightening and his breathing only getting louder. 'Either join us or get back to Gwen – there's a good man,' Isaac continues, turning to pick up his drink.

I feel like I'm watching a car crash in slow motion. The tension in the atmosphere is palpable, Michael doesn't know how to react. The tables closest to us have stopped their conversations entirely to watch this spectacle. I put myself between the two rivals, gently placing my hands on Michael's chest both to calm him and create a little more space between them.

'Maybe you should just leave it, Michael.'

It doesn't work. He grabs my wrist and twists, and I wince with the sudden pain. Even though I try to prise at his fingers to loosen his grip, he easily holds on. I freeze. In times gone by I would brace myself – to take a blow, to my face or body. To be submissive until the anger dissipates. It's the only way I've survived such aggression before. I keep my eyes down as Michael moves his level with mine, spitting his words at me.

'I told you – I won't let anyone come between me and Gwen!'

I feel Isaac brush past and launch Michael away from me, in one forceful push.

'Get the fuck away from her!' he growls, hands clenched, standing guard in front of me.

I cradle my sore wrist, unable to think quickly enough to intervene in any meaningful way. My whole body is tense with fear. I watch helplessly as they start pushing each other back and forth, bumping into other patrons' tables, sending drinks crashing to the floor. The distraught onlookers are clearing the area, not wanting to be caught up in the violence about to erupt. Thankfully, to my right I can see two bartenders rushing over.

'Oi! That's enough!' one yells as they roughly pull them apart.

Michael starts running his hands through his hair and straightening his tailored shirt and tie, whilst the bar staff warn him and Isaac about calling the police. Isaac turns away at this point, leaning on our table, taking deep breaths to calm himself. His knuckles are turning white from how hard he is gripping the edge, his head down avoiding any kind of communication.

'You need to leave mate,' the bartenders continue, facing Michael, blocking his path to us.

His eyes widen, ready to protest, but as if coming to his senses he backs away, looking first at me and then at Isaac.

By now the entire bar has quietened, watching the scene with keen interest.

'You alright miss?' The other barman turns to me.

All eyes are on me now. I open my mouth to respond but nothing comes out. With this, Michael's shoulders lower with the tension visibly leaving his body, presumably relieved that I'm not going to create more of a scene than he already has. When he speaks his voice is much calmer – a controlled hiss that sends chills through me.

'I'll speak to you later, Isaac.'

Before any reply can be made, he turns and storms out of the bar. Who is this man? Once again I've seen the Mr Hyde to the Doctor Jekyll Gwen knows, except this time he was even more frightening. There is a hush in the room, with people looking and whispering. The bartender offers to fetch me another drink but I shake my head, instead edging towards my coat and bag. I just want to leave.

'That was a little dramatic, wasn't it?' says Isaac, forcing a laugh. However, it fades when he sees how tearful I am, still cradling my wrist. He reaches for me, but I flinch.

'Please, let me see. Do you need some ice? Or a doctor?'

I don't want him or anyone else near me. I don't know what has just happened but he's hiding something from me. Why would Michael behave that way?

'I just want to go home,' is all I can muster.

Isaac looks like he wants to say something more, but he resigns himself to simply, 'I'll get you a taxi.'

He helps me to put my coat on, the feel of my sleeve sending a twinge through my injured wrist. It's been a while since I've felt pain like this, the ache dragging my thoughts back to years of covering bruises. I hate Michael for making me feel this way but if nothing else, at least I know now that I'm not being paranoid. There's definitely a dark side to him, and I'm sure Isaac had never seen it before either. When we step outside Isaac manoeuvres in front of me, but I can barely look at him.

'I'm sorry you got caught up in that. Please let me see your wrist.'

'Caught up in what?'

Exhaling, he steps back, keeping his eyes firmly on the floor. 'Look, after what you said, I realised I didn't really know much about Michael's past…'

'So…'

'So I started looking into his companies' records, just to see how he got started.'

In my impatience I almost forget the pain shooting up my arm. I'm hanging on every word, sensing that at last, I might find out something important about Gwen's future husband.

'He must know what I was doing, what I found.'

'What did you find?' My heart is racing in anticipation.

'He changed his name a couple of years back – he used to be called Michael Wood.'

I am dumbstruck. Could that be why I didn't find anything about him online? Between the throbbing of my wrist and what finally feels like some kind of breakthrough, I can't find any words. All I can do is nod slowly.

'I don't know why he reacted so badly though, Vic. I'm sure it's not unusual to change names really. Sometimes people with money change theirs so they can carve their own lives away from their families. That would seem reasonable considering Michael's entrepreneurial enterprises.' He sounds less than convinced by his own theory, 'Look – I'm sorry.'

He steps forward, wrapping his arms around me. I can't reciprocate but I don't push him away either, instead resting my head against his chest. I know he is trying to comfort me, but I don't feel it. My mind is whirring, from flashbacks of crying in pain alone all those years ago, to wondering if Michael has ever put his hands on Gwen.

'I just need to go home,' I whisper, gently pushing Isaac away.

He's looking at me with such sadness in his eyes. Nevertheless he hails me a taxi. Holding the door open as I climb in, he pauses. 'Victoria. If you need anything, please call. I really am sorry for tonight.'

I try to manage a smile – this isn't his fault after all – but I can already feel the familiar trickle of tears on my face as my cab pulls away.

My head is filling with a tornado of suspicion, anxiety, stress, and a tirade of questions. Why did Michael change his name? Why is he so angry that Isaac knows? Why is he so angry that Isaac has told *me*? Surely if it was to be his own man like Isaac thinks, he wouldn't mind that we know? I need to talk to Gwen, make sure she is safe. I know she won't answer her phone tonight, not whilst she's busy at the exhibition, but I text her now, whilst I still have the nerve.

> We need to talk. I'm coming to yours tomorrow morning.x

I must seem so rude, barely acknowledging the driver as he drops me off, but I need to just be in my house, away from the world. As soon as I get inside, I feel myself sliding down the wall into a heap on the floor, floods of tears escape me as I relive the events in the bar. Sometimes I feel like I have come so far in my life, but those few moments made me feel just as helpless as I did at my lowest.

I'm not sure how long I sit there before the throbbing of my wrist persuades me to get up and fetch some ice. I'm standing in the kitchen, wrapping some frozen peas in a tea towel when my phone buzzes and I balk, worried that Gwen has already responded when I'm not ready to talk to anyone.

Just checking you got home OK? x

Isaac. I sigh. I feel sorry for him, he hasn't done anything wrong. Far from it. Deep down I wonder, if all of this wasn't going on, how might the night have ended?

Home OK. Heading to bed. Speak soon. X

I turn my phone to silent and lay it down on the island. My wrist is turning a deep blue-purple colour, which only serves to remind me of Michael's ruddy face, contorted, close to mine. I concentrate on my breathing, trying to make my anger dissipate but it simply channels into determination. I stride to my study, armed with his real name. It is about time I start having some of my questions answered.

As I move through the house, it still feels different. This is the first night I've been alone since the break-in. Every shadow seems more sinister somehow. I turn on every light downstairs and open every internal door wide so I can see and hear everything around me. I check that each window is locked as I move through the house, closing the curtains as I go. Only then do I feel comfortable enough to go through to my study. Though it takes only seconds, I am impatient as computer fires up, pressing the buttons aggressively and repeatedly until the bright search page opens. This is it.

Carefully typing in Michael Wood into the box, I click my mouse. Instantly thousands of results come back. My heart sinks at having to sift through them again, but I click onto the Images page and there he is. With slightly different hairstyles and a variety of ages, but several of them are definitely him.

I frantically click on one image after another – there is an overwhelming amount of information to take in. His university sports team pictures, old social media images. Link by link, I try and absorb as much information as I can, motivated by each breakthrough. My eyes are beginning to sting from the brightness of the screen, but I keep going. Scrolling and scrolling until I see her. I stop to stare at the stunning brunette a much younger Michael has his arm around. I hold my breath – could this be the mystery woman I have been hunting?

I click on the link. In the seconds it's taking to load I steady my breathing, readying myself for what may come next. Maybe proof that Gwen shouldn't marry Michael. Or maybe nothing. I rap my fingernails on the desk, watching the buffering icon spin round and round, leaning closer in anticipation. Then the screen fills with pictures and text, but this is not what I imagined. My jaw drops in disbelief. This woman isn't the one I saw at the party, but someone who looks incredibly like her. No, the woman on my screen cannot be her – because this woman is dead. The news headline reads:

'Accidental death. Fire kills devoted wife. Widower becomes recluse.'
Article after article, witness statement after police statement.

'Serena Wood dies in tragic accidental fire.'
Serena Wood, as in Michael Wood? Surely… it can't be? She was his wife. I never knew Michael had been married before. But if Serena is dead, who the hell is the woman I saw him with? More to the point, why is Michael so desperate to hide all of this – surely there's nothing here for him to be afraid of? Unless there is more to this accident than the reports are saying.

Chapter Twenty-Two

The Ex

I don't know how to take in all of this information. I try to take stock of what I know: Michael has been married before, his wife died in an accident, he changed his name. Now I don't want to overreact, but when I add these facts to the way I've seen him behave, to how careful he is to never disclose too much about himself, I have to wonder what else he is hiding. Or with his obvious temper, what he is capable of.

I wrestle with what to do next. If he is an abuser, or worse, and I go to Gwen without a fool proof plan for keeping her safe, it could put her in even more danger. Also, I have to bear in mind that even when faced with this, she may somehow try and defend him. I know all too well how easy it is to defend someone who you know deep down is truly a monster. Fear clouds any rational decision making.

To me it seems obvious: Gwen is about to marry a dangerous man. On the other hand, could there be a logical explanation – a way he would explain it all away? Perhaps he's changed his name to escape his tragic past? And he's guarded because he cannot bear to think about a love that he's lost? And then there's the possibility that Gwen already knows about this past marriage, but if she did, I'm sure she would've told me – wouldn't she?

I'm not sure how long I've been sitting at my desk, staring at these screens. How long I have been sat trying to understand why Michael has been hiding such a huge part of his life. All this time I have wanted evidence that he's not the man he portrays himself to be, and here there is reams of it, all at once. I must organise my thoughts and what I have found though, so as not to overwhelm Gwen when I tell her.

I start writing key details onto sticky notes, scribbling furiously. Anything that might be helpful: his previous address, when the fire happened, and some facts about Serena. Detail after detail; I scribble furiously, sticking each note to the wall behind my screen as I go. Next, I turn my attention to printing some pictures and pin them to the wall too. One of Michael and Serena, and another of the remnants of their home. It's hard not to stare at the photo of them together – it's the same as any happy couple picture. It's not lost on me that in some of the photos he is looking at his late wife much in the same way he looks at Gwen. Perhaps Gwen doesn't need to see these. But I continue to print some of the news articles and even the pictures on my phone. All for my wall.

I know, to an outsider, I may look a tad obsessive here, but seeing the evidence in front of me is a huge relief. My instincts were right all along. Gwen will have to listen to all of this. Casting my eyes over each note, I still don't know how this links to the mysterious brunette, or why she seems to have disappeared. The ache in my temples and wrist are telling me I need rest, but when I look down at the swelling and finger-mark shaped bruises on my arm, I know now isn't the time. Every minute Gwen is with Michael is a minute too long.

I fetch myself a fresh cup of coffee to help keep me going as I trawl through local news articles. I'm not sure I understand some of the finer details of the fire, but I can research those separately.

Just as I feel I'm about to give in to my pain and weariness, I find it – I find her. A picture of Serena's family, dressed in black. There, next to what I assume are Serena's parents, is the mystery brunette. Searching for details within the caption, I finally get my answer.

'Anna, sister of Serena, mourns her tragic loss.'

There's no doubt about it. Deep brown hair, beautiful face, it's definitely her. I can feel the truth scratching inside my skull. I just can't make all of this link up. I will though and one way or another, Michael's past is about to catch up to him.

I absorb every line of the article: the pain and loss that was felt at the funeral. The loss to the community that their Serena had been such an active part of. She sounds like she was the ideal woman, using what they describe as an 'incredible wealth' to help those in need.

Just as I am about to close my computer down for the night, satisfied I have gathered enough information, I see one last link on the page. It leads to a video, recorded by the press camped outside the grieving family's home. As the family repeatedly make 'no comment' responses, I feel for them – how can these journalists harass people in such agony? Until Anna does something unexpected. The family are walking away but she turns back towards the journalist.

'Why didn't she wake up when the fire started? That's what I want to know. Why didn't she wake up?'

Then she's cut off, dragged back to the house by her mother. I pause the clip as Anna looks into the camera. Anguish and anger mingling on her face. What is she getting at?

My stomach drops when I finally start to make the connections. What I saw and heard between her and Michael. The tampered question at the party. The secret she wants revealed. Could Anna be implying that her sister's untimely death was no accident?

I have to stop. I can't read any more right now. It's one thing for me to be deeply suspicious of Michael, if not afraid of him, but do I really believe he could cause someone's death? This is so far from the evidence of an affair I thought I would find. And that would be so much easier to explain.

My heart is pumping so hard as I storm back to the kitchen for my phone. Gwen's reply to my message reads:

Brilliant night. Off to bed. Speak later. xx

It's past 3 a.m. now. She'll be asleep. I'll wait the few hours until daybreak and then I'll see her. I might not have all the answers yet, but I have to share with her the picture they are painting as soon as possible.

Before I take myself to bed, I go back to the study, stand back to stare at the array of notes on the wall. It's a disorganised mess – pretty symbolic of my thoughts right now. I take my large wall planner and pin it over the top, so the post-it notes and pictures are completely hidden. I wish I could shift my paranoia but I have to be sure that if it is Michael coming into my home, he doesn't see what I now know.

The morning seems to come in the blink of an eye. I don't even remember falling asleep but rather than my usual slow roll out of bed, I dress quickly, with purpose. As I brush my teeth, there is no way of hiding how drawn my reflection looks in the mirror – with huge dark circles under my eyes, traces of mascara still smudged on my cheeks, but most disturbingly, the bruising on my arm, which has darkened as I slept. A reminder that I don't want to face Michael. I desperately need to speak to Gwen, but how to get her alone?

I reach for a long sleeve top to cover my wrist and text her, then sit fidgeting, waiting for a reply. As the minutes tick by I make a cup of tea and some toast – anything to help the time pass and settle my stomach, raging with nerves.

I can't help but pace back and forth as I eat, spilling crumbs everywhere. I go back to the study and move the wall planner aside so I can read over some of the notes I made last night – my handwriting had definitely worsened the more tired and frantic I got, but the messages are clear.

Not only is Michael not the person he portrays himself to be, but there is every possibility he is even more sinister than I had ever imagined.

A twinge in my wrist brings the interaction between him and Isaac back to me in painful detail. The anger, the aggression. I should regret dragging Isaac into this, but I wouldn't have all of this without his help. At least now he too can start to see Michael for what he truly is: at best, unstable. As I set down my empty mug on the desk, my phone vibrates at last. I had expected Gwen's name to pop up on the screen, but freeze when I see it's not her. It's Michael.

My heart races, my eyes darting back to everything written on the wall. Is it possible he knows what I have found out?

> I'm sorry, I can explain. Please don't tell Gwen.

I can feel my grip on the phone tighten. What does he mean? That he doesn't want me to tell Gwen about what he did to me and Isaac last night, or that he realises what Isaac must have told me? My fear seeps away as a growing fury takes over. How dare he contact me as if we're friends, as if he has some say in what I will and will not divulge to Gwen. I throw my phone back onto the desk, resolute that I'm not even going to respond. However, as I pace back and forth, fuming, an idea comes to me.

> OK. Meet me at the café across the park.
> 30 minutes.

I have no intention of meeting him. But while he's out of the house, waiting for me, I'll be getting some quality time with Gwen – we've got a lot to catch up on.

OK.

His reply is immediate. Perfect. I hurry out of the house, still pulling my jacket on as I reach the street. I won't take my car, I'm too jittery to drive safely. I'll make it to Gwen's on foot in time.

It doesn't take long for me to feel breathless from the pace I am trying to keep up, the cold air stinging my lungs, but I can't slow down. Only when I'm approaching Gwen's front door do I realise I have no idea what I'm actually going to say to her. I have rehearsed in my mind telling her about last night, how Michael has made me feel and what I've found online. Now I just have to find the courage to start any of those sentences. I'm starting to feel sick with fear now. How will she react? Will I even manage to get the words out? My mouth is already feeling dry and my hands sweaty as I press her doorbell.

Looking around as I wait, I notice something that makes my stomach drop. There are still two cars parked on the street outside. I hear the door unlatch from behind and a wave of dread washes over me as I turn to see who has opened it. Michael.

Chapter Twenty-Three

Love Hurts

Just over 3 weeks until the wedding

His look of shock must be a perfect match for mine. For a second we stand in silence gawping at each other. I watch as his expression changes to one of concern. Rather than letting me in, he gently pushes me back down the front steps, pulling the door to behind him.

'Why are you here?' he whispers, checking over his shoulder, eyes wide waiting for my answer.

I try to step back to put some space between us but he keeps edging closer, lowering his voice even further. 'I was about to leave. Go, I'll meet you there. Please.'

Where is the rage I was on the receiving end of yesterday? The intimidating figure who grabbed me is now hiding behind hushed tones. I can feel that anger building inside of me again. Who is he to push me away from Gwen's house? I'm not sure where my courage is coming from but rather than letting him usher me back any further, I lunge towards him, forcing him to retreat.

'I know all about you,' I hiss.

We are so close I can smell the coffee on his breath. My body is so tense I'm shaking, but I'll be damned if I am going to show that I'm scared. I half expect him to retaliate, meet aggression with aggression, but unexpectedly he stutters wordlessly, until Gwen's voice drifts out to us from inside. 'Who's that at the door darling?'

Taking advantage of his current daze, I shove past him, crashing my way through the door.

'Just me!' I announce loudly before he can stop me.

I hear Gwen running down the stairs to greet me. Behind me Michael pretends to cough, to get our attention.

'Shall I drive you home Vic? You look tired,' Michael asks.

'Don't be silly, she's just got here,' Gwen replies, giving me another smile and leading me to the kitchen.

'Yes, don't be silly Michael, Gwen and I have lots to catch up on. It was quite a night last night,' I reply, turning to look him in the eye.

I want to show him he's not the one in control now. Again, I expect his anger to resurface. Instead, he is almost slumped against the wall, looking utterly defeated. I wonder if he will follow us, give her his side of the story, but instead he grabs his car keys.

'Just got some errands to run then. I'll see you ladies later.' And he is gone.

I watch Gwen busy herself with making coffee, complaining about still being tired. It's all just an echo to me. This is the bit I had been dreading. How do I even start the conversation about Michael? I need to warm up, fill the silence.

'You must be pleased with last night's turnout?'

She spins around to look at me with a glint in her eye, changing the subject immediately. 'Shouldn't we talk about you and Isaac first? Give me the gossip!'

This isn't like Gwen. She usually likes to monopolise the conversation. It's not something that bothers me – she likes to talk and I like to listen. I wonder if she still feels guilty about doubting my sanity over the break-ins, trying to make me feel heard now. Seeing the huge smile on her face, pain swells in my chest. I don't want to be the person to take that smile away. Gwen hurls question after question about Isaac, but I don't respond. My nerves getting the better of me.

'We can talk about him later. The exhibition looked like a huge success. Did anyone buy anything?'

Thankfully Gwen takes the hint and soon gets lost in relaying every part of the evening. There's a look of pure glee on her face as she regales me with every detail of the who's-who that attended and their interest in the way she curated the show. She truly lights up. This is making it worse. I should've just come out with it. I will, the next time she stops to take a breath.

'I'm sorry I didn't stay until the end but...'

'But Isaac was nicer to look at than the artwork?' Gwen winks and laughs at her own joke.

I feel my cheeks flush a deep shade of crimson. 'It's not like that.' Well, it kind of is but I don't want us to get distracted when there is so much I need to say.

'Why not? He's gorgeous and he clearly likes you! So...' She nudges me melodramatically, making kissing noises. 'You never answered, where did you go?'

Michael definitely hasn't told her anything about last night, then.

'We went for a drink, at that little bar around the corner.'

She huddles closer, expecting some flirty gossip. I close my eyes and swallow hard. It's now or never. I begin to explain that I enjoyed the start of the evening, how easily conversation flowed and how I do feel reluctantly drawn to him. She is squeezing my uninjured arm with excitement. I'd forgotten how we used to talk like this, before she met Michael. We'd sit and chatter about the awful dates she'd been on. From men who droned on too much about themselves, to those trying to hide wedding rings. In return she'd dry my eyes many a time when I recounted my past with Dylan, never pushing me to jump back into the dating scene. It feels like old times. I wish it were old times, then I wouldn't have to break her heart. I can feel that I'm stalling. I'm wasting whatever time Michael is granting me.

'He knows how to make a woman blush, that's for sure. I know you can handle him though, Vic!' Then she wiggles her eyebrows ridiculously. 'So… did you… you know?'

I can't bring myself to smile, instead pulling my arms free of her hold.

'What?' she asks, puzzled. 'What happened Vic, you don't look well.'

'No, that's not how the evening ended.' I carefully explain. 'Gwen, there's something I need to tell you and I need you to just listen.'

The colour drains from her face as she straightens herself in her chair. 'You're frightening me Vic,' she murmurs, taking my hand again. Then her phones rings. It's Michael.

'Don't answer it – please?' I beg.

Without question she sends his call to voicemail and promptly turns her phone to silent. I'm relieved to have her undivided attention, but my stomach is churning.

'It started at the engagement party.'

She already looks taken aback. 'You and Isaac? I know, you told me that already.' Her eyes wrinkle with confusion. I shoot her a look and she realises she's interrupted. 'Sorry, you go.'

'I saw Michael, talking to someone. Away from the party. A woman.'

Gwen's mouth drops open, but she remains silent.

'I took a photo,' I continue, trying my best to plough on.

'Show me,' she gasps.

I open my phone, my hand trembling as I hold it out to her. Without a word she zooms in, bringing the phone closer to her face.

'It's the same woman I saw him in the park with. Both times he seemed upset with her.'

'Go on,' she ushers, clearly trying to hold back a barrage of questions.

'Then Michael came to my house to bring those flowers. Do you remember?'

She nods silently.

'I think he knew I'd seen him with her, and it really angered him, Gwen. He didn't want me to tell you about it. He said it would ruin things and I really didn't want to ruin anything for you.' My voice cracks. Even though my eyes are stinging, I want to be clear in what I am saying. I hear her breathing hitch too.

'And last night?' she asks, a single tear falling down her cheek, which she swiftly wipes away.

'I was just talking to Isaac. I wanted to ask him about this mystery woman.'

'And did you? Did you ask him?' Her voice is far more intense now, her grip on my hand uncomfortably tight.

'No, Michael interrupted us.'

'When? He was with me at the gallery…' Her face screws up as if she's suddenly seeing the evening in a whole new light. '… He was so agitated. I thought he was just tired from a long day at work.'

'It must have been before that. I don't know how he knew we were there, maybe he saw us through the window, but he came in and he… he…'

'He what?' She leans forward, and rather than telling her, I pull my hands free to raise my sleeve, revealing the bruise on my arm.

'He was so angry that I hadn't listened to his warning to stay out of his business. I tried to tell him to leave but…'

On her face is a look I hope never to see again. One of anger and disbelief but most of all, she looks hurt. Gently running her fingers over the bruise, she says quietly, 'But why… why would he do that?' Then she gets up and marches away from the table, pacing the room at such speed that she's beginning to frighten me. 'Please tell me this is a sick joke.'

'It's all true,' I hear the voice from behind me say. There in the doorway stands Michael. 'We need to talk – all of us.'

Chapter Twenty-Four

We Need To Talk

The silence is palpable. I stand, staring at a crestfallen Michael, his eyes sunken as he slumps against the doorway. The next instant, though, his eyes widen in shock and his hands move to defend his face as Gwen's coffee cup shatters on the wall, barely missing him. Shards of it rain down onto this seemingly helpless man. Neither of us have time to react before she throws the cafetière too. I turn to see she is grabbing anything she can reach to keep the projectiles flying.

'Please… listen!'

Michael edges tentatively towards her, one arm outstretched in surrender, the other still shielding his face.

'Look what you did to her!'

Both of their eyes fall on me, moving down to my battered arm. He begins to stammer an apology but before he can form the words Gwen stands between us like a demon possessed. She does not want him near either of us, and launches my half-filled cup directly at him to prove it.

'Another woman Michael? You're seeing another woman? How could you?'

Her eyes are filled with rage, her breathing so heavy. I've never seen her like this before. Michael won't let up though, he starts towards her again. The sound Gwen makes next is something I will never forget. An incredible shriek of frustration and pain. Her hands are so tightly clenched and tears are streaming down her face. I have to protect her. Mustering all the confidence I can I step forwards, between them.

Locking eyes with Michael I shout, 'Just get out!'

He pauses, his eyes darting between Gwen and me. I hold my breath, unsure of how he will react. This approach didn't work well for me last night and now there aren't any bar staff to come to our aid. He edges a little towards Gwen, clearly hoping she will still talk to him, but she has already turned away, sobbing as she leans over the sink.

It's up to me now. I step closer to him, as close as he was to me last night, and look him directly in the eyes.

'I told you to fucking leave!'

Even I am surprised at the level of venom piercing my words. He almost stumbles backwards. Then, with a sigh and one last look at Gwen, he turns to go. Reaching for his coat he pauses in the kitchen doorway, leaning on the frame to gather his strength. We can barely hear him mutter.

'I really am sorry Vic, and I really do love you, Gwen. I didn't mean for this to happen.'

With that, he disappears through the front door, slamming it behind him.

Gwen and I stand in silence for what seems an age. There's still so much to tell her but she clearly isn't ready.

This is more than enough for her to try and understand right now. Instead, I begin to pick up the larger pieces of glass and ceramic scattered across the floor. I hear her mumble that I should leave it, but I feel less awkward while I'm doing something. What else can I do? Comfort her? Tell her everything is going to be alright? No, I know that isn't the case at all. Far from it. I think things are only going to get worse from here. When I can find the courage to tell her the rest of what I have to say that is.

'I said leave it,' she says more forcefully this time, storming over and pulling me up from the floor, careful not to touch my wrist. We hug. Silently. Endlessly.

'I'm so sorry Gwen, I hate having to upset you.'

Standing back to face me, she seems almost calm. 'You have nothing to be sorry for Vic. You're a good friend–'

Perhaps I should at least make it clear that the woman from the park is not a mistress. Give Gwen some peace of mind. 'Gwen, about the woman, I don't think–'

'Please Vic, I don't want to hear any more right now.'

I need to be alone for a bit if that's OK? I'm going to have a lie down upstairs.'

All I can do is nod. She's going to need time, and probably a long cry into her pillow.

'I'll be here when you come back down.'

She manages a half smile through the tears still streaming down her face. I help wipe them away and offer to run her a bath or make her tea, but she just shrugs and walks slowly from the room, leaving me standing alone.

I return to picking up the fragments of porcelain and wonder how our lives have come to this. When is Michael coming back, and more frighteningly, what he is going to say or do when he does?

To keep busy I continue to sweep and mop the mess left on the floor and walls, and when I've emptied the dust pan into the bin, the kitchen is as close to its pristine self as I can get it. Almost as if nothing has happened. I tie the bin liner to take it outside, sharp pieces of glass starting to protrude so I quicken my pace. The chilly breeze makes me shiver. Standing outside, I let the bin lid drop, and stop to take a second to let the fresh air rush through my hair. It feels refreshing but I know I need to get back inside in case Michael returns.

I pull the chain across the front door so if he does come home, I'll be able to hear him trying to get in.

I walk into the front room and happen to look out of the front windows. Across the street I can see something. A person, I think, hidden amongst the parked cars and low hanging branches. Unmoving I feel a shiver down my spine. I don't wait to see who it is. Now is not the time to fixate on anyone watching us from outside – whether it's a stranger or Michael, so I draw the curtains and turn on the lamps. Each highlights various photos on the walls and shelves. I smile at those featuring some of the girls' nights out, a gorgeous one of all of us enjoying the sun last summer. I stop at a frame with a picture of Gwen and Michael. She's framed the rose petal picture from when he proposed. Once again, I find myself ruminating on the kind of person Michael is.

It seems he thinks the only thing that Gwen and I have talked about is his angry outburst from last night and the brunette, but there was no mention of who she is or his name changes. He must know I know about his name though, after the way he reacted to Isaac. And as for Anna, she is still the key to all of this, I can feel it. Now I know who she is and possibly where to find her, maybe I need to speak to her myself. Then I might find out more about why she questions the way in which her sister died. And why she tracked down Michael. *If* Serena's death wasn't an accident, Gwen's life could also be at risk. I need to wait, and go to Gwen when I have as much information as possible, then there would be no way she would stay with Michael. Although after today, perhaps they are already over?

Flopping onto the sofa there's not much I can do right this second. So I take out my phone to text Isaac to cancel our dinner date tonight. Hopefully he will understand, given the chaos of last night. Part of me wants to tell him everything about this morning too, but at the same time, I'm not sure dragging him into this nightmare any further is fair.

> Are you alright? Sorry but think I need to take a rain check for dinner tonight. xx

I watch the little dots appear.

> I understand – as long as you're OK. x

Before I can respond another text pops up.

> I wish I could see you though. x

I let out a groan, imagining being in his company, laughing and flirting.

> I'm with Gwen now. Can I call you later, make it up to you? x

The three dots appear and then disappear. I wonder what he is thinking, then a brief response.

> Sure, whenever you're ready. x

This whole situation is a nightmare, but one good thing is starting to come from this – with Isaac I'm feeling able to let down some of my walls finally. It's odd considering how little time we've really spent together, but he has such a warmth and tenderness about him. He's different. Just the kind of person I need and want in my life.

The hours tick by and to my surprise Michael doesn't come back. It's night-time before I hear Gwen come down the stairs, her eyes puffy and skin looking sallow.

'Gwen, I–' Before I can offer any comfort, she interrupts. 'I need to speak to him, Vic.'

What? Is this what she has been thinking about when she was alone upstairs – how much she misses Michael?

'But Gwen, what if he gets angry?'

Her eyes lower to my swollen wrist before looking back at me. 'I have to, Vic. I need to know what's going on. Why he did this.'

My head is shaking instinctively. I'm not sure I could let her be alone with him if I tried.

'I promise I'll check in with you,' she says, 'so you know I'm OK.'

I sit and watch her type a message to him, before she crumples onto the sofa next to me, leaning on my shoulder. She pulls her tissue into little strands waiting for his reply – which comes quickly.

'He says he'll be here in twenty minutes,' she murmurs, scrambling to pick up the tiny strips of paper littering the floor.

She doesn't say it, but I know she wants me to leave before he arrives. I gather my things and order a taxi – it is far too dark to walk home alone. It irritates me when I notice Gwen fixing her hair in the mirror above the fireplace, then I feel a pang of sympathy. She's confused. Focusing on her image is instinctual for her, and Michael is the man she loves. That cannot just stop, not yet. I wonder how much of this she's really taken in yet. The sick sense of dread I'm feeling only worsens when I open the door to leave, and see Michael already pulling up outside.

I take one last look at Gwen as she fidgets in the doorway, before turning to walk towards him. He is almost bracing himself as I move closer. What a strange shift in dynamic; he is intimidated – by me? His eyes are red and his usually impeccably neat shirt is stained with coffee, missing its tie. I want him to know I'm watching him.

'I'll be speaking to Gwen later, to make sure you haven't hurt her,' I say. 'I won't hesitate to call the police.'

He doesn't reply, just nods and shuffles past. What's he going to say to Gwen? Knowing him, he'll try to explain this all away. But will Gwen believe him? As he reaches the door, his attempt to kiss Gwen is met with her stepping back turning her face away, which he accepts without argument. The tone is set for their meeting. Whatever happens next, whatever he tells her, doesn't matter – I hope.

I will get back to my study as soon as I get home and think clearly enough for the both of us.

Chapter Twenty-Five

Forsaking All Others

As soon as I get home I head straight for my computer. Sitting at my desk I text Gwen.

> Waiting to hear from you. Let me know how you're getting on. X

Then I pull the large wall planner from the wall to reveal the enormous web of neon notes behind. It is quite the sight, and it takes a moment for my eyes to adjust and follow each scribble. As the disturbing details jump out at me, that nauseating feeling washes over me again. What kind of man have I left Gwen with? On one hand he might be an innocent widower, on the other… It doesn't bear thinking about. What I'm most interested in now is the picture of Anna. Dressed head to toe in black at her sister's funeral, her face is full of such sorrow, not contorted with anger like in the video I watched.

I fire up my computer, and thanks to all the invasive journalism around her sister's death, she's instantly searchable online. Her social media profiles are set to private, so I can't reach out to her directly, but in a matter of minutes I've learned that she still lives in the same town where Michael lived with Serena: a wealthy looking seaside town, only a couple of hours' drive from here. There's also the odd picture that her friends have tagged her in, including one of her posing behind a bar, pouring wine from a bottle. She must work there. Zooming in on the stack of menus on the bar, I make out the name: The Oyster Bar and Restaurant. There's only one thing for it, I have to go to her, in person.

I call Becky to tell her I need a few days away, and she works her magic on the appointment schedule and arranges some cover. I'll have to think of how I'll explain my sudden absence to Gwen, but I will handle that when she eventually contacts me. For now, I turn my attention to organising my notes, copying down any points that might be useful to ask Anna about, scribbling questions so I don't forget anything.

Hours later, I wake on the sofa. I must have dropped off while waiting for Gwen to message. Looking at my phone, there's still nothing from her. Panic rises inside me – I don't want her to think I'm not respecting her privacy but she really should've checked in by now. Michael could have done anything to her. My thumb hovers over the call button but before I can press it, I hear a screech of tyres outside. I peer out of the window and see Gwen making her way to my house. Running to the door, I open it before she even has a chance to press the doorbell, and she stumbles into my arms.

I cannot put into words the relief I feel that she is here, and safe. We sit down silently on the sofa, and I wait for her to speak first.

'Can I stay here tonight?' she asks, looking more lost and vulnerable than I've ever seen her before.

'Yes, absolutely. You don't have to ask.'

Bringing her knees up, she wraps her arms around them and sobs. I'm taken aback. I have dealt with so many clients who have acted in the same way but normally Gwen is a force to be reckoned with. The strong one of the pair of us. To see her like this makes my heart ache.

'I'm just so tired…'

I reach for one of her hands. 'C'mon, let's get you some PJs.'

I get up to pull her to her feet, but then I notice that the study door is still ajar. I can't let Gwen see what's inside. I gently turn her towards the hall and quickly rush to close the door before she even realises I'm not right behind her.

Upstairs, I rifle through my drawers to find her some nightclothes, making ridiculous small talk about my favourite pyjamas just to fill the painful silence as she sits catatonic on my bed.

Finally, she says, 'I'm sorry, Vic.'

I spin to look at her. Her eyes are glassy and seem to look straight through me.

'For what? None of this is your fault, Gwen.'

She breaks down again. This isn't like her at all. Every part of me wants her to just spit it out, tell me what has happened since I left her house – what he said. She notices the framed picture from our holiday on the nightstand, and gestures weakly at it.

'Life was so simple then, Vic. I'd do anything to be back there now.'

'Gwen,' I have to ask, 'what's happened?'

She lets out a huge sigh. 'He's been keeping so much from me.' She collapses back onto the bed, pulling a pillow towards her to hug. I begin to lean towards her, to try to comfort her.

'She's an ex!' she blurts out.

I stop short. 'What… who?'

'The woman at the party. She's been trying to get back with him and he never told me – he should've told me though.'

I'm floored. He's done it again. Fed her lie after lie, and she's falling for it. Anna being an ex would certainly serve as a simple explanation for what I saw at the party and in the park, but I know so much more now.

'He's been so stressed about the wedding and her – that's why he's been getting so irritable.'

I recoil at her tone. Irritable? He wasn't irritable, he has been threatening. Deliberately intimidating. Surely she cannot be so easily won over. Gwen's wide eyes focus on mine.

'He never meant to hurt you, Vic. He's just so frustrated with how unsupportive Isaac is being with the wedding, and when he saw that he wasn't at the exhibit either, he just lost it.'

I am flabbergasted, sliding back on the bed to put some distance between us. I examine every part of her face, her puffy eyes, her attempt at a smile. This is what she wants to believe. It's a perfectly constructed lie. I'm so angry that she would allow him to talk his way out of hurting me, after all I've been through, but she's well and truly under his spell. Plus, she doesn't know what I know. Hasn't read the articles I've read. I contemplate the idea of telling her now, making her see what a manipulative monster Michael is, but how can I when all she wants is for me to tell her everything will be OK?

'You've gone quiet. Please. It would mean so much to me if you two can make up.'

I tense at the very suggestion. Make up? What a phrase. Like we're a couple of kids that have had a spat. Her rose-tinted glasses are proving her to be beyond deluded. If Gwen were a client of mine I would be helping her to recognise the toxic hold he has on her, but still I hold my tongue.

'He's just so stressed out by it all,' she goes on. 'It would mean a lot to him too, if we can just put this incident behind us.'

I grip the duvet, trying to hide my anger. The bruising on my arm will take longer to fade than her wrath towards him. I move further back from her, pretending to tidy away some of the clothes I've previously thrown on the floor, so that I don't have to look at her.

'Vic, speak to me.'

She stands up, reaching for my hands, but I flinch as she catches my wrist. Not that she acknowledges it – I guess she can't. If she checks how my wrist is, it would be like admitting what Michael is capable of and she clearly wants to pretend all this never happened. I want to lash out, scream and shout at her, but I have to remain calm.

'Gwen, what he did to me is not OK.' My voice is low, my eyes focused on hers.

'I know, he feels awful…'

She looks at me with such hope, with that smile again. Perhaps this is partly my fault. I've always let her have her way, so it makes sense she thinks she can help me decide on how to react to this situation. It's clear that the more I speak the more she will defend him, and I just don't want to hear it.

'Just be careful Gwen, he's…'

'He's what? It was a mistake Vic, he's not a monster.'

Her defensive tone is more than I can stand.

'Isn't he?' I blurt out before I can think.

I can tell from how quickly her eyebrows furrow that I should've stopped myself.

'Vic, don't ruin this for me.'

Her tearfulness has stopped as quickly as it started. I don't want to think of her as self-centred, but right now she isn't showing me any empathy at all.

'I'm not trying to ruin anything. I just want you to be careful.'

'Maybe if you were in love you'd understand.'

Ouch. I can see she already wants to take back the words, but it is too late. They have landed on their target. I've always known Gwen has a bitchy side, but this is the first I have been on the receiving end of it. We stand staring at one another for what feels like the longest time. She knows why I've been single for so long. What I've survived. I want to believe her words were born from raw emotion, tiredness and being manipulated, but right now I feel like she doesn't value me at all.

'I'm sorry. I don't know what I'm saying.' Gwen collapses back onto the bed, fresh tears falling. This rollercoaster of emotions is too much for me. This is his doing, and I hate it. Sitting next to her, I half-heartedly try to comfort her, gently rubbing her shoulder, but it feels like a blade in my back when I hear her whisper, 'I love him, Vic.'

That's enough – I can't take any more tonight. I encourage her to get some sleep, telling her I'll be in the spare room if she needs anything, and turn off the light as she pulls the duvet up around her.

Who's to say that even when I tell her the truth as I know it, she won't still stand by his side? Clearly it doesn't matter how he acted, how he made me feel, how he hurt me – he's managing to twist this so that if I hold any kind of grudge, I'm somehow the bad guy. And he thinks he has gotten away with it. I can't let that happen, whether she forgives me for it or not. I return to my study to cover my investigations and close my computer. All of this shall remain my secret – for now.

Chapter Twenty-Six

The Mood Board

It's nearly lunchtime, but Gwen is still asleep. When I check on her, the sheets are ruffled and a pillow has been hurled on the floor – clearly she's had a restless night. I'll make her breakfast before waking her – that'll give me time to think of a way to tell her I'm leaving for a few days. Still half asleep myself, I'm only halfway down the stairs when the doorbell rings. Looking at the silhouette in the door's glass panels, I try and make out who it is – can it be Michael? Holding my breath, I edge closer and call out, 'Who is it?'

'It's me, Isaac.'

I exhale and open the door. The warmth of his smile is such a welcome relief. He steps inside, gripping me in a tight hug that I melt into. I didn't realise how much I need this. When we part his eyes dart to my wrist, flashing with sympathy and a hint of anger. He runs his fingertips tenderly over the bruise until he is holding my hand, his other hand reaching to stroke my cheek.

'Victoria, I…'

'Morning, love birds!'

Impeccable timing as always. Gwen's leaning over the banister, looking down at us. I watch her carefully as she comes downstairs – she's already dressed, no longer emotional and weak. She seems to have completely flipped back into her stride, as if yesterday didn't happen. I feel a pang of fear, worried she is covering her true emotions and putting on a brave face for Michael's sake.

'Sorry, I didn't mean to interrupt. I think I'm going to head home, Vic,' she adds sheepishly.

'What? No, we still have so much to talk about. Please at least stay for breakfast?'

'Sorry, Michael and I have a lot to talk about too.'

She pulls me away from Isaac to give me a hug goodbye, but I notice her winking at him over my shoulder.

'Anyhow, looks like you have a breakfast date already.'

Although she is smiling, I am not. All of this still feels so wrong. As she moves to kiss Isaac on the cheek before opening the door, I try one more time to convince her to stay, but it's no good.

'It's fine Vic, promise,' she says over her shoulder. 'Speak soon yeah?'

She pulls the door shut before I can protest any further, leaving Isaac and me standing silently in the hallway.

'Did I interrupt something?' His eyes search my face for some clue as to what he's just walked in on, but all I can do is roll my eyes.

'It's fine. Tea?'

He follows me to the kitchen, eyeing my every movement, shuffling nervously in his seat when I place his cup in front of him.

The last time I saw him was traumatic, but Gwen's willingness to so easily believe Michael's lies somehow feels worse. As Isaac fidgets with his watch strap, I wait for him to say what he is readying himself to.

'How are you, Victoria?'

There's such sadness in his eyes. I reach for him, cupping his face in my hands. I feel the warmth of his hands covering mine.

'I never knew he would hurt you. I should've stopped him sooner.'

'This isn't your fault, Isaac. None of it.'

Although he smiles, he looks no less deflated. Kissing my injured wrist, he strokes it tenderly.

'I'm sorry, that's all.' His face falls even further. 'Vic. About that night. Michael's not been acting himself.'

My ears prick up. 'What do you mean?'

'He called. It's like he wants to pretend it all never happened but I'm ready to tell him to shove his wedding.'

A huge part of me is relieved that someone feels the way I do, that someone understands the severity of Michael's actions. But I cannot let Isaac's anger interfere with my plan. I don't want him to confront Michael until I'm ready.

'Don't do that,' I interrupt. 'Please. Just go along with it for now.'

His eyes narrow as he stares at me. 'What? I would've thought you'd be feeling the same – if not more angry. What's going on?'

I desperately need someone to talk to – someone to tell everything I've found. I would have preferred it to be Gwen, but perhaps Isaac will be a more sympathetic ear.

'Can I trust you? I mean really trust you?'

It's a rhetorical question really, but he answers anyway. 'Of course.'

He pulls me close, kissing me delicately, whilst running his fingers through my hair. Even when we part, he stays a matter of inches away from my face, his eyes locked on mine.

'Talk to me.'

'Michael has a past that he seems desperate to hide from all of us.'

He doesn't seem surprised. 'I figured, with the name change and all.'

I pause, then with a deep intake of breath, I take him by the hand and lead him to my study. When I pull down my wall planner for him to see my work – the many, many notes and pictures of Michael, Serena and Anna – he lets out an audible gasp, stepping back to take in the sight before him.

'What the… what is all this?' he murmurs, trying to take in every note and scribble, his eyes darting in every direction.

'You'd better sit down, let me explain.'

Still open mouthed he sits himself in my chair, slowly moving his eyes from the wall to me. I perch on the desk beside him as I detail what I have found, who Michael really is and even what I think he may be capable of – murdering his late wife.

By the time I've finished playing him the video with Anna, he is cradling his head in his hands, unable to look at me. My heart sinks. This is all too much for him. I kneel in front of him, gently moving his hands away but instead of looking at me, he collapses back into his chair, still focusing on the wall. It seems an age before he speaks.

'Vic, this is Michael we're talking about. It can't be possible.'

I understand. It's one thing to believe a friend has an anger issue but this is a whole other level of deceit. His face is screwed up with concentration.

'I know it's a lot to accept, but this is why he changed his name, so we wouldn't find out about all of this. That he's been married, that his wife died. I can't help but wonder why he just wouldn't be open about it all? Unless…'

'Unless what?'

'Unless, and I don't have any proof yet, unless he had something to do with his late wife's death.'

He pushes my hands away, standing up to pace back and forth in front of me.

'Come on. Michael? A murderer? You can't be serious.' I try to reach out to him but he recoils from me. 'Why isn't he in jail if he did it?'

'That I can't answer.'

'No, this is ridiculous.'

He can't even look at me. His head is shaking, perhaps to disagree with me or to shake off the very thoughts I am putting in his mind. I have to keep going though – if I can't convince *him* to at least finish listening to me, what hope do I have with Gwen?

'Isaac, do you remember this picture?' I ask, pointing to the one of Anna and Michael at the party. He focuses back in, nodding and listening intently. 'He's told Gwen that she is an ex who showed up to the party. You've seen the video yourself. You know that's not true and so do I.' I scroll through my phone. 'Here's the picture that shows her putting that question you asked in the box. Why, Isaac? What secret does she want revealed?'

He starts rubbing his temples, lowering himself back into the chair. 'Does Gwen know?'

'No. I think it's safer that way, until I get proof.'

Isaac's breathing suddenly gets quicker as he faces me. 'What do you mean – get proof?'

'I'm going to go and find out about the fire myself. I'm going to find Anna.'

Standing up, he pulls my hands so I'm standing directly in front of him. 'This isn't right. If he's as dangerous as you think then he's not going to like you digging around like this.'

'That's why I haven't told Gwen and I need you not to tell him either. OK?'

He closes his eyes, resting his forehead on mine momentarily, before stepping back. 'No, this isn't right. I know Michael is a lot of things, but a murderer isn't one of them. He's my best friend, Vic – or was my best friend.' He lets out an exasperated sigh. 'I don't know what to think.'

I feel a horrible mix of anger and panic – he's not going to believe me either. What is so special about Michael that no one around him will listen to reason?

'What about all of this then?' I point to the wall, equally exasperated.

Isaac won't look at it. 'There'll be a reasonable explanation for all of this, I just know it.'

I feel like I'm losing him. Is that a look of disdain creeping onto his face?

'I'm sorry Vic, I need some air.'

With that he walks away. I feel so alone. Confused by what has just happened. The slam of the front door sends a jolt of pain through me. First Gwen, now Isaac – they are both choosing Michael's lies over my truth.

I can't help it though. As I collapse into my chair, a pang of guilt ripples through me too. I hadn't thought about how much this would be for Isaac to take on, and I have no idea how I would react if someone suddenly decided to tell me such a wild story about Gwen. It's only been a matter of minutes and I'm conscious that my emotions are yo-yoing faster than I can rationalise them, but I feel the need to make amends, so I call him – it goes straight to voicemail. I take the hint – he doesn't want to talk to me right now, but I send him a message, so he can respond when he wants to.

> I'm sorry I dumped so much on you. Please can we talk? Soon? xx

His response comes a few minutes later.

It's OK. I need time to think. Speak after the hen/stag dos. xx

I have totally lost track of the wedding schedule. The hen do is tomorrow! I don't have the first idea how I'm going to fake a celebratory mood. What happened between myself, Michael and Gwen does not feel resolved at all, merely swept under the carpet. I know I can't miss the hen party but I hate the thought of listening to her enthusing about the wedding, no doubt oblivious to how I am feeling.

I have to work out how I will tell her I'm having a few days away. I'll wait until the hen do is well underway, when she's relaxed and I'll have had a chance to make it clear that the wedding will still be on track without me.

As for Isaac, how will he cope on the stag do with Michael? Will Isaac still be angry, or will Michael cast his manipulative magic on him too? All I can hope for right now is that Isaac doesn't let slip to Michael what I am up to. The thought of how he would react to that sends a shiver up my spine.

Chapter Twenty-Seven

The Hen Do

The next day

'If this doesn't make you feel better, nothing will!'

I half smile at Jessica as I climb into the taxi. I know she means well – she's left me alone these last couple of weeks and that's been a gift in itself. It's the first time Samira's seen me since the exhibition opening and although I've made a real effort to wear make-up and straighten my hair, she looks aghast.

'You look dreadful, Vic. Are you sure you're up to this?'

'Of course she is! We all need this, don't we?' Gwen interjects, holding my hands between hers. I can't tell if she's asking me or telling me. Either way, her usual easy charm is grating on me. How is she OK already?

I find it easier to just remain quiet for the drive, listening to the excitement for the big day around me with gritted teeth. I try to calm myself by watching the water droplets racing down the windows. The beautiful colours of autumn are long gone, and all I can see outside are rows of bare trees. Every so often I catch Samira looking at me, her eyes flitting between suspicion and sympathy, but I make sure to look away before she can ask me any questions.

We pull into the sprawling gardens of the spa, and Gwen's eyes light up at the sight of it. The paved pathway is glistening in the rain, leading to the oversized glass doors, between formidable stone columns. Even through the drizzle there is no denying that this place screams exclusive luxury. Inwardly I sigh at how much effort this day will be – all I want is to curl up on my sofa and catch up on some sleep, to save my energies for my quest to find Anna.

We step from the cold and damp outside, into the most pristine foyer. The staff stand to attention in neat black tunics, with their professional, bright smiles. A tray of slender glasses filled with cucumber water is placed in front of us as we're checked in, the receptionist making sure to divulge every detail of the exquisite treatments that await us.

The gentle sound of running water from the fountain behind them does emanate a sense of calm, but it will take significantly more than a water feature and some twinkly music to help me relax. I lean against the reception desk, inhaling the sweet smell of the flowers at either end while Jessica finalises the details.

I hear the arrival of more of Gwen's friends behind me, followed by numerous air kisses. At least they'll serve as a buffer between Gwen and me. Watching Gwen flick her hair as she talks, it dawns on me that my resentment towards her is really starting to fester. She's living in a perfect world of her own making: she's wonderful, Michael's wonderful, the wedding's bloody wonderful. Then there's me. The outsider who knows this is all built on selfish mistruths at best, or villainous lies at worst. After all this has come to whatever conclusion it comes to, I'll have to find the right time to talk to Gwen about this tendency she has to ignore the less than positive things in her life. It's simply not healthy and downright frustrating – which is probably why we're in this mess right now.

'This way please.'

We all follow the smiley receptionist, the others giggling excitedly as we take in every inch of our extravagant surroundings. Heels clicking on the polished, tiled floor as we walk past the floor-to-ceiling windows – each offering a relaxing view from every direction of perfectly manicured lawns and rows of evergreen trees.

Turning a corner, on one side the windows now overlook a pristine swimming area, lined with heated stone loungers. The gentle bubbling of the hot tub only just visible behind the ornamental waterfall, pouring into the pool. I hear the group gushing about their eagerness to slip into the heated water, but I find myself slowing down, walking just behind them so as to avoid being involved in the conversation.

Then we reach what I assume is the treatment area. Rows and rows of glistening, wooden doors, a different piece of art hung between each, which naturally Gwen feels the need to comment on as the others discuss which treatments they've chosen.

When we reach the changing room, I feel as if I am on auto-pilot – my body here, but my mind elsewhere. I feel a tug on my hand as Samira leans in close to whisper to me.

'You're not OK, are you? If you're not feeling well, we can leave.'

I shake my head and keep looking straight at the back of our host's neatly coifed head as she leads us to the wooden benched area.

'Fine, but I'm going to keep checking on you,' I hear her say, squeezing my hand again.

The changing room is empty apart from us – Jessica arranged this after all. A sign of her snobbery. Not that I'd admit it to her but actually, the peace and quiet of not having too many people around us is comforting.

'Your robes and slippers are in your lockers. Once you're changed you are welcome to relax in the calming area until your therapists collect you.'

Calming area? I can't help but chuckle to myself. If only a hot tub and some vegetable-flavoured ice water was the only cure I needed for my inner turmoil. I follow Samira's lead, putting my bag down on one of the large benches by the lockers, sitting down to brace myself for all the superficial conversation to come. Without warning, Samira launches a bath robe at me, partly covering my head and nearly knocking me off the bench.

'If you're staying, best get in the relaxing mood!'

She wastes no time in changing into her bikini. I follow suit, yanking my one piece on.

'But I meant what I said, I'll be keeping an eye on you…'

I turn to see why her voice has trailed off, following her eyes to my wrist.

'Your arm! What the hell happened?'

Damn it, I forgot she doesn't know about that. Without thinking I say, 'I had a few drinks the other night, lost my balance.'

'When you were with Isaac? Did he do that?'

She places her fingers in the same places as the bruises – it's obviously a handprint. I can't have her thinking Isaac did this.

'No, I fell walking out of the exhibit. Stupid heels.'

I quickly wrap my bathrobe around me so she can stop looking at the purple and yellow shapes on my arm. I don't know why I don't just tell her the truth. Maybe because I was used to covering up when Dylan would leave me covered in similar injuries. Or maybe because I know she'd confront Gwen, make a huge scene. Then she'd have no fear in confronting Michael too – and that's not what's needed right now. Thankfully, the sound of Jessica urging us all to hurry up stops her from continuing her interrogation. She clearly has something she wants to say but there's too many people around us now, so we just silently join the back of the group.

They are congregated in the hot tub, so I slip in quickly before anyone can notice my bruises. I must admit, the feel of the warm water and bubbles is soothing. I slide down until the water is nearly to my chin, closing my eyes to try and shut out the endless chatter. I don't even pretend to be part of the conversation happening over my head.

'It was so hard to choose a gift from your registry Gwen. Everything is beautiful,' Jessica simpers. I listen as others concur what fantastic taste Gwen has, whilst she laps up the compliments, not noticing my silence. That's probably for the best as I haven't even thought about buying anything –

I'd feel guilty but saving Gwen from this marriage is my priority.

The conversation eventually turns to whose roots need doing before the big day, whose accessories and nail designs are going to match or clash. I'm probably expected to join in, to remind them of the colour schemes and styles Gwen has chosen but I don't care.

'Speaking of hairstyles, have you thought any more about that makeover we talked about?'

I open my eyes when I feel Jessica run her fingers through some loose strands of my hair. I guess the being nice to me phase is over, then. Between having my home invaded, being manhandled and wondering if my best friend could be marrying a murderer, no, I have not thought about my hair! What I wouldn't do to say that out loud. I'm really not in the mood for her today.

'Leave it Jessica, you never know when to give it a rest!' Gwen has noticed how uncomfortable Jessica is making me, whilst thoughtfully neatening a few stray hairs around her own face. I'd be pleased, but it smacks of irony that she will stand up for me against a tactless comment but does nothing when her fiancé puts his hands on me.

'I was just suggesting that the wedding would be a nice time to show off a new, more polished image, that's all,' Jessica says. 'No offence meant.'

To Jessica's credit she's backed down far quicker than usual, but her sly eye roll to some of the other ladies as they smile back is infuriating. I look over at Gwen, smiling at me as if she has done me some kind of favour. How have I never noticed how completely selfish she is? I've never questioned her, after all she helped me rebuild my life after Dylan. Things have changed since I questioned her relationship with Michael. Maybe her superficial reaction to that is the real Gwen, and I've been blind to it all along? Perhaps it's not just Jessica who has a touch of narcissism.

I shake my head. What am I saying to myself? She's my best friend. I'm tired and stressed. I should be saving my rage for Michael. He's the one manipulating her right now. It's not her fault.

At the sound of flip flops on the tiled floor, we turn to see that our host is back.

'Ladies, if you're ready, please follow me. I'll take you to your treatment rooms.'

Each of us clambers out of the tub, following her as she separates us into our smaller rooms. Samira and I are sent into a candlelit room together. Laid on our separate masseuse tables, the feeling of warm oils and hands massaging my stresses away is bliss. I close my eyes, listening to the delicate music in the background. It should be easy to drift away, get lost in the relaxation, but I can't. There is simply too much whirring through my mind.

'You're holding a lot of tension in your shoulders,' the surprisingly strong masseuse informs me, kneading deep into them. The sensation turns quickly from painful to soothing. It's easy to see why Jessica is so fond of coming here. I can hear Samira giving a little more direction to her therapist about where her aches and pains are. It's rare she ever gets this amount of time to herself so I'm glad she's making the most of it.

The masseuses ask us to turn over – it's time for our facial. The feeling of one exotic fragranced lotion and potion after another cleaning and massaging my face is heavenly. Even the bristles of the soft brush as the warming papaya face mask is applied feels delightful. When all of whatever this situation is with the wedding is over, I need to come back here sometime with Samira.

'We're going to leave you for a few moments, while the masks set.'

Placing a cooling mask over our eyes, the masseuses leave the room.

'Vic… Vic… Are you there?'

Of course Samira can't just lie there quietly.

'Yeah, I'm here.'

'What's really going on with you and Gwen?'

I turn my head to look at her, lifting up the edge of my eye mask. Samira has already taken hers off to look at me.

'Nothing's going on.'

'Liar!'

'Just leave it, Samira.'

'No, I'm not going to leave it. You're looking at her differently. Is this linked to that bruise on your arm?'

I can feel my breathing get heavier as I weigh up the risks – can I be honest with Samira? I can, but should I be? Knowing how protective she is, can I trust that she will keep what I tell her to herself?

'It's just the wedding, she's turning into a bridezilla.'

Samira rolls onto her side to stare directly at me. 'It's more than that. You're keeping something from me, I know it.'

I have to look away, I hate that she feels I cannot be open with her. She deserves better than to think that I don't value her. I roll over to meet her eye, completely removing my eye mask too. 'Please… when I'm ready to talk about it, I promise I will come to you.'

Her brow furrows, she's not sure how to respond but before she can, we hear footsteps leading back to our door. Both of us return to lying flat on our backs, replacing the eye masks before the masseuses return. It's hard to enjoy the invigorating sensation of the warm, wet cotton wool removing the mask, not when I know that as soon as she finishes with the serums and creams, Samira will be waiting to talk to me again.

Chapter Twenty-Eight

Girl Talk

'Take your time to sit up ladies. You may feel a little dizzy so please, stay here for as long as you need. Then join your friends in the calming area when you're ready.'

As soon as they leave I sense Samira sitting up. I look over at her. Her face is unusually stoic. I have to tell her something.

'Fine. Look, me and Gwen had words.'

'About what?'

'About this wedding happening way too quickly. I mean how well do any of us really know Michael?'

Samira looks puzzled. 'What?'

'You must admit, it's been a quick engagement.'

She pauses. 'Yeah, I agree, it's just… I thought you were going to say you're pissed off she's pretending like the break-ins haven't happened. I mean we all seem to be acting like you should already be alright about it all.'

She's right. I've been so focused on everything I've discovered about Michael that the break-ins – whether he was involved or not – have only played a minor role in my thoughts.

'If it's not that, then what?' Samira goes on. 'Is it Michael? There's something off about him isn't there. Like he's a bit too good to be true.'

My eyes flick to meet hers – I never realised she thought so too. 'It's more than that. I don't like him. Not as a person and not for Gwen.'

Samira nods in agreement. 'I take it you told Gwen? Is that what's weird between you?'

'Yeah, I just think she's making a mistake marrying him.'

I don't realise that I've been subconsciously holding my wrist until Samira's eyes widen.

'Did *he* do that to you?'

I try to look away, I hadn't wanted to confess this to her but she leaps from her table, making sure she stays in my eye line. 'It *was* him! But why?'

'Look it's complicated, please don't say anything.' I can tell from the way she is pursing her lips that she is gearing herself up to go into battle for me. 'There's just so much going on. It's not safe.'

I see her recoil at my last comment. Before she can question me further, we hear the sounds of laughter outside. Everyone else must be making their way back to the calming area.

'Please Samira, I'll tell you everything, just not here.'

From the way she silently hands me my robe, I can tell that she is willing to be uncharacteristically patient. I squeeze her hand as we share a smile. I've perhaps already told her too much, but I cannot risk dragging her into this until it's over. Whatever *this* is.

When we get back to the others, they are deep in conversation about their fantastic treatments. Gwen is wiggling a fresh manicure at everyone – any excuse to show off her ring again. I watch her, hoping to see her show any hint of embarrassment at the charade she is putting on. Some kind of recognition that life is not as perfect as she's implying, but no. Nothing. She is loving every second of being centre of attention and nothing else, including me, matters.

Next, we are led through to the dining room for afternoon tea. The table is beautifully decorated with white china cups and three-tier plates with delicate flowers painted on the edges. Rows of finger sandwiches and cake slices fill each dish. I roll my eyes that we cannot start eating until everyone has taken 101 photos, but by the time we get to touch the food I can't actually bring myself to eat.

I wish I knew what was happening at the stag do right now. I check my phone for any messages from Isaac but there's nothing. Once again, I am forced to listen to Gwen gushing about her gown, and the guest rooms at the wedding venue. I can feel my stomach turning as I get lost in my own thoughts. It's surreal. My home has been violated, and I've been threatened by someone who may be capable of murder, but all is well in Gwen's world because we have a wedding to look forward to.

'Vic, are you alright? You look really pale.'

Samira touches my hand delicately. Everyone stops to look at me and all of a sudden, I don't feel like I can breathe, not here, not with them. I leave the table abruptly and hurry back to the changing rooms.

I'm splashing water on my face at the sink when Samira and Gwen come rushing to my side. Neither is speaking but I see the looks of concern they give each other.

'You're not well. Let me take you home,' Samira offers.

'She's fine,' Gwen says abruptly, almost pushing Samira out of the way to hand me a towel.

I can see in the mirror that Samira is readying herself to put Gwen in her place, but I shoot her a pleading look.

'Please can we have a minute, Samira?'

She pauses. Even though she nods, she doesn't take her steely gaze from Gwen. There's no way she will be able to hold her tongue if I disclose everything about Michael to her. She's too protective to just stand by and let me investigate him.

'Fine, but if you need me, I'll be right outside.'

She makes sure to give Gwen a wide berth on her way past. Not that Gwen reads Samira's body language at all. Instead, she turns to me, her practised smile on her face.

'Oh Vic, I thought today would relax you, but you don't look well at all. Are you OK?'

I bite my tongue. What a ridiculous question. She above anyone knows I'm not. I can only hope, when she is rid of Michael and thinking for herself, that she will be able to forgive herself for how she is treating me right now.

'No, I'm not OK,' I say, rage building inside me. 'I'm tired. Tired of trying to cover my wrist so your friends don't see what your fiancé is capable of. Tired of pretending like he isn't terrifying and tired of watching you act like none of this is happening.'

There's an uncomfortable pause where she just stands there, open mouthed at my fury. I've never spoken to her like this before – I'm making it crystal clear now that I've had enough, which is clearly taking her by surprise. Instead of apologising or taking any kind of responsibility, Gwen says something that shocks me.

'This my hen party and I don't want anything to ruin it. If you're not enjoying yourself, perhaps you should leave.'

'Enjoying myself?' I know my voice is raised but I cannot stop. 'How can I enjoy myself? I would do anything for you, and you can't even be bothered to acknowledge what I have been going through the last few weeks.'

Stepping back, Gwen flicks her hair over her shoulders and smooths down her robe. When she looks at me next, it's as if there is no light behind her eyes. She is unrecognisably cold.

'Like I say, if you are not enjoying my party, then I suggest you go home. I'll just tell everyone you're feeling sick or something.'

She turns to leave. I feel such rage that I pick up the closest thing to me, a bottle of soap, and launch it at her. I miss, hitting the door frame next to her. When she turns I half expect her to return my anger but she simply looks me up and down before shaking her head and walking out. I don't waste any time changing back into my clothes. I won't stay where I am not wanted. I head to the reception desk to call me a taxi but Samira catches me in the hallway.

'Where are you going?'

'I just need to get out of here. I'll call you, I promise.'

I keep moving before she can talk to me any further, my hands shaking with fury.

At home I try to pack a bag for my trip, but I feel like the walls are closing in, sweat forming on the back of my neck. I'm still furious, and every part of me feels painfully tense – so much for that massage. I just need some fresh air before I spend hours driving in the car.

Without even grabbing a coat, I walk straight out onto the cold, empty street. The faces of Gwen, Michael and Isaac circulate my thoughts. My jaw is aching from gritting my teeth too hard, my nails leaving indents in the palms of my clenched hands. The clouds burst with cold, heavy rain, soaking my clothes within seconds. I don't care. No matter how much I shiver, I just want to keep moving, wherever my feet are taking me. I don't even know where I'm going, until I turn a corner and realise that I am at Gwen's closed gallery.

The streets are empty as I stand facing Gwen's exquisitely designed workspace. The rain is blurring my vision but the gallery looks perfect, just like everything in Gwen's world does. Standing in the cold, I am appalled that Gwen is risking all of this, everything she has built – for him. Why won't she listen to me? That's when I catch a glimpse of my own reflection. The tear-stained face of someone pathetic and alone in the darkness, with only the streetlights for company. No wonder she doesn't listen to me, look at me, I don't belong in her world.

Without a second thought I lash out at my reflection, striking the window with all of my might with my uninjured arm. The sharp pain of hitting the glass feels refreshing against the dull pain in my chest.

That's when I hear it. A crack.

I step back and watch as a long, jagged line starts to run across the window, before fracturing into hundreds of tiny lines spreading outwards. The cracking grows louder and louder until the entire pane shatters, sending fragments of glass crashing to the ground. I manage to step back in time so that it doesn't rain down on me. I look at my still-clenched fist dumbly – what have I just done? This place is Gwen's pride and joy.

The anger leaves my body, swiftly replaced by sheer panic. What will Gwen say? With everything that's happened, would she believe it was an accident? I want to run, the streets are deserted and no one will know it was me, but I can't. What if someone took something from the gallery? She would never forgive me. I freeze, with no idea what to do. I start to imagine police sirens wailing and officers rushing over to arrest me.

The only person I can think to call is Isaac. He must still be at the stag do, so I just hope he isn't too drunk to answer the phone. My wet, shaky fingers make it hard to unlock, but I feel such relief when it doesn't take long for him to pick up.

'Vic, I'm so glad you called, I–'

'Isaac, I need your help.'

He stops talking immediately to listen.

'I'm outside Gwen's gallery. Please… I need you.'

There's a pause.

'OK, I'll make some excuse to leave. I'm on my way.'

That's all I need to hear. Hanging up on his last word, all I can do now is stand here and wait, looking at the mess I've made.

Chapter Twenty-Nine

Love Lies

10 days until the wedding

It feels like an eternity but is perhaps a matter of minutes until Isaac pulls up behind me. When he climbs out of the taxi, he takes off his coat and wraps it around me. Seeing the taxi driver gawping at the scene he takes a wad of notes from his wallet, and whispers something to him. Whatever he said, the driver speeds away without looking back.

'What the hell happened?'

'I… er… I… didn't mean it. One minute I was…' I can't get the words out, and my chattering teeth aren't helping.

I see him look down at the blood trickling between my fingers. I'm so cold I didn't even feel any pain from the impact or from the rain, turning to hail, now bouncing off my body.

'You have to get out of here before the police come.'

I stare at him, not fully understanding.

'I'll need to call them, to protect the gallery.'

He already has his phone ready to dial.

'But what will you say to them?'

'Don't worry, I'll think of something. You need to go. I'll handle this.' He lowers his face to look me directly in the eyes, 'Can you get yourself home?'

'Yes but…'

He kisses me on the forehead before sending me on my way. I feel so dazed and confused, I do as I am told without saying a word, turning towards home and not looking back. Half running, half stumbling.

By the time I get to the house, I'm shaking violently from the cold. I take myself upstairs, dropping my soaked clothes and Isaac's jacket on the bathroom floor, before washing my bloody hand under the tap. I watch intently as the blood is diluted and leaves in a swirl through the plug hole, then sit on the edge of the bath to steady myself. How has it come to this? Did I mean to break that window? I know I was angry, but I think it was an accident.

Inside my head is pure chaos. Wrapping myself in my dressing gown I check my phone – nothing from Isaac. Just a few messages from Samira, checking on me and telling me she wishes she could leave the hen do too. I quickly text her back to tell her I'm OK – I can't have her coming over tonight. How would I explain all of this?

The doorbell rings, startling me. For a split second I half expect the police to be on the other side of the door, or even worse, Samira or Gwen. I peer down the hall, wiping my face with my sleeve, and see Isaac's familiar silhouette.

I rush to let him in. He spills inside, water spraying from his hair as he tries to shake himself from the cold.

'Let me get you a towel.'

He follows me silently as I pull one from the dryer, then ask him, 'What did you do?'

His eyes weren't focused on mine. He is looking at my injured hand, holding the towel. 'Do you need a doctor for those cuts?'

'No, they're not deep. Please, what did you do?'

'I called Michael.'

'You did what?' My heart sinks at the thought of facing his wrath.

'I called, said I was passing by on my way home and saw the window had shattered. I managed to persuade him that it doesn't look like anything has been taken and that I would take care of it.'

'Did he believe that?'

'No reason for him not to. Nothing is taken and it did just look like the glass had shattered, maybe from the hail, rather than been vandalised.'

I lean back against the island to steady myself. Isaac moves closer, and I melt into his arms as they wrap around me. I let myself cry on his shoulder. He waits for me to calm down before speaking again.

'Vic, I'm worried about you. What happened?'

'It was an accident. I promise. I was just… I…'

I begin sobbing again. He squeezes me a little tighter. I want to stay here, feeling warm and safe, but then I remember that Isaac should still be at the stag do. Stepping back from him, I ask, 'What did you say when you left the party?'

'I told them we'd had an argument. That I couldn't stop thinking about you or enjoy the party until I sorted things out with you.'

'And they believed that?'

'Why wouldn't they? It's the truth.' His honesty – or is it charm? – is so disarming, I don't know how to respond. 'I am sorry you know. For the way we left things. It was just so much to take in.' There's that pang of guilt in my chest again. 'Why don't I make us a hot drink and we can sit and talk?'

All I can do is nod and let him walk me to the living room. He wraps me in a blanket before returning to the kitchen. When he comes back, he slides under the blanket next to me, pulling me to lean into his shoulder as he forms a protective cocoon around me.

'I'm the one who should be apologising,' I begin. 'I shouldn't have told you all that stuff about Michael, not when I have no proof. And now I've ruined your night – again.'

'You haven't ruined anything, I wasn't in the party mood anyway,' he says. 'To be honest after what you told me, I really started to notice how little any of us know anything about his past. Everyone at the stag do has only known him as long as I have or less. That's odd, right?'

I stare blankly at him. I don't think I can think about everything much more tonight. Isaac notices my pained expression. 'I'm sorry, it's been a long day for you. Shall I go?'

I don't want him to go at all. But what will asking him to stay mean? Perceptive as always, Isaac breaks the awkward silence.

'Vic, I know this isn't the time but at some point we should talk. You know, about where we stand with one another. Like sometimes I feel we're clicking but then you feel so distant.'

'I know, you're right.'

'Am I missing something? If this is one sided, you can just tell me.'

'It's not one sided.' I pause, taking in how intently he is looking at me. 'My last boyfriend wasn't the nicest of people.' I hold my wrist out, Michael's bruises dark under the overhead lights. 'Stuff like this happened a lot.'

I see Isaac wince at the realisation of what I am getting at, his jaw tensing. 'I would never…'

I know better than to say that I know he wouldn't, I don't. 'I never thought Dylan would either. He was so charming, so kind, to begin with. The more I let him into my life, the more he took from me.'

Sitting back into the sofa, I can see Isaac adding up all that I'm saying. 'Do I remind you of him?' There's a pause before he leans forward, taking my hands in his, saying again, 'I would never hurt you.'

'I want to believe you. I know I shouldn't punish you for Dylan's actions but…'

'You need time. To get to know me. To trust me?' I nod. 'I understand.'

He lifts my chin with his fingers, kissing me gently before pulling me into a hug. We stay, in silence, in this moment. A few seconds of sanctuary in the complete pandemonium that is my life right now. When he shuffles back from me, he moves the hair from my face, tucking it behind my ear.

'You look exhausted. Why don't you have a lie down and I'll make us something to eat.'

I begin to protest but as he stands, ready to cover me with the blanket, I realise I need to listen to him. It will do me good to rest.

By the time I wake up, it's dark outside. The smell of pasta, I think, is wafting under the door. I sit up feeling woozy, my stomach growling, and let my legs hang down the side of the sofa to help propel me upright. Just as I put a foot on the floor though, I stop – I think I can hear voices coming from the kitchen. Moving closer to the door, I freeze. It's Michael. How can that be – he should be at his stag do? I reach for the handle, trying not to let it click as it opens.

'I'm worried about her. You need to get Gwen to back off with all the wedding stuff – she needs a break,' I hear Isaac say.

When I emerge from the doorway, Michael spots me. 'Fine, I'll talk to Gwen,' he says to Isaac, pretending he hasn't seen me. 'She'll will be home from the spa soon.'

I feel cold as he walks towards me, reeking of alcohol – closing the kitchen door behind him. 'Perfect timing,' he whispers. 'We need to talk.'

I can feel the knots forming in my stomach, watching Michael stand emotionless next to the living room door, inviting me to go back in. I want to refuse, call to Isaac, anything but go into that room alone with him, but I want to know what he has to say. At least if I scream I know Isaac will come to my rescue.

The way he shuts the door behind us makes the hair on the back of my neck stand up.

'Can I sit?' he asks, already on his way to the armchair.

I stay stood up, looking at the door, just in case I need to make my escape.

'So, you've had an eventful day.'

I don't respond. I don't know what he knows.

'Don't worry, I won't tell Gwen.'

'Won't tell Gwen what?'

'That you'd rather be here with Isaac than at her hen party. Though it's probably for the best, since she seems to think you don't like or trust me. I hear you even told her about my ex in the park.'

My brow furrows, he thinks I believe the whole ex story. At least that means he doesn't know I've been looking into his past.

'Well why aren't you at your own stag do then?' I ask defiantly.

His mouth curls up on one side. 'Can you believe that a window on Gwen's gallery was *accidentally* smashed? I didn't want her hen do to be interrupted. Not with all the stress she's been under with the wedding planning and well... everything. She needs to relax. I thought it best that I deal with it and then be on my way back to the party.'

He knows it was me. I can tell. Before I can protest, he relaxes into the chair, his smirk even more pronounced.

'Look, we all have our secrets. I know you certainly have yours.' My heart and head are racing. Did Isaac tell him I smashed the window? Why would he do that? 'I mean how would Isaac react if he found out what happened to your ex. Dylan, wasn't it?'

I'm taken aback. 'I've told Isaac about him,' I respond aggressively.

'Even that he's dead? That you let him die?'

I audibly gasp, which prompts Michael to smile widely.

'Ah, I guess he doesn't know everything then. Yes, a very sad story that one. I should probably warn Isaac to stay away from you. After all, falling for you seems to be what led to poor Dylan's demise!'

'I didn't… I didn't…' I try to find the words.

'You didn't kill him? That's not what I heard.'

I can feel the hot pricks behind my eyes as I try desperately not to cry in front of him.

'But we're friends though,' he purrs dangerously, 'and friends keep each other's little secrets, don't we? You don't need to tell Gwen any more of mine, and I won't tell Isaac yours.'

I am stunned into silence. How things have changed since the last time I saw him. He's back to his arrogant, smug self.

He doesn't wait for any further reaction, walking close enough that I flinch as he leaves. I hear the front door close and the kitchen door open.

'Oh you're awake – I was just about to dish up,' Isaac announces.

He pauses when he sees the fear in my eyes.

'What? What's happened?'

I try to respond but the room starts spinning. Isaac moves quickly towards me but as I reach out to him, everything goes black.

'Victoria? Victoria…'

Isaac's voice sounds so far away. I open my eyes to see he's laid me on the sofa, kneeling on the floor next to me, stroking my face. I try to sit up, but I still feel so woozy.

'Just stay still,' Isaac says, gently helping me to lay down again. 'You gave me quite the scare.'

'What happened?' I ask, closing my eyes to try and stop the dizziness.

'You fainted. I'll go and get you a glass of water.' I can feel him start to stand up.

'No,' I open my eyes and grab his hand, 'please just stay here with me.'

Clasping my hands in his, he perches on the edge of the sofa, his kind eyes are looking down on me. I should tell him everything – about Dylan, about how he died – but would it change how he looks at me? I don't see how it couldn't – it changed how I looked at myself for a long time. Even after years of my own therapy, deep down I do still feel responsible for Dylan's death. Gwen is the only person I've ever told. And now she's handed that information over to Michael, to use it against me. Why would she do such a thing?

'Victoria, maybe we should get you to a doctor–'

'I don't need a doctor,' I snap, feeling immediately guilty for the bitterness in my tone. 'Sorry, I didn't mean to raise my voice… I'm not ill.'

'Then what is it? Let me help you.' Isaac's voice is still calm and soothing.

I think back to the conversation we had when he asked me if he reminded me of Dylan. Moments like this show them to be nothing alike. I dread to think how Dylan would've reacted if I had spoken to him like that. Isaac's kindness is genuine and unending. He doesn't expect anything in return.

Dylan on the other hand took everything from me, my happiness, freedom, and towards the end – nearly my life. I had to leave him to survive. He'd manipulated me so much in the past that, even when he messaged saying he was giving up – that he had nothing left to fight for – I ignored it. I didn't believe this or any of his other threats of suicide. Not until his neighbours found his body did I realise how much he needed me. Would Isaac believe that I didn't ignore Dylan's cries for help out of malice? Sometimes even I wonder if that's the truth. That I didn't feel some relief when I knew he was dead. I can't tell Isaac all of this, at least not now.

'It's nothing,' I lie. 'I just haven't really eaten all day.'

I can see his eyes narrow but he doesn't push me. Taking my hands, he helps me to the kitchen, where I watch him dish up a huge plate of spaghetti bolognese in front of me. It looks and smells fantastic but I'm just too tired, mentally and physically, to eat. I can feel him watching me as I push it around my plate. I hate that he's silently staring, it's making me feel claustrophobic, even though I know he means well.

'Isaac…' He puts his fork down to listen. 'I've decided I'm going to take a few days' break from here.'

He leans back in his chair eyeing me suspiciously. 'You're still going to try and find Anna, aren't you?'

There is no point lying to him.

'I need to know, I have to go to where the fire was. Please though, keep it between us. I'm going to tell Gwen I'm going back to mum's for a few days to relax.'

He rests his elbows on the table, his shoulders hunched under the weight of whatever he is feeling. 'I know I have no right to say this,' he murmurs carefully, 'but I don't want you to go.' I reach over and rub the back of his neck, until he eventually looks up at me. 'Maybe I can come too? For support.'

That's a tempting idea, but as I think it through briefly, I have a better one. 'Or if you stayed here, you could keep an eye on Michael. Would you mind? Until we know Gwen is safe with him.'

He sighs, leaning back. By now he knows I'm too stubborn to be dissuaded. 'Just make sure you come back in one piece. I'm still waiting for that date.' His warm smile relaxes the tension I'm holding in my shoulders – I reach for his hand, interlinking my fingers with his. If things were different I wonder where we would be as a couple right now, but until this nightmare is over, I can't think further than Michael. 'When are you planning on going?'

'Tomorrow. As soon as I wake up.'

'You probably want me to leave so you can get yourself together – but please, keep in touch, so I know you're safe?'

I can tell he wants me to ask him to stay. The way he strokes my face as he gets up sends an electric shiver through me. I place my hand on his chest to stop him leaving. He clasps his hands, delicately – remembering my earlier injury – leaning down to kiss me. This time longer, deeper than ever before. I find myself getting lost in him, wrapping my arms around his neck to pull him closer. His hands grip my waist. It feels like seconds and eternity at the same time. I step back, taking him by the hand again and making my way towards the stairs. Even if for only one night, I want to just think about us.

Chapter Thirty

Mr & Mrs

I pack my case quietly whilst Isaac sleeps, leaning to kiss him goodbye, savouring the smell of his cologne. When this is all over I will give him so much more of my attention and then, when I'm ready, I'll come clean about Dylan. Right now, I have to get going. I drag my case as quietly as I can downstairs.

I shoot Samira a quick text to let her know that I'll be going to my mum for a few days so she doesn't worry when she sees I'm not home. Now the only thing left to do is tell Gwen.

The wedding is barely a week away – the rehearsal dinner even sooner, so no doubt Gwen will react badly – but after yesterday, I'll be glad to be away from her. Not only for her complete lack of empathy but knowing she has told Michael about Dylan's death. Part of me wants to confront her, find out why she would betray my trust like that but the last thing I want is another slanging match like yesterday's. With a deep breath I press dial.

'Vic, I'm so glad you called. Did you hear about the gallery?'

My heat sinks as she reels off the many tasks she now has ahead of her to have the window replaced – completely focused on herself, again. No mention of the hen party. No mention of how triggering this might be for my own break-in. Although it's difficult to blame her for that, bearing in mind it was me who smashed her window.

'Yes, sounds awful. At least nothing was taken.' If Gwen was paying me any real attention she'd hear the lack of concern in my voice. 'Gwen… I need to take a break.'

'From what?'

From what? The audacity of the question!

'From everything. Work, the break-in, the wedding, it's all getting on top of me.' I know better than to throw Michael's name into the mix right now. There is a long pause.

'Look Vic. If this is about yesterday, then let's just forget it. I've put a lot on you and I'm sorry about that. Are you going to have the day to yourself then?'

I am in shock. How does she still not get that this is about more than wedding planning? I should challenge her behaviour, but not now. I have to stay focused.

Taking a deep breath to rid the annoyance from my voice, I say, 'Actually, I'm going to go away. A few days of mum's home cooking will do the trick.'

I can hear her breathing, shallow and irregular, but otherwise there is silence. 'You *are* still coming to rehearsal dinner? And the wedding?' Her voice is breaking.

'Sure, I'll be back. Promise.'

Her sigh of relief is so loud I probably would've heard it without the phone. I'd like to believe it's because I'm important to her but I wonder if she just doesn't want to explain my absence.

'I think that sounds like a great idea then. Everything's on track for the wedding because of your hard work. I can take care of the rest now the exhibit is over.'

Hanging up is a massive relief. I can't hear Isaac moving around yet, so I grab some paper and a pen to leave him a note, and pour him some juice. When I take it upstairs he looks so peaceful, so I place the drink on the bedside cabinet and lean on the windowsill to write him a message.

> When I get back, how about we finally have that dinner - at your place? I'll bring the wine. xx

It's about time I made the effort to visit him as much as he comes to me. In fact, I look forward to making *us* more of a priority when this is all over. I slide the note under the orange juice before kissing him lightly on the forehead.

I close the door as quietly as I can, before making my way back to the study. I quickly take photos of each part of my wall, putting a few of the more pertinent post-it notes into my suitcase, so I can refer to them later. With one last look at Anna, I take my suitcase and head out to find her. The wrath on her face in the still from the video, and the sadness in the funeral photo could mean she might be just the ally I need.

I barely notice much of the drive to Anna's quaint seaside town. One motorway after another, until the roads started narrowing and winding. Just as my eyes are getting tired from the never-ending hedge and stone wall-lined lanes, I catch a glimpse of my destination ahead. It's simply breath-taking. Waves crashing on the horizon, a jigsaw of green fields in between us. Each new turn brings another incredible view, until I start to make out the town.

The roads widen, revealing beautiful, detached houses, sat back behind mature gardens and wrought iron gates. Then expensive looking boutiques, mixed with charming looking cafes until finally, I see my hotel. A grand, glass-fronted building in what feels like the centre of the sea front. If I wasn't here for such an important purpose, this could have been an incredible place to have a lovely weekend away. I cannot wait to park and stretch my tired legs, but as soon as I get out of the car it hits me, there's no turning back now.

My room is far more luxurious than my usual taste, modern art lining the walls, odd sculptures adorning the many glass shelves. Even the furniture strikes me as being more for show than comfort, stiff and oddly shaped. It was the only hotel I could find at such short notice, and it feels safe, which is the main thing.

I'm far too physically and mentally exhausted to wander the streets right now, so even though I'm desperate to start my search for Anna, I know I need to rest. Moving a ridiculous amount of throw cushions to make space on the bed to lie down, I toss and turn until I eventually fall asleep.

Waking a few hours later, I don't waste time unpacking – laying out the few things I've brought from my study on the poorly remade bed, plus a map I picked up from the hotel foyer. I need to decide where to begin. There is only one place I can think to start: Michael's old house, where his wife died. I can at least drive past it tonight, get my bearings.

My satnav finds the street with ease but where the house used to be, there is a large garden with raised flower beds. Perfectly maintained shrubs are symmetrically placed around a wooden bench, illuminated by the streetlight.

I check the sat nav again, this is definitely the right place. Parking up, I decide to take a seat on the bench and enjoy the evening breeze whilst I plan my next move.

The street is mainly quiet except for the odd passing car and lights peeking out from around curtains of houses nearby. I walk towards the bench and spot a plaque on it. I run my fingers over the small, engraved lettering.

In memory of my dear wife Serena. The world is a little less bright without you.

This is a memorial garden. There is no house, which means no current tenants who might have some useful information about Anna. Michael has donated the space for this. I roll my eyes as I slump onto the bench. What did I expect? To be some TV detective who manages to unravel a clue left in a house years after a murder? This isn't some docu-series. If I want answers, I'll have to go looking for them elsewhere.

Out of the corner of my eye I spot a curtain twitching across the street. I check my phone for the photos of my notes, and review the names of some of the witnesses from the fire – what if the curtain twitcher is one of them? I talk myself into going and knocking on the door, holding onto a tiny piece of hope that someone might be willing to talk to me about this fire. Curtain twitcher clearly spots that they have caught my attention, flicking off their lights and closing the gap in their drapes. Clearly they don't want me to go over there and as expected, when I ring the doorbell, there's no answer.

I feel a surge of determination, I've come all this way and if that means I need to push myself out of my comfort zone to get someone to open their door to me, then I will.

I do the only thing I can: press every doorbell on this street until I find someone who remembers the fire, Michael or Anna. Yet not one of the few that answer their doors can spare the time to talk to me – even when I show them a photo of Michael on my phone.

Just when I'm about to accept defeat I spot a woman, across the road, watching me from her front upstairs window. I wait for a car to pass before crossing the road to her. I'm expecting her to turn her lights off to hide away from me like so many have already but instead, when I start walking towards her house, more lights flick on. The upstairs hallway, downstairs hallway and finally the porch light. It's as if she's beckoning me to her.

I press the bell and a second later she appears at the door. A small, elderly woman, with perfectly coifed white hair, hunched over a cane. I lift the photo of Michael and start my now practised spiel about being a friend from out of town. This is usually the point at which the doors close on me.

'Are you a reporter?' she asks, her eyes narrow as she looks me up and down.

'Er, no. No, not a reporter, a friend, I–'

Before I can continue with my lie, she turns her back on me and slowly walks into her hallway, the cane clicking on the floor as she walks. Frozen, I'm not sure what to do.

'Well do come in dear, you're letting all the heat out.'

I follow her inside, careful to wipe my feet on her welcome mat and close the door tightly behind me. Her vast house is immaculate, with professionally framed pictures on the walls, and a vase full of fresh flowers on the side table. I keep walking, following her voice until I find her again in her kitchen.

'I'm Mrs Morgan but you can call me Alice, dear. Join me for a cup of tea won't you?'

I awkwardly sit myself at the kitchen table as she silently fills a teapot, before carrying a tray of tinkling cups and saucers to me. I offer to help but she declines.

'Biscuit?'

I eagerly take one from the china plate she is holding towards me. I haven't eaten today.

'So, who are you, dear?' I stop mid-bite to answer, repeating my friend from out of town story. 'And what is it you're so desperate to know?'

I hadn't actually planned what I was going to say if I got this far. Starting to choke on some crumbs, I sip some of the sweet tea to clear my throat.

'I lost touch with my friend. I just want to look him up whilst I'm in town.'

She looks at me suspiciously, not even looking down at the image on my phone, her eyes transfixed on my lying mouth.

'Shall we waste more time with your tales my dear, or perhaps you'd like to ask me the questions you really want answered – why else would you be going door to door in this weather?'

I open my mouth to protest but Alice raises her hand to silence me. Who am I kidding? I've never been a great liar and let's face it, she is seeing straight through me.

'Fine. I want to know what happened to the house that was there before,' I say, gesturing behind me in the direction of the garden.

'Why?'

I don't know what to say. Avoiding her gaze, I fidget with my cup.

Alice persists, perfectly calmly stirring her tea whilst watching me squirm. 'It would likely work in your favour to just tell the truth. I'm not getting any younger.'

What do I have to lose with the truth?

'The man who lived there. I think he lives near me. But I can't be sure.'

Her eyes widen. 'Michael?'

'Yes, Michael.'

We both sit silently. She sips her tea, still staring at me.

'Where is he now?'

'A few hours from here. He's marrying a friend of mine.'

Her eyes grip mine as she places her teacup down rather abruptly into her saucer. Without a word she leaves the room. I don't know if I'm meant to follow this domineering lady or stay here but before I can decide, she returns with what looks like a photo album.

'It's old fashioned I know, to print pictures out, but I do love to look at them. My late husband was quite the photographer.' She smiles as she begins to flick through the cardboard pages in front of her. Then she pauses. 'They were a beautiful couple. The wedding was perfect – hard to believe it was only four years ago.'

Four years? With all of my research it hadn't occurred to me to find out when Michael and Serena were actually married. He's gone from married to widowed and engaged to be married again in the space of four years?

She turns the book to show me the picture she has stopped at.

'That was Michael and Serena's wedding. Serena invited us, the whole street actually. She was such a wonderful soul. I thought that by now there'd be tiny feet running around their house.' She looks wistful at the thought. My heart leaps – finally a real person is acknowledging what I found online – Michael's been married before.

'What happened, to Serena I mean?'

With a sigh Alice slams the book shut, before answering in a very matter of fact tone. 'There was a fire. Serena didn't survive.' Lowering her voice as if sharing some secret, she adds, 'As for Michael. Some people believe he had to leave, that the thought of being near where he had a life with Serena was too much for him.'

'And what do you think?' By now I am leaning forward, hanging on every word.

'I don't like to gossip, but some people say they were having problems. That her death may have been suspicious.'

I feel a surge of adrenaline, this is why I've come all this way, to find out what Michael is truly capable of. 'Why would some people say that?'

'Well I was never one to pry, dear, but when she died, he inherited her money – there was a lot of it too. She's from old money you see. Then he just disappeared. And now you tell me he's marrying again. So soon.'

I can feel my heart beating quicker as she shakes her head in disappointment at my news. She is starting to confirm my wildest fears. 'So, if some people believe that, why didn't the police get involved?'

'Oh they did my dear, but he had answers for everything. He was at a local charity event when she died. Hundreds of people in attendance, myself included. They concluded it was an accident, so that's that.'

No, that isn't that. I want to ask so much more but I can see from the way Alice begins to tidy the table that I am about to overstay my welcome.

'I'm sorry dear, it's starting to get late – I must get my beauty sleep,' she smiles, standing from her seat. 'I'm glad to know what happened to Michael after all these years. I have wondered.'

I start to follow her to the door, wondering how I can make an opportunity to ask her about Anna but she stops at a table where her landline is placed, fiddling with a rolodex – I didn't even realise people still had these in their homes any more.

'Ah, yes, here it is,' she mumbles to herself as she copies the number onto a flowered piece of notepaper. She pauses before handing it to me. 'It's never sat right with me, you know. That he just left after she died. What is it you are trying to find out – really?'

There's no point in me lying, Alice is far too perceptive.

'I want to make sure my friend is safe. That Michael's wife's death was really an accident.'

Her eyebrows raise. 'Then do what you must.' She hands me the folded piece of paper. 'Perhaps call this young lady, she may be able to help you.' She offers a comforting smile. 'This is Anna's number. Serena's sister. Understandably she took her death incredibly hard. She certainly has things to say about Michael.'

I am in awe of this woman, who has single-handedly offered me more than I could've hoped for already.

'I'm not sure how willing she will be to go over this, mind. Her family own the restaurant across town so if she doesn't answer, you can find her there.' That makes sense, the picture I had found online of her behind a bar – she was posing at her own restaurant. I step outside, turning back to offer Alice my gratitude.

'Please be careful, Victoria. I don't like to speak ill of anyone but I never liked that Michael. There's something about his eyes.'

Her words echo in my ears as I walk back to my car, my eyes firmly fixed on the piece of paper I'm gripping in my hand. It's too late to call her now but at least I know how to find Anna. I'm convinced more than ever that she is the key to all of this.

Chapter Thirty-One

RSVP

4 days until the wedding

I'm completely exhausted by the time I get back to the hotel, but when I try to lie down to get some sleep I cannot relax, fixating on Anna. I'm not sure when I drift off but when the steward knocks on my door to bring me my room-service breakfast order, I wake up still feeling utterly wiped out. The pile of toast and jam is what I need, and the tea is hot enough to burn the back of my throat a little, just the way I like it.

When I'm revived enough to face it, I retrieve the piece of paper from Alice and dial Anna's number before I lose my courage. Anna picks up within a couple of rings but by that time, I've already lost my train of thought.

'Hello… hello… is there anyone there?' I can hear her asking.

I want to hang up. How do I explain why I'm here, in her town? What made me think she would want to talk to me?

'Who is this?' Her voice sounds almost panicked now. 'Michael?'

Hearing his name is like a shot of adrenaline. Why does she think it's him? 'Er no, Hi. My name is Victoria.'

She remains silent, clearly waiting for me to explain the purpose of my call but I pause for too long.

'I don't know any Victoria. Sorry you must have the wrong number.' She hangs up.

Damn it. I ready myself to press redial, contemplating more thoroughly what I will say. She picks up just as quickly the second time.

'Please don't hang up, it's not a wrong number. My best friend is about to marry Michael and I think you know why that scares me.' I barely take a breath trying to get my words out before she can end the call again.

Her breathing is heavy on the end of the line.

'What do you want from me?'

I can hear the fear in her shaking voice.

'I've come to town to find you. I just want to talk – ask you a few questions about Michael and Serena.'

'Look, I can't talk right now. I'll text you where and when to meet me.'

She doesn't wait for me to answer before hanging up again. I don't know how hopeful to feel that she will stay true to her word and text me, but I know where to find her place of work if she doesn't.

At 3.47 p.m. I'm sitting in a café, feverishly awaiting Anna's arrival. I'm early, but it's felt like an age since Anna's message came through – Bellissimo's 4pm. Sit at the table by the door – and I couldn't stay in the hotel any longer.

Every time the bell above the door rings I look up sharply to see who's arrived, so when Anna walks in, her face strained, shoulders huddled, I spot her instantly. Her eyes darting around us and the way she keeps making sure her hood isn't sliding down is far removed from the feisty, confident woman I saw at the party and in the park though.

I wave to her and she slides into the chair opposite me, resting her elbows on the table, without taking her coat off or even lowering her hood. With her face partly hidden, she must look odd to everyone around us, we're inside after all. I can't help but wonder why she is so concerned with keeping her identity concealed, who will care if she is seen with me?

'Look,' she says forcefully, without any kind of greeting. 'Before you start. Michael threatened my family. I just can't risk getting involved with whatever it is you're doing here.' Her eyes are wide, constantly flicking to the doorway. That certainly explains her paranoia at being seen here. 'If he finds out I've spoken to you...'

'He won't, you have my word.'

I touch her hand to reassure her, but her eyes are still restless, darting over both of our shoulders before she leans in and lowers her voice. 'You need to learn who you're really dealing with. Protect your friend – and yourself.' She slides a manilla envelope from her bag across the table. As I touch it, she grabs my hand and pulls me forward so I can hear her whisper. 'You have to stop him, before it's too late. I wish I had. Then maybe Serena would still be here.' She slides her chair back and starts to walk away.

'Wait!' I protest. 'Please, I have so much to ask you. If you're worried about being seen here, we can go to my hotel?'

'No, I can't–'

'Please, for Serena?'

I hadn't planned to tug on her emotions like this, but I can't just let her leave. Not when I have come all this way and with Gwen's safety at stake. She nods. I don't waste time, grabbing my things I head for the door. I look down at the envelope in my hands, my mind whirring with what might be inside – and why Anna is so afraid to be seen. There is no doubt there must be proof here, something that will make Gwen finally believe me.

Anna's paranoia, however, is contagious. I slide the envelope into my bag as we cross the street, suddenly feeling vulnerable in this town I don't know, filled with faces I don't recognise. I can feel my pulse racing, echoing in my ears – I just want to be safely locked inside my hotel room. I yank my own hood up and try to blend in with hustle and bustle of the high street. Soon the voices and traffic fade away behind us, until it sounds as if only our hastening footsteps are echoing on the pavement, but the further I walk, the more sure I am that I can hear someone else's behind us. Tightening my grip on my bag, I look over my shoulder, but there is no one there.

By the time we've closed the short distance to the hotel, my lungs are burning from swallowing the frosty air. We dive into the lift and no one comes in behind us, much to my relief. As we make our way to my room, I can feel sweat beading on my forehead and running down the back of my neck.

'Quick, shut the door,' Anna commands as she pushes her way into my room.

I hang the 'Do not disturb' sign on the handle before locking the door behind us, and Anna moves to close the curtains.

'So, what do you want to know?' She is straight to the point.

'Tell me everything. I need to know what happened to Serena and why Michael left so soon afterwards. Why did he change his name?'

'He murdered her.'

I gasp. It is something I have feared but hearing someone else say it out loud sends a new wave of horror through me. 'I know it, but I can't prove it,' she continues.

I sit down on the bed, Anna pulling up the desk chair to face me.

'Why do you think that? Most witness reports at the time say how devastated he was, how in love they were.'

'What do they know? They didn't see my sister crying when she thought he was having an affair. They didn't see how much anger that man had when he was questioned about it.' Anna aggressively gesticulates as she speaks with such fury.

I can already feel myself tense at her words. This all feels too familiar. That is the very same fear Gwen has, that he might be having affair, and I have certainly seen how angry he can get.

'The last time I spoke to her she was worried he was going to leave her, then she was dead. He did it, I don't know how, but he did.' Her voice exasperated. 'You have to believe me…'

'I do.'

Silence.

'You do?' Surprise in her tone.

I fill her in on his relationship with Gwen, her fears and mine. How manipulative and frightening he's been. She sits, absorbing my words. Her body seems to almost relax as I relay my fears.

'I came to see her you know. At their engagement party.' Her tone is much more matter of fact now.

'Did you? Why?' I feign ignorance so she will explain.

'I'd always known where he'd gone, that he changed his name. I paid an investigator to keep tabs on him to begin with. I'd never given up on getting justice for my sister, and I think I was just waiting for him to make a mistake. When I found out he was engaged, I knew I had to warn her, your friend, of the kind of man she is marrying.'

'Why didn't you speak to her?'

'He stopped me. Threatened my family. Until that point I had no proof he was a killer but from the way he spoke to me, I knew he would kill me too. I have young children. I can't risk them getting hurt, so I left. I have to put my family first.' Finally, the pieces of the puzzle are slotting together. That's why she disappeared after I saw her in the park. 'Your friend, she has money, doesn't she?'

'Yes.'

'Then she is in danger too.'

I'm gobsmacked. It's one thing for me to fear that Michael is a murderer but to have someone who knows him say the same is another thing. I have to put a stop to this wedding.

'How can I prove it?' I question.

Anna nods towards the envelope in my lap. I swallow hard as I peel it open and tip out its contents: a pile of papers, newspaper clippings and photos fall onto the bed. I gently spread them out so I can see them more clearly, focusing first on the clippings. Each is reporting on the fire that caused Serena's death. Most of them seem to repeat what I have already seen online, that she was trapped alone inside the house and was unable to get out before succumbing to the smoke. A tragic accident.

One clipping however is attached to an official looking document. Sliding the paper clip off, I examine the heading: *Sunrise Insurance loss adjuster's report.* I start to read, failing to understand much of the jargon, ignoring Anna pacing up and down the room in front of me. Page after page of references to fire alarms and emergency service response times. Then I finally reach the bullet pointed conclusion.

- Fire appears to have been started in the kitchen due to an electrical fault.
- Faulty fire alarms meant the occupant did not wake until the fire had completely overtaken the ground floor.
- The deceased was found on the first-floor landing. Pronounced dead at the scene, succumbing to carbon monoxide poisoning from the fire.

I don't understand. This isn't proof. Nothing in this remotely suggests Michael had anything to do with Serena's death. My heart sinks. So far there isn't much more here than what I'd been able to find for myself on the internet. I push the pages aside and move onto the next official looking document. A prenuptial agreement. This makes me sit up a little straighter. I read through the details of Serena's finances – her wealth was staggering. She, Anna and their parents, were the only living heirs from the wealth their maternal grandparents had accrued. Shares, trust funds, houses… the list seems endless. Anna leans over.

'Read that bit,' she insists, pointing to a highlighted section.

Whilst Serena and Michael were married, he could live in her home and earn a small number of shares in one of her companies. Should they divorce, regardless of reason, he wouldn't stand to gain any more of her fortune. In fact, the only way he would be able to secure her fortune for himself is if she were to die. I sit back, catching Anna's eye.

'You see?' Her eyes are so wide, so desperate.

'No, I don't see Anna. This is a motive for sure, but hardly proof that he ended her life.'

Anna's eyes flash with rage, and she kicks the chair. There's no point me pretending I feel differently. I think over every time he has boasted to Gwen and me about what a self-made success story he is, how he started out with nothing. I guess mentioning that his money actually came from his dead wife would have been far less impressive. Would this be enough to convince Gwen to cancel the wedding though? I'm just not sure.

'Look, Anna. I believe you, I really do. But if this was proof, you'd have been able to go to the police with it.'

The speed in which she turns to me, her face livid, is frightening.

'Don't you think I know that? Do you think I haven't tried to make him pay for what he did to her?' Taking a deep breath, she wraps her arms around herself. 'Look, I should go. I hope you can protect your friend but this is as far as I can help you.'

My heart sinks with the realisation that I had put all of my hopes into Anna being the key to cracking whatever it is that Michael is hiding – but she isn't.

'Do you want to take your things back?' I gesture to the pile on the bed.

'No, I've spent years looking at those. Maybe it's time I stopped.'

I can see in her eyes that she is still scared. Just as she passes through the doorway I realise I what I should have said much earlier.

'I am truly sorry, Anna, for your loss.'

She tries to muster a smile, whilst pulling her hood up again. 'He robbed my family of a truly special person. I'll never forgive him from that. Proof or no proof.'

When she leaves I make sure to lock the door again, before tidying the documents back into the envelope. I may not be able to prove that Michael killed his wife, but I can prove that he has based his whole new life on a lie. I just have to hope that is enough to convince Gwen he is not the person she thinks she is in love with. If somehow he is responsible for Serena's death, I have to do what I can to save her from suffering the same fate.

I reach for the last of the photos that had tumbled from the envelope: seemingly happy photos of Michael and Serena. They look so in love, not too different from the photos taken at Gwen's engagement party. It doesn't matter how many people are in the frame, the adoring couple only have eyes for one another. There are so many – it looks like they knew each other all the way back to their teenage years, maybe they were even childhood sweethearts? Then, just a few short years after their marriage, she was dead. I just don't understand how he has got away with it – so far.

Chapter Thirty-Two

The Makeover

3 days until the wedding:

I'm trying to get some rest before my long drive home, but my mind is wide awake. The sky is still dark outside – it's early in the morning – but there's no point staying here any longer. The sooner I get back, the sooner I can speak to Gwen.

I stare over at my bag, hoping the envelope inside will be the ammunition I need to destroy the trust Gwen has in that man. I do wonder though if our friendship will be collateral damage. It's odd. I cannot imagine her not wanting me in her life, but she's shown me such a different side to her lately that perhaps we do need to reflect on what our friendship is really based on. I have had to find such an inner strength these last few weeks, which seems to be bothering Gwen. Perhaps she prefers it when I am in her shadow, in need of her strength?

I shake that thought from my head. I can address my hurt when this is over. I peek inside the envelope again and flick through the photos once more. Serena was a part of so many key events in Michael's life. How has he managed to hide this all from Gwen?

I stare at her graduation photo, him kissing her cheek as she holds onto her certificate. The women around them looking incredibly jealous at the romantic gesture. There is something so familiar about this photo, but I can't place my finger on it. I roll my eyes – I've looked at these pictures so much I'm starting to imagine things.

I repack the envelope and start planning how I will tell Gwen. By the time I've driven home she'll probably be getting ready for work. I know she has a couple of loose ends to tie up before the rehearsal dinner tomorrow, thanks to my act of vandalism. I can call her when she gets to the gallery, maybe meet her there, or bring her back to my house – to make sure Michael isn't around.

The street is fairly empty when I step out into the hotel carpark, but the hairs on the back of my neck are tingling. There is that feeling again. That I'm being watched. Spinning around, I don't notice anyone behaving strangely. A handful of people are walking and talking, the odd car or two hurrying along the road. This is Anna's doing, it's her paranoia I'm feeling. Even so, I still take quicker steps to my car, placing the bag with the envelope on the passenger seat next to me. I don't want it out of my eye line.

I'm glad to be heading home, back to the familiar. I feel my shoulders relax when the engine begins to roar, and soon see the coast fading into the distance behind me. The road ahead is peaceful, the rising sun casting beautiful shadows on the tree lined lanes ahead. Barely any other cars pass by. My eyes are starting to feel a little heavy and part of me wonders if driving on so little sleep is a good idea, but it's worth it for what I'm bringing back to Gwen: proof that Michael is a liar.

It's only 7 a.m. when I get home, so I go straight up to my room, taking my bags with me. I need to wait until Gwen gets to work – when she's there Michael won't know I'm calling her. Right now, I just need to lie down, my back hurting from driving so much the last couple of days. I set my alarm so I don't over sleep, savouring the feeling of my bed welcoming me home. I'm so exhausted that it doesn't take long for my eyes to feel heavy again and sleep to find me.

I wake with a jerk, the high pitch beeping from my alarm clock reminding me what a huge thing I need to get up and do. Still aching from the drive, I turn onto my side to switch it off, then pause. Something feels odd. My bedroom door is open, but I'm sure I closed it behind me. Beside the bed, my handbag's contents are scattered on the carpet.

I shudder and sit up, holding my breath, listening for any sound. This can't be happening again. I rush to close the bedroom door, but as I turn to look back over my bedroom, something strange catches my eye. On my pillow, there is a halo of something brown.

That's when it dawns on me. Normally when I wake I have to brush my hair out of my face, but this morning I didn't. I reach up to run my fingers through it but I feel nothing – then shorter strands. Bringing my hand round to look, chunks of long hair are tangled around my fingers. I frantically grab at my scalp but pile after pile of strands come away in my hands.

My breathing becomes fast and shallow as I stagger to the mirror to see what has happened. Stumbling back, I see my blunt lipstick laying on the edge of the sink, but my eyes still fixate on the mirror ahead. Not on my reflection, but on the words written in red across the glass.

I told you, if you don't look after yourself, I will.

I fall back against the door frame, desperate to get away from that message. Michael must know what I've found. He must be trying to scare me away. What if he is still in the house?

I go back to the bedroom, but the sight of my hair-covered carpet makes me stop in my tracks. I don't know what to do. Grabbing my phone, I rush for the stairs, nearly missing one as I throw myself down the last few steps. Without stopping to see if anyone else is in the house I run straight for the front door, out onto the street. Looking back over my shoulder I run straight into a pair of dog walkers, who are bewildered by my appearance or manner or both. I think I hear one of them ask if I need any help, but I don't respond. I just keep running, barefoot, to Samira's house and bang on the door with my closed fists. Through the frosted panels of the door, I see her figure rushing towards me.

'Oh my god, what's happened to you?'

I step into her house and fall into a heap at her feet without waiting for an invitation. She kneels down beside me and says, 'Vic, let's get you inside properly.' But I can't move. I can't cry. I just feel fear. Sheer fear.

'Samira, who was at the door?' I can hear Raheem shouting, stopping as soon as sees me. I watch his face change from shocked to concerned before he lifts me and carries me to the sofa.

'Mum, I can't find my coat,' a small voice echoes from the kitchen.

'I'm going to get the kids to school and then I'll be right back,' Raheem says. He and Samira exchanging worried looks before he leaves us alone, closing the door behind him.

'Vic, please, you're scaring me. What's happened?'

I can barely string a sentence together, as I try to understand what's happening myself. Samira carefully wraps a blanket around me – only then do I realise how much I am shaking. 'Who did this?' She runs her hands through what is left of my hair.

I can just about mutter through my silent tears. 'I don't know. I think it was Michael. He left a message.'

Her sympathy turns to anger. 'We need to call the police.'

I don't have the energy to argue. She takes herself to the hallway and I can hear her muffled voice on the phone. Then Raheem's voice as he comes back from the school run. I feel so numb. I can't even think straight. I can hear her and Raheem talking, bickering about what to do with me. I stand to look at myself in the mirror above her fireplace, to finally take in what he has done to me.

Chunks of my hair are cut haphazardly at different lengths. Before it hung below my shoulders, and now it falls barely to my chin in some parts, even shorter in others. On one side I can even see patches of skin where there is little more than stubble left. I pull at different sections frantically to see how much is missing. Each cut section representing Michael holding something sharp near me. A knife? Scissors? I just don't know. If I weren't so exhausted I'm sure the feeling of him being near me would've been enough to wake me up.

Samira walks in, putting a mug of steaming tea on the table nearby. She sits down on the sofa, patting the empty space next to her, beckoning me to sit. I dutifully flop down, and start to explain the scene I woke up to, but it's not long before I start to cry.

Thankfully the police arrive quickly. Everything is such a blur, it isn't until the officers sit down on the sofa opposite me that I realise it is the same pair from the first break-in.

'Can you talk us through what happened?'

I wonder what the point is, they'll only judge me again. I just sit and stare at my cup of tea.

'Someone broke in, did this to her hair,' says Samira for me.

'Is that right, Victoria?' I look up. Officer Kerr actually looks sympathetic, so I nod. 'It would really help us if you could talk us through what happened. Take your time.'

Samira slides next to me, smiling and nodding for me to go on.

'I don't know what happened. I went to sleep and woke up like this.'

Officer Larson furiously scribbles in her notepad. I wonder what they're thinking. Do they think I did this to myself? That I'm making it up?

'Tell him about the message, Vic.'

Both officers look up, waiting.

'There are words. On the mirror,' is all I can muster before needing to look back at my tea. I watch it ripple as a single tear spills into it.

'What does the message say?'

I shake my head, I don't want to say it out aloud.

'OK, we're going to go and take a look if that's all right?' Officer Larson asks gently. I nod as Samira takes off my spare key from her bunch, drawing immediate attention from Officer Kerr. 'And how long have you had a spare key?'

Samira frowns, not understanding the purpose of the question. 'Erm, for years, why?'

The officers exchange a glance, ignoring her question. 'And where were you last night?'

Samira and I shoot one another a look of disbelief. They cannot believe she was involved in the attack?

Sliding the key towards them defiantly, Samira answers. 'In bed with my husband. You can ask him if you like?'

'Thank you. I'm sure you understand, we just need to follow every avenue of investigation.'

Samira's silence screams that she does not understand at all. But the police don't know what I know. They don't know about Michael.

The officers take the key and make their way to my house. Samira and I watch them through the window, until they are out of sight. It feels like an age until they come out. Officer Kerr is talking into his radio whilst Officer Larson makes her way back to us.

'We're going to wait for forensics to come. Do you have any family you can stay with nearby?' she asks me.

'It's fine, she can stay here with me,' Samira responds.

'Perhaps you would be more comfortable with family?' Officer Larson persists, her eyes flicking between me and Samira, clearly unhappy with me being under the same roof with a potential suspect. Samira folds her arms, clearly reading the situation in the same way I have.

'I think it would be best for me to stay here, with Samira. I feel safe with her.'

With a sigh, the officer nods. 'Once forensics have finished you'll be able to go back and get a few things.'

I look at my dirty feet and creased clothes, before running my fingers though what's left of my hair. What on earth can I collect that will make this ok? Then I remember, the envelope and the image of my handbag on the bedroom floor. That's all I need, to check for the envelope. I stand up, dropping the blanket behind me.

'I need to get back into the house!' I try to push past the officer but she doesn't budge.

'You really should stay here Victoria, just until…'

'No, I have to go now!'

I can see the confusion in her face as I try to outmanoeuvre her. Samira tries to calm me, offering to lend me her clothes so I can change, but that's not the issue here. I need to get back to check that Michael hasn't taken that evidence of his lies. Without it, how will I convince Gwen?

By now I am pleading and more officers are arriving. They look at one another, clearly considering giving in just to calm me down.

'Look, we can take you back but we're going to have to stay with you, OK?' PC Larson says.

I nod. They don't need to know what I am going back for. Wrapping the blanket back around me and stepping into Samira's slippers, I walk back to the house with them. With a gloved hand Officer Kerr opens the door, encouraging me not to touch anything that I don't need to.

First I make my way to the study, and gasp at what I see. My wall planner is ripped and on the floor. All of my notes and photos have gone. There is nothing on my desk either. An empty space where my computer once stood. I cannot comprehend what is happening. I dive towards the stairs, I need to get to my handbag, but I am blocked by Larson and Kerr.

'Please, I just want my handbag... I need to check my purse is still in it. Or if I need to cancel my card,' I lie.

They talk amongst themselves before going upstairs for me. A man with a camera follows closely behind. It seems an age until they return with my bag.

'Your purse is still inside. Cash and cards too,' Officer Larson says.

I know she is trying to be comforting but I couldn't care less about that. I quickly rifle through but I think I already knew – there's no envelope. I begin to feel dizzy, grasping at Samira to steady myself.

'Right, this is too much for you, we're going back to mine.'

I don't argue as she leads me out of the house. Michael has defeated me. He has everything I was going to show Gwen and with the rehearsal dinner only a day away, I am running out of time. The only thing I have are the photos on my phone – which thankfully I left in the car – but that won't be enough.

Samira and I walk back to her house in silence, her arms around me, helping to steady me. In the comfort of her living room, I sit and look at the photos on my phone whilst she hovers around me, fearful of leaving me alone I think. The more I sit and stare at my phone, the more resolute I become. I've come too far now to let Michael scare me away – I have to tell Gwen what I've found, whether she chooses to believe me or not.

I try to call her. Straight to voicemail. Damn. I leave a message asking her to call me back as soon as possible and message her as well.

We need to talk. Urgently.

I don't care if Michael knows I'm contacting her. He clearly knows what I'm up to and I won't let him win. I'd rather just take the risk and talk to her than one day be stood at Gwen's funeral thinking I should've spoken up – or for her to be stood at mine.

Chapter Thirty-Three

Preparing The Speech

When Gwen finally returns my call, the joy in her voice is grating. Part of me is glad to hear she is safe and well but the other part of me can't believe that she hasn't once asked after me, despite everything I am going through, for her. After all, we haven't spoken since I left for my so-called break. I want to just say what I have to say but before I can get a word in, she floods my ears with talk of the last wedding dress fitting and the rehearsal dinner.

'Gwen please, I need to talk to you.'

'Sure, why don't you pop round. Michael is working from home today but he won't be a bother.'

I clench my fists. There is absolutely no way he's going to leave me alone with her, not with everything he knows I know.

'I'd rather it was just you and me, Gwen.' There is a frosty silence.

'Please stop this Vic. We need to concentrate on moving forward. This wedding is happening. I love him. You can't keep avoiding him.'

Before I can ask if there is another time for us to meet up she cuts me off, her tone abrasive and abrupt.

'It's going to be a really busy day today. Why don't we just talk at the meal tomorrow? Anyway, must dash, the venue has left a message for me. Speak soon.' Then she is gone.

I sit in shock, still holding the phone to my ear. She is right about one thing though: I will speak to her at the meal. If it's the only opportunity I have to tell her everything I know about Michael, then so be it. He won't be able to stop me, not with so many other people around. In fact, maybe it isn't just her I need to speak to. Maybe everyone who is under his spell needs to know who he truly is. It dawns on me that there will be one opportunity I have where Michael won't be able to silence me: my speech. The fact that I don't have all the evidence won't matter. All I need is to sow a seed of doubt in enough people so that Gwen can't ignore it.

Samira comes in with snacks and yet another cup of tea, bringing me back to the here and now. I join her as she watches the comings and goings on our street. People in white overalls are coming from my house, carrying kits and clear bags filled with bits and pieces from my home. I'm too far away to see what exactly, but there is definitely one filled with brown hair – my hair. I instinctively reach for the few longer strands still hanging at the back of my head and near my neck.

Earlier in Samira's kitchen, one of the forensic team had me stand there as they took photos of me from all angles. I haven't really thought about my hair since. I can't go to the rehearsal dinner like this though. I need Gwen to think that everything is normal until I can get the whole room's full attention.

Samira notices me twiddling my hair anxiously around my fingers. 'Look Vic, say no if you want to but, shall I try and help fix your hair?'

Samira tried to cut her eldest daughter's hair once, and made such a disaster of it that it has been expensive hair salon appointments for her household ever since. What other choice do I have though? Even if I could get an appointment at such short notice, if I go to a salon I will no doubt be met with a barrage of questions as to why my hair is in this state and I can't deal with that right now.

I sit as still as I can on the stool in her kitchen, a towel wrapped around my shoulders, as she chops away with the kitchen scissors at the random longer strands. She has to use Raheem's beard trimmer on one side as there simply isn't enough hair left to style.

'I'll just try and shape it a bit, OK?' she says, and the look of concentration on her face is a comfort. Here's someone who undoubtedly cares about me.

She has given me a mirror to hold, so I can watch and speak up if I'm not happy, but I don't care about the hair really, it'll grow back. What I can't get over is Michael being in my home as I slept, sending me a message that he can get to me whenever he wants? How did he do it, even after I've had the locks changed?

More hair falls past my face but I just feel numb to it. I won't let him get away with thinking he can control me.

'That's it, all done! Not bad if I do say so myself!' Samira steps back, looking at me this way and that. 'What do you think?'

I reluctantly look in the mirror. To her credit, the cut isn't terrible. An asymmetric style, shaved on one side, longer on the other – far more synonymous with a young actress than a thirty something therapist, but certainly an improvement from where she started.

I don't look like me though, and in an odd way, how I looked a few minutes ago better reflected how I feel right now, but I don't have time to dwell. We both spot the time on the clock. Her children will be home soon.

'Thank you. Samira, I think I might book myself into a hotel tonight.'

'I won't hear of it! If it's the kids you're worried about, Raheem is taking them to his mother's for the night.'

I try to muster a smile. 'I'm sorry, I never wanted–'

'Stop, has anyone ever told you that you apologise too much? Why don't you maybe have a lie down. I'll get some food ready.'

I know there is no point arguing with her when she puts on her mum voice, so I wander up to the spare bed, avoiding looking at myself in the dressing table mirror. It's still a strange sensation, not feeling my hair on my back or having it fall inconveniently across my face. I won't let the sadness overcome me though. I want to keep the anger simmering inside, I need it to make sure I do what I have to do at the party tomorrow.

I search for the maid of honour's speech saved on my phone. There was so much back and forth with Gwen about this speech, to meet her exacting standards. Yet I can barely read through all the absurd script about their happiness and their future together. Instead I start furiously typing what I actually want to say. The secrets. The betrayal. The danger.

Once I've said all of this, there will be no going back. Not only will Michael not be able to do anything about this but neither will Gwen. I have no idea what mix of emotions she will feel and it will all be so public. She will hate me. That thought scares me a little. No matter how badly she's treated me, I hate knowing that I am about to rip her life apart. I just have to hope that eventually she will forgive me. I'd rather her angry and alive than living in some warped, Michael-shaped reality, and in danger.

My notes disappear as my screen lights up with an incoming call. It's Gwen. My heart sinks as I pick up, preparing myself to listen to more of her happy, unsuspecting chatter.

'Hey Vic. I'm sorry about earlier. The stress of the wedding is making me snappy.'

I bite back the emotion waiting to spill out of me. I have to save it for the meal.

'It's OK, you were right, this is a happy occasion and I don't want to spoil it for you,' I lie.

'Vic, are you OK? Samira texted me – she says something's happened and you're at her place.'

I can feel my grip tighten on the phone. I'm not OK but I don't want her here and I certainly don't want her bringing Michael.

'I think someone was in the house again when I was away. It's fine though, I'm staying with Samira until we know for sure.'

I try to keep my breathing and tone steady. I'll have plenty of time in the future to tell her the whole truth.

'Do you need me to come over? I can be there soon?'

'No, it's fine. Samira and Raheem are looking after me – and the police are taking it more seriously this time. Which is a good thing.'

'Are they? Is there something else you're not telling me, Vic?'

Yes, so much. 'No, of course not.'

'Vic… I know I keep saying this wedding is everything to me, but if you don't feel like you can make the meal or anything then...' Her voice trails off.

My sharp intake of breath speaks volumes at what she is implying – doesn't she want me there?

'I'm not saying don't be at the wedding, you're a huge part of that, but the dinner is just a rehearsal, and you've been through so much.'

I can feel myself fighting back tears, I want to believe that Gwen is finally showing some semblance that she cares but it feels more like she's pushing me away.

'I'll definitely make it. I wouldn't miss it for anything.'

Silence.

'If you're sure?'

I'm one hundred per cent sure. My entire plan to stop the wedding hinges on me being there.

The rest of the evening feels interminable. The police come and go, with very little to update me on. Later, dinner with Samira and Raheem is strained. Feeding me has always been Samira's way of making sure I'm OK – I've never come for dinner and not left with a Tupperware filled with leftovers – but it's not the same today. Despite her and Raheem's best efforts to lift my spirits, it all just feels like a countdown until tomorrow. Samira's need to try and continually cheer me up must be exhausting for her, so I excuse myself to bed for both of our sakes. I lie down, staring at the ceiling, fine tuning my speech in my head and texting Isaac.

When I do attempt to close my eyes, I see Michael standing above me, my hair in his hands. I roll into my pillow, hugging it tightly for the faintest bit of comfort. One way or another, this will come to an end tomorrow.

Chapter Thirty-Four

Speak Now Or Forever Hold Your Peace

2 days until the wedding.

Today is the day. The day I say my truth. The day I ruin this wedding.

I push the sweat soaked blanket off me, nauseous at the thought of what I am preparing to do. I struggle to push myself up to sitting, my arms wobbling under the strain. For a minute I just want to be in my own bed, pull the duvet back over my head and ignore the world, but I have to go through with this. For all of our sakes.

I scrape the hair, what is left of it, from my clammy forehead, change quickly and shove my clothes into my hold-all, not wasting time to fold them. Break-in or not, I'm going home. I need to get my dress so everything appears normal when I first arrive at the meal. I need to see if I can contact Anna too, check if there's any evidence left that I can salvage. I try not to make too much noise as I make my way downstairs but my bag gets caught on the banister, and before I have a chance to sneak out, I hear Samira's door open.

'Where are you going?'

She rushes to tie her robe as she follows me down the stairs but I don't stop, quickly pulling on my shoes before turning to answer her. 'I need to go home.'

'Wait, I'll come.'

I want to argue but at this point Samira calls out to Raheem. 'Vic wants to go home, we need to go with her to make sure everything's OK.' Turning to me, she says in her bossiest voice, 'Wait here until we're dressed.'

I do as I'm told, sitting on their stairs whilst they get ready.

They walk on either side of me to my house. A police officer is still sitting in their car outside. Raheem takes the lead through the front door, and there is a quiet sense of fear in all of us as we move cautiously through to the kitchen. Everything just feels so still.

'Shall we get the kettle on then?' Samira says, doing her usual job of breaking the painful silence. Poor Raheem still looks half asleep as he slumps at the kitchen table, waiting for his caffeine fix. Samira stops mid-sentence, her gaze wandering just over my shoulder to the remnants of white powder on the door handle where the police have been.

'We should probably give this place a once over when we've had breakfast,' she says, already head deep into the fridge. 'Let's see what we have to work with – not a lot it seems,' she tuts. She has an amazing talent of being able to whip up culinary works of art from next to nothing, so she's in her element right now.

'I'm just going to take my bag upstairs,' I say.

They look at each other, then me. There's no way they're letting me go alone.

Each step sends a cold wave through me as I relive the last time I was in my room. My pulse is quickening but I don't want Samira to see my nerves and make me go back to her house. More remains of white powder lie scattered on various surfaces.

I hold my breath as I open my bedroom door. The bed is stripped, with just the bare mattress on display. I exhale, thankful not to have to see that hair left on my pillow again.

'Where are your spare sheets? Let's get this remade.' Samira pushes past me, but then stops suddenly, blocking my path. 'Er, maybe we should have breakfast first.' She's trying to nudge me back towards the door.

'What are you– why?'

I yank myself free, craning my neck to look at where she is pulling me away from: the en suite bathroom. Still emblazoned across the mirror is that red writing. Spinning me back to face her, Samira's eyes are wide with the realisation of just how intimate my intruder's visit has been.

'I'll get this cleaned up, you finish making the tea.'

I nod, emotionless. Perhaps I'm not as ready to be here as I had thought.

Thankfully Samira isn't long. She doesn't mention the writing again, instead making herself busy in the kitchen.

'Pass the eggs will you, Vic.'

I wander to the fridge but as I pass them to her, my hands start to shake uncontrollably, rattling the box open.

One egg falls to the floor before Samira manages to grab them from me.

'Maybe you should just sit? I'll clear up and bring you some food.'

I don't protest, sitting and watching her and Raheem cook and clean as they go. We sit quietly through breakfast too. I wish they didn't feel obliged to stay, to do all this for me.

'I'm going to get some rest before the party tonight, maybe you should get to your mum's, see the kids?'

'What? You can't seriously want to go to the dinner? Not when you think Michael did this to you?' Samira's voice is raised, gesturing in exasperation at my hair.

'I have to talk to Gwen, face to face. She has to see this.'

Raheem reaches out to squeeze Samira's hand, and her shoulders relax as she looks to him. They give each other such strength.

'This is a bad idea, Vic. But if you're going to go, we'll be right next to you.'

I feel like crying again but we smile at one another before going back to eating. Neither Raheem nor Samira are in a rush to go but with some persuading they eventually leave, if only because the squad car is still outside. As soon as they go, I make my way back to my study. The bare walls still break my heart, after all the time and effort I had put into my investigations. Now I have nearly nothing to show for it.

Before I can sit down, the doorbell rings. I expect it's Samira, changing her mind about leaving me alone, but it's Isaac. He moves to speak, stopping when his eyes fix on my hair. I feel so self-conscious, using my hands to try and pull it into some kind of shape.

'Your hair, er… it suits you short.' I can tell he's lying.

'You don't have to… it's a long story.'

He notices my eyes filling, and steps in to hug me tightly. I really need this. We stand in the open doorway silently holding onto one another.

'Really though, your hair… it looks nice,' he murmurs, running his fingers across my bare neck. 'You're not hiding behind it anymore.'

I let out a sigh before leading him into the study, ready to explain everything. He sits, dumbstruck as I relay my time with Anna. Except for the odd question to clarify, he makes no other comment.

'It's true then? Really?' He seems so disillusioned.

'I'm sorry Isaac. I know he's your–'

'Was,' he interrupts.

'What?'

'You were going to say friend, but he isn't, not anymore. He *was* my friend. The Michael I knew was a great guy – hard-working, decent, you know? That's why I went into business with him. I don't know who this Michael is.' He pauses, resting his head in his hands, before looking back at me. 'Can I see it, the envelope?'

My heart sinks. I watch his eyes widen and his hands clench as I finish my update. He stands to run his hands through my hair once more, before turning away and slamming them on the desk. Adrenaline courses through me as he makes his way towards the door, muttering, 'I'm going to fucking kill him.'

'No.' I stand in front of him, blocking his exit. 'If you go for Michael, Gwen will just defend him. She has to hear – everyone has to hear and see what he's truly like.'

He grimaces, clearly confused. I push him gently backwards until he falls back into the chair. As I reveal my plan – the rehearsal dinner speech – he remains silent, brooding.

'Are you sure this is a good idea? He's dangerous. Just tell the police.'

'Tell the police what? What proof do I have it was him last night or any other time? He's too smart for that. I need him to show his true colours in front of everyone. I want everyone to see the monster he is.'

I can tell from the way Isaac is twiddling his fingers, unwilling to look at me, that he's not happy, but I can't let this shake me. Kneeling in front of him, I lift his chin.

'When all of this is over, you and I are going to have that date. OK? We just need to get through tonight.'

He can't help but smile as my forehead rests against his. 'If this is what you have to do, count me in. Shall I get my taxi to pick you up for the dinner?'

'Don't worry, I have a few things I need to think about. If I drive myself and stay sober, it will help clear my head.'

I can see from his pained expression that he would prefer us to go together, but he relents. 'Fine, but I'll be right by your side at the meal.'

Between him, Samira and Raheem, Michael won't be able to stop me. The way he strokes my face, so gently, so intimately, gives me so much courage, like we're in this together. I don't want to let myself think past tonight but when this is all over, I *will* make him more of a priority.

I walk him to the front door but he hesitates, turning to me. 'I'm going to go round to see Michael. Keep him company today.'

I'm taken aback. Why would he want to spend time with him after everything I have just said? 'If I'm with him, then he can't be anywhere near you. Do what you need to do.'

As he walks to his car, I don't know how to feel. Isaac is truly loyal to me but I am still so scared of what lies ahead – will he be safe with Michael? I can only hope so.

When he's gone I return to my desk, wasting no more time in messaging Anna. To my surprise, she calls me instantly.

'What have you done?' she asks right away, her tone desperate and searching. 'Does he know you know?'

'I think so.'

'What do you mean, you think?'

It pains me to go through the details of last night again. Each time I feel the hairs on the back of my neck stand on end. I move around the house as I speak to her, opening each of the doors wide. I'm not sure what I would do if someone was behind one of them, but I can't help checking that I'm alone.

'What are you going to do now?'

'Do you have any copies you can e-mail me? Wedding photos – anything?'

'I can do later, text me your e-mail. She pauses. Are you sure you want to do this? There'll be no turning back.'

My blood runs cold. I know she's right. I have been resisting truly thinking about what will happen after my speech. But I cannot let the immediate consequences cloud my motivation – it's too late for that.

I make my way up to the bedroom. Time to start getting ready for tonight. Taking in my new reflection I don't even know how to feel. I don't recognise myself. I've skipped so many meals that my weight has changed dramatically – unhealthily so. My skin looks gaunt and my hair, well, I can't bear to even look at my hair again. I can just imagine what Jessica will have to say about it.

I take a few deep breaths, doing the best I can with the make-up I have. Then I pull out the other dress she lent me. A deep blue, backless midi dress. The colour only making my complexion look even more washed out. It's so tight I wonder how it would've fitted if I hadn't lost so much weight. I shake my head to try to rid myself of the negative thoughts. At least it has long sleeves, to hide the now yellowing bruises from Michael. None of that matters though. Only my speech does.

Chapter Thirty-Five

The Rehearsal Dinner

I hate driving on country lanes, not least in the rain when the roads are slippery, but Gwen wanted the meal to be in part of the sprawling estate where the wedding is to be celebrated. Eventually I can see the grand entrance ahead, leading to an incredible gothic building I recognise from the brochure Gwen showed me. My stomach feels tense with anxiety. This is really happening. I can see a few taxis have arrived before me, and Isaac's just stepped out of one of them, which offers me some relief. I park and take one last look in the mirror before exiting – mopping the sweat from my brow, cursing my nerves. The air outside is bitterly cold, which takes my breath away, but at least feels refreshing against my skin.

'Vic!' Isaac comes rushing over to me. 'Are you OK?'

I nod, rubbing my arms against the cold.

'You don't have to go through with this you know, we can find another way.'

I do have to though. Who knows how much longer Gwen will be safe with Michael?

'I'm fine. Are they here?'

He nods. Taking a deep breath in, I ready myself to pretend to be fulfilling the role of the dutiful maid of honour, at least until there are enough people there to make my speech worthwhile.

Isaac puts his arm out for me to link through as we walk into the dining room. The ceilings are high and swathed with white silk ribbons, from the chandeliers to the walls. I chose that shade of white, I think to myself. In fact, looking around, I made so much of this happen. The twinkle of the candlelight across the crystal glasses is simply stunning. Each seat is laid immaculately, with their single roses and name tags. I run my fingers across one, remembering how long it had taken me to do the same for every place at the engagement party. So much has happened since then. That night changed everything. If I don't act tonight, then this is where Gwen and Michael will be sitting down for their wedding breakfast in two days' time.

'Shall we get a drink?' Isaac drags my attention back. I nod as he grabs two flutes of champagne from a passing waiter. I want to gulp the entire glass in one go, anything to steady my nerves. Knowing I have to drive home, I resist.

Isaac squeezes my hand. 'I'll be right here with you.'

I look at him, someone I truly adore. I can't imagine how I would feel if I found out he isn't the trustworthy person I feel he is. So how will Gwen feel when I tell her about Michael? I lift what's left of my drink, trying not to dwell on the short-term pain her safety will cost.

'*What* have you done to your *hair*?' I spin around to see Jessica's usual disapproving scowl. She reaches out to try and change the way my hair is styled but I lean back to escape her clutches. 'Seriously, you know the plan was that we'd all have our hair up for the wedding! Now I'll have to call the hairdresser and–'

'Just do what you have to do, I don't care!' I spit back at her. I don't mean to be so abrupt but I just need her to stop talking. She recoils, probably in shock that I've actually spoken up for myself. Before she can react I see Gwen and Samira rushing over.

'Vic!'

Gwen budges Jessica to the side so she can greet me. She stops short of her usual hug as she sees my hair too. 'Oh, erm. Wow. That's a change. It suits you.'

As she stands there, trying to be kind to me, all I can think about is how I'm going to rip her life apart. More guests arrive to take her attention away, leaving me with Samira.

'As soon as you want to leave, we will leave,' she whispers.

I can tell she's holding back her concern as best as she can, but it's written all over her face. I look over to Gwen welcoming her guests, looking even more radiant than normal. Her hair is literally glistening in the light, swaying as she urges each newcomer to mingle.

That's when I see Michael coming. As if in slow motion, he pulls Gwen close to him, kissing her hands, then looks over her shoulder at me. His smile falls a little before his gaze refocuses onto Gwen. Is he surprised I'm here? He must have thought he'd scared me away. The thought of him looking over me as I slept, blade in hand, comes back and reignites my anger with a vengeance.

My turbulent thoughts are interrupted by a much more civilised tone. 'Ladies and gentlemen,' a rather well-dressed maître d announces, and the room falls silent, 'dinner is served.'

We all move towards the tables, everyone looking for their seat. I feel unsteady on my feet, using the back of my hand to pat away the sweat that has inevitably returned to my forehead. On a good day, standing in front of so many people and giving a speech would be hard enough for me but this speech... I can't bear to think about it.

'We're over here!' Samira yells to me, pointing to the seats close to Gwen. Isaac pulls my chair out for me, trying to offer me a reassuring smile as he watches me sit down, but all I can do is stare at Michael. I watch him sneak a kiss on Gwen's neck, looking mischievous as she pushes him away. Her face is radiating happiness and contentment. I'm not sure how I can sit and watch this for much longer.

As everyone tucks into their starters the room fills with joyful chatter. Michael cracks some witty joke, making Gwen's mother laugh while Gwen looking adoringly on. My stomach is churning, the pungent aroma of the chicken liver and cognac pate not helping, so I push the plate away.

My nausea continues on hearing the other guests compliment what a well-matched couple they are and what a beautiful bride Gwen will be. I know I'm not supposed to make my speech until after the main course but before I even know what I am doing I pick up a spoon, and gently tap my glass. The room hushes. I can't seem to quite take the deep breath I so desperately need, and my heart is pounding. But when I look at Isaac, his nod is all I need to stand up. I swallow hard against the faint taste of vomit already rising in my throat.

'Good evening, everyone! I'd just like to say a few words.' My mouth feels so dry.

'Oh, the speeches aren't planned for until the end of the meal,' Michael interrupts, laughing uneasily. He shoots me a look that is frighteningly cold but it's now or never. I look to Gwen.

'Please Gwen, I'd like to speak now.'

She looks confused and uncomfortable.

'Yes, let's hear it Vic!' Samira's encouragement forces Gwen to nod with a faux smile. I try to reach for my water but my unsteady hand knocks the glass over on the table. I can hear guests muttering that they think I'm already drunk, their hollow laughter echoing. I grip the edge of the table to steady my nerves.

'Perhaps you should just sit down, Victoria? You don't look well,' Michael says, tightly gripping his napkin in his closed fist. He looks as if he is about to walk around the table to me. Before I can respond Isaac stands up too.

'She's fine.' He turns to look at me, his face close to mine, whispering, 'I'm right here. Don't be scared.'

I take a deep breath and turn to face Gwen again, Isaac sitting but still holding my hand.

'No, what I have to say I have to say now. Gwen, I love you–'

'And I love you! Cheers!' she shouts back, lifting her glass so that everyone takes a sip of their drink. Michael gets up from his chair and starts moving towards me. I feel flustered. I just need to get the words out.

'–but you can't marry him!'

The collective gasp from across the room halts Michael in his tracks.

'He's not who you think he is.'

Gwen's eyes are wide with shock, before they silently plead with me to stop. But I have to keep going, holding tighter onto Isaac's hand. I catch Jessica standing out of the corner of my eye.

'Sit down, you're embarrassing yourself,' she commands.

Undeterred, I continue. 'Gwen, he's been married before and… look I have proof.' Fumbling for my phone in my handbag, I can barely make my hands do what I need them to, dropping it on the floor. Isaac reaches for it.

'Look, you need to get some air and sober up.' Michael manages to get past the now distracted Isaac, gripping my already bruised arm painfully tight.

'Get your bloody hands off me,' I yell, pushing him hard, Isaac manoeuvres to stand between us.

'Don't you dare touch her!'

The two men square up to one another as Isaac thrusts my phone at me. Yet just as Michael is about to open his mouth, Gwen breaks the low-level chatter now filling the room.

'Vic, what are you doing?' Her eyes are filled with tears. The other guests all fall silent, waiting for my reply. Her look of disappointment breaks my heart but this has to be done. She'll understand soon.

'Please Gwen, look at this photo.'

I struggle to unlock my phone and by the time I look up, Gwen's mother is leading her out of the room crying. Her father is angrily walking in my direction.

'You need to leave.'

'What? No, you need to listen to me, she's in danger!' I protest, still trying to get someone, anyone, to look at my phone.

'No young lady. I don't know if you're drunk or just jealous but you're making a fool of yourself!'

He grabs my phone, throws it back in my bag and starts to lead me towards the door. No matter how much I object he won't let me turn around. Over my shoulder I can see Isaac trying to make his way to me but Michael is blocking him. Samira and Jessica are arguing on the other side of the table. We reach the fire exit, Gwen's father commanding me to stay away. By the time he leaves me I can see Michael making his way to me too.

'What have you done?' he growls. 'I told you before, I won't let anything come between me and Gwen – least of all a stupid little bitch like you.'

I want to shout at him, but everything's spinning. This isn't going to plan at all. I need to get out into the fresh air. I stumble to the door, spilling out into the darkened car park. It's raining and it feels like my chest is being crushed under the weight of the secrets I'm so desperate to get out. Behind me I can hear Michael's voice becoming hoarse as he screams my name but I know now isn't the time to rest. I need to get away from him. I haven't told everyone enough to keep me safe from him.

Running for my car, I fumble with my bag to find the keys, but my eyesight is blurry from tears and my tremor is now out of control. I can hear his footsteps, splashing in the puddles as he gains on me, but my heartbeat is even louder. The keys slip through my wet hands, tumbling to the pitch-black tarmac. I know I have to move quickly – he is getting closer and closer, his voice angrier and angrier. By the time I stand up, he is right in front of me; grabbing my arm he wrenches me backwards, spinning me to face him. His face so close I can feel the heat of his breath. His eyes are wild with rage.

'You need to come back – fix this! Tell everyone you're sorry that it's a stupid drunken joke. Then leave and don't bother coming back.' The words spew from his gritted teeth.

I struggle against the pain of his tightening grip, wriggling and pulling until one hand slips free. Summoning the little energy I have left I swing for his face – my palm connecting across his cheek. For a split second we're both stunned into silence. As he recoils from the sting, his eyes wide in shock, I push him away, scrambling to unlock my car and dive in. I barely manage to press the lock button before he starts yanking the passenger handle. The taste of bile burns the back of my throat as the panic continues to rise within me. I momentarily look at his face, contorting as he yells my name. He bangs on the window and the full horror of the situation hits me: there is no one else around. He could do anything right now and who could stop him? Time to get out of here.

I frantically wipe the tears and rain from my eyes and jam the keys into the ignition. I just can't make my hands stop shaking long enough to slide it into place. Using one hand to steady the other, I manage to turn the key and the sound of the engine roaring through the deserted carpark is a small relief. I take one last look at him banging his clenched fist on the window, and floor the accelerator. The squeal of the tyres echoes in the darkness as I swerve out of the carpark and onto the lane back to town. I watch Michael get smaller in the rear-view mirror, glad I have managed to get away. The drive will at least buy me some time to rethink my approach.

When the estate finally disappears from sight, my breathing starts to slow to a normal pace, my chest hurting from how hard my heart is beating. The country lanes are now jet black, my headlights catching on the rows of trees in the otherwise deserted night, my window wipers flailing back and forth to clear the hammering rain.

That's when I notice the bright headlights behind me. The speed at which they are gaining on me is unnerving so I move to the left so they can overtake. They don't though. The car just keeps gaining. Faster and faster, swerving to stay directly behind me. They accelerate so fast they nudge my bumper, jolting me. I lurch forward before my head slams back against the headrest. I clench my jaw at the pain shooting across my skull, squinting to try and see the driver in my mirror but I struggle to make out the silhouette in the rain and brightness of their lights.

What is happening? It must have been an accident. They hadn't managed to slow down before hitting me on the rain-soaked roads, surely? Yet instead of moving away from me or slowing down, all I can see are the lights getting closer – bumping me again. This is no accident. I'm in trouble.

It has to be Michael. I floor the accelerator again, checking in my mirror to see how he reacts. Within seconds, he is right behind me. My fingers are white from gripping the steering wheel so tightly. I urgently search the road ahead for someone to help, somewhere to turn, anything. This lane seems to be a never-ending tunnel of darkness. I veer left and right, trying to stay on the winding road but before I can act, the third strike hits. My car begins to spin out of control. I can hear the screech of my tyres skidding across the road, but the brakes are no longer responding. Closer and closer, the trees are hurtling towards me, before my ears fill with the sickening sound of metal crushing around me. The shock is instant and intense.

The metallic taste of blood fills my mouth as I push myself back away from the deflated airbag. Everything is hurting as I try to take in my surroundings, my vision blurry. Even blinking hurts. Every breath feels laboured and shallow. I reach for the source of my pain, wincing as I touch my forehead, the blood trickling into my eye. I can barely move but I hear the screech of brakes behind me, from the road. Michael's coming.

If he were to kill me now, it would look like an accident and there is a room full of people who will vouch that I was drinking and behaving strangely. The similarity to Serena's death being ruled an accident isn't lost on me. I won't let this happen.

I try to reach for the handle but there just isn't enough strength in me to force the crushed door open. I can feel myself start to lose consciousness, as I see a figure in my wing mirror start to walk from the road down to me. Just as they near me, more headlights hurtle towards us. The figure turns. My eyelids are growing heavier – I can barely keep them open, my head falls against the door.

A small flame begin to grow from the side of the bonnet. The distinct smell of smoke reaches my nostrils just before everything goes dark.

Chapter Thirty-Six

In Sickness And In Health

It takes me a moment to gain my bearings. I squint against the bright lights above me, then realise I'm not in my car anymore. I'm lying down, and something is secured to my face – an oxygen mask. I'm lying in an ambulance.

I try to sit up but I feel a strong hand push me back down. The comforting eyes of a paramedic next to me seem so concerned. I can't remember being put in here. Who called them? I can just about make out an array of blue lights through the open doors: police officers are blocking the road, and firefighters are hosing down what looks like my burnt-out car.

'Has she woken up?' That's Isaac's voice.

I want to sit up but my head's spinning, my body racked with pain. Have I broken something? The paramedic is busy looking at a variety of machines next to me, I'm not sure what she said next but I feel his strong hand grasp mine as he sits next to the gurney, before everything goes dark again.

When I next open my eyes I'm already in hospital, wires attached to my arms and fingers, the gentle hum of the beeping machines next to me. I have no idea how long I've been here. Painfully I try and look around. Isaac is sitting, looking down at his phone, unaware that I'm awake. He looks exhausted. I reach my hand out to touch him, but the intense pain in my shoulder is instant, forcing me to recoil.

'That's where your seatbelt has bruised you,' the nurse I hadn't noticed was there explains. Isaac stands to move towards me and I in turn try to sit up. 'No, no, you lie down. You've been in a nasty accident,' the nurse continues.

Isaac silently moves his chair next to me, stroking my face tenderly, saying, 'You had me worried.'

'He's been sat here for hours you know,' the nurse says, smiling at Isaac and then me. 'I'll get the doctor. The police will want to speak to you too – when you feel up to it.'

I nod as best as I can and we both watch her leave. Isaac sighs, taking my hand in his. 'What happened?'

Everything feels so hazy but I do my best to tell him what I remember. 'I know it was Michael. He was so angry at me.' Isaac sits back in his chair, releasing my hand. Biting his lip, he is staring at the floor.

'I'm sorry that I let him out of my sight, but the other guests were blocking me…'

'It's not your fault.' I wait for him to look back at me, offering as much of a smile as I can muster. 'What happened after I left?'

'People were saying you were drunk. I tried to tell them you were telling the truth, but they threw me out too. That's when I got a taxi and found you. There was no one else in sight.'

Before I can think about it any further the doctor arrives. He looks intently at the chart at the end of my bed before plastering a professionally friendly smile on his face.

'You're very lucky. Other than slight concussion and a great deal of bruising, you're in one piece.'

I don't feel lucky. 'So can I go home?'

'We'd like you to stay until the morning, just to keep an eye on you, OK?'

He's acting like I have a choice but I don't think I do. 'You're going to have to be left to get some rest though,' he goes on, looking at Isaac. I hold his hand tighter. 'He can come back in the morning to take you home.'

Isaac does as he's told, releasing my hand and kissing me on the forehead. 'I'll be here first thing in the morning, OK?'

'Will you ask Samira to put a few things in a bag for me? She has a spare key. Let her know I'm OK?' He nods, pulling the blanket up to my chin before he walks out with the doctor.

I lie there, listening to the comings and goings of the ward, before focusing on the many wires attached to me. So many questions are rattling around in my mind. It must have been Michael in the car but how did he manage to leave the party unnoticed? Was he trying to kill me or scare me? I can barely string my thoughts together, the pain in my head is now pulsating. Thankfully the friendly nurse comes to my aid again.

'Take these, they'll help with the pain.'

I don't stop to ask what they are before swallowing the tablets and closing my eyes. Thankfully, whatever they were relieves the pain enough that I am able to fall asleep.

The next thing I'm aware of is the sound of a trolley, and the smell of eggs and toast wafting across the ward. It makes my stomach turn. I try to roll onto my side, but there are too many wires attached, forcing me to stare up at the ceiling.

'Morning, how are we feeling today?' Another friendly face paws at my tubes and scribbles on the chart at the end of my bed.

'I'm fine thanks. Can I go home soon?'

'As soon as the doctor says you can go. You have a visitor waiting. A handsome young man!' he says, winking at me.

I feel a wave of relief. I can't wait to see Isaac. I push myself up to sitting, and the nurse helps to readjust my pillows before going to fetch him. I smooth down my hair – goodness knows what I must look like.

Yet it isn't him that walks in. To my horror, Michael moves slowly towards me, his face cold and emotionless. My eyes dart around the room – there are so many people walking by, he can't do anything to me here, can he? Without a word he pulls a chair up to the bed and sits down. I'm in so much pain but I'll be damned if I'm going to let him see that I'm scared. I speak first. 'I know you did this to me.' I don't break my stare as I wait for his response.

'I don't know what you mean, Victoria.' Before I can argue, he's ready with his cover story. 'I'm sure if that's what you tell the police, they'll be able to check my alibi. Much like you had them check where I was when you were getting that haircut. I had an alibi then and I have one now. There was close to one hundred people all focused on me trying to smooth things over after the mess you made last night.'

I'm dumbstruck. He is so confident – but how is that possible? I try to regain my concentration. 'What are you doing here then?'

'Just delivering a message.' His steely gaze is uncomfortably intense. 'First of all, Gwen no longer wants you to be at the wedding.' I feel a sharp pain in my chest. She hates me. And what if it's all been for nothing? 'I have a feeling though that you'll try and gate-crash, to make a scene like you did last night.'

'You can't stop me,' I spit back through welling tears.

'Look, I don't know what you were playing at last night but if you have something to say, say it now. Ask me anything.'

'What?' I can't tell what he is trying to do. Find out what I know? The way he leans back casually into the chair, as if he doesn't have a care in the world, completely throws me. With a shrug of his shoulders, he says, 'Ask me anything. I don't know what you've been told or by whom, but they are misleading you. I'll answer anything if it keeps you away from the wedding.'

My rage is about to spill over at last. Fine, I think. I don't care if he knows what I know, he can't stop me telling Gwen too.

'I know about Serena. I know about the money. I know you killed her.'

He chuckles slightly. 'And if I did, why haven't I been arrested? Can it be because, just like last night, I had an alibi and just like last night, there is no proof at all?'

I clench my fists, ignoring the searing pain of the cannula digging in deeper. I would do anything to be able to claw at him right now. I watch him as he leans forward, relaxed and in total control. 'Look Vic, I know you care about Gwen. What she wants is to enjoy her wedding and she can't do that with you there. I'm asking you nicely, to stay away.'

I dread to think what he will do if I don't.

'What the hell are you doing here?' Isaac is towering behind Michael.

'Not to worry, I'm just leaving.' Michael stands calmly to face him. 'Goes without saying, I won't be needing you to be my best man anymore.'

The smile he gives Isaac is alarming. He knows he's bested us. Worse than that, he has Gwen completely wrapped around his little finger. I can see Isaac breathing hard, trying to hold back his temper as Michael barges into his shoulder on his way out. Isaac doesn't react, instead stepping to my side.

'Are you OK? What did he say?' He drops one of my bags on the floor.

'He says he has an alibi for last night, just like he did when his first wife died. And that I can't go to the wedding.' Isaac cradles me as I begin to cry.

What is frightening me the most is that he never denied killing her, like he never denied running me off the road, but there is no proof. That's when I really feel the tears stream down my face. Even if Anna has emailed me enough evidence, I have no idea how I can get to Gwen now.

'It will be OK.' Isaac's voice is soothing and calm.

'How will it be OK?'

He sits silently on the bed, holding me close as I cry into his chest. Then it comes to me. 'I have to go and see Gwen, talk to her, explain what I was trying to do last night.'

Isaac pulls away from me, concern etched on his face. 'She'll never speak to you. It's the day before the wedding, she'll be concentrating on that. Let alone the fact that Michael probably won't leave her side.'

He's right of course. I just hope that deep down she'll want to talk to me. We've been best friends for years. No matter what she says, she'll be devastated that I'm not going to be at her wedding. 'I'll call her, tell her I need to apologise. Can I have your phone?'

Isaac reaches into his pocket but stops short of passing it to me.

'Are you sure you're meant to use one, with all this equipment around?'

I follow his eye line to the various beeping bits of machinery next to me. 'I'm sure it will be fine… please?' He sighs as I hold my hand out, checking around to make sure the nurses are nowhere to be seen.

I put the phone on loudspeaker so he can hear but it goes to voicemail. I ring again and again but it's the same. This time I leave a message: 'Gwen, I know what I did last night was awful. Please let me apologise. I will stay away from the wedding if you want me to but I want to hear it from you.'

As soon as I give the phone back to Isaac, I pull back the bed covers, trying to swing my legs out.

'Where are you going?'

'Gwen's house, I have to see her.'

Before he can try and argue, the doctor returns to my cubicle, noticing me trying to take the various tubes out of my arms. 'You're up – how do you feel?'

'Fine,' I lie unconvincingly.

His eyes narrow as he notices I'm still clutching the bed to help me balance. 'Do you have someone at home to help look after you? You really should be resting.'

I look to Isaac, pleading with my eyes.

'Yes, I'll be there to look after her.'

'Fine then, I'll discharge you, but be prepared for some discomfort – over-the-counter painkillers should do the trick but any problems, your GP will be able to prescribe you something stronger.'

I can sense Isaac looking at me but I avoid his gaze, focusing my attention on the nurse removing the needles from my arm and taping cotton wool over the pin pricks of blood they leave behind. Both of my arms are covered in fresh bruises but I can still see the fading yellow ones that Michael left behind. I can't dwell on it, so I muster a smile to confirm I'm well enough to go home, dropping it as soon as it's only Isaac and me in the room.

I try to reach the bag Isaac brought but can't quite manage it. He rushes to my side to help. 'You're going to need a hand getting dressed, aren't you?'

I feel a sense of such caring as I watch him thread my arms with difficulty – trying to avoid hurting me – through an oversized sweater, before gathering my jogging bottoms into two small rings that remind me of when my mum used to dress me as a child. I step inside each neat hoop as he pulls them up, before he slips on my socks and trainers. Watching him tie the laces, I feel incredibly lucky – bizarrely. Isaac is being the friend I've needed for some time.

'That's a beautiful smile,' he comments when he finally turns to look at me. I hadn't realised I was.

'Thank you – for everything.'

He leans in to kiss me but I flinch from the sudden pain as he touches my face. 'I'm sorry, I–'

Before he can finish his sentence I walk into his arms, where I feel safe.

'How are you going to make sure Michael isn't around?' he asks. I hadn't thought of that and I don't have an answer. There's that sigh of his again. 'Look, shall I call him? Do the same, ask to see him at the office maybe – to make peace?'

'But what if he realises there's something up? He's dangerous, Isaac.'

'I'll be fine.'

A sense of dread fills me. This doesn't feel right, but I have no other option. I watch as he texts. To my surprise Michael responds and they arrange to meet. Issac's face is serious. 'Right, I'll drop you off and then go to the office.'

As we walk out hand in hand, I can only hope this plan works.

Chapter Thirty-Seven

The Fire In My Heart

Isaac pulls up to the end of Gwen's street, a sense of dread returns to me. We park up, just out of sight of her house.

'When you're ready I'll go and meet Michael,' he says. 'If I need to get in touch, I'll call Gwen's phone and ask for you.'

Giving him one last kiss, I stumble out of the car, each movement slow and painful. We had already agreed that he would pull away before I knock on the door, so she won't see him. The walk up the drive feels enormously long. I haven't planned exactly how I am going to say it, but I am going to tell her everything.

I knock on the door – no answer. I cup my hands around my eyes to look through her front window but there is no sign of her. So I start the mile or so walk to her gallery, cursing myself for not having asked Isaac to fetch me a jacket.

When I get there at last, out of breath and aching all over, she isn't there either. By now I am slowing down, desperate to just get indoors, somewhere warm. I'll have to go home, at least there I can get a jacket and figure out how to contact her.

The walk is getting steadily more painful. As I turn the corner onto my street, I can just make out a gentle glowing light. That's strange. It seems to be emanating from my garden.

Quickening my pace, I near the end of my drive. The glow is now even brighter and seems to be moving.

Fire.

My mouth drops open. Flames are licking at the windows of the ground floor of my house. Their brightness as they ravage the front door and curtains is hypnotising. With each second the flames climb higher, but all I can do is stand there, watching, even as the blaze leaps up into my bedroom window.

The living room window explodes, sending hot shards of glass scattering across the driveway. The sound shatters the peace within the street. My neighbours come rushing out of their houses, some of them reaching for their phones and dialling 999, others simply standing aghast, gasping at the sight in front of them.

More people come pouring out onto the street, gathering around the spectacle that is my home, burning to the ground. Samira comes elbowing past them to get to me, her eyes wide as she takes in the injuries on my face.

In my peripheral vision I notice something in one of the upstairs windows – the spare bedroom. Fighting through the dark smoke, a hand on the window, slamming over and over against the glass. I locked all the windows before I left yesterday. Whoever they are, they won't be able to open them.

'Someone's inside,' I can barely whisper.

'What?'

'Someone's inside!' This time I shout, pointing to the window.

I edge closer, looking at that hand hitting at the glass. Then a face, coughing, trying to breathe despite the thick, black smoke. It is hard to make out in the shadows of the fire but it's a woman. No, it can't be, is that… Suzie? She sees me as she pushes her face to the glass, banging on it with both clenched fists. How did she get in? Why is she here?

'We have to do something,' I cry, trying to run for the front door. I'm not sure what I think I can do but I have to try and help her. Samira tries to grab my arm to hold me back but I slip past her. I don't make it anywhere near the front door though; the intense heat pushes me back, and the billowing smoke makes my eyes and lungs sting. I don't have the strength to persevere.

Samira catches up with me, pulling me back to the street. I wince from the pain so she loosens her grip, leading me by the hands, my eyes are stinging so much I can barely see. Then I hear the sirens.

'There's someone upstairs!' Samira yells to the fire fighters as they rush past us.

When I am able to look to the window again, I can't see Suzie any more. No hands, no anguished face. Just dense, black smoke.

As Samira and I are ushered back by police officers, the very window I had seen Suzie at explodes outwards. The police force the panicked group of onlookers even further away for their own protection. We stand amongst the crowd, looking on as the firefighters do their best to quell the climbing blaze. There is so much smoke and water. The sizzling sound as the hoses fire at the base of the flames blares above the hysterical chatter of the on-looking neighbours.

Finally we see one firefighter climb a ladder to the first floor. Then we wait for what seems like forever. Eventually, I see him emerging from the window, Suzie laid lifeless over his shoulder as he descends the ladder. We watch on as she is placed gently onto the awaiting paramedic's gurney. Like worker ants they swarm around her.

'She's breathing,' I hear one say.

After placing an oxygen mask on her face and attaching countless other wires to her, they start rolling her back to the ambulance. I push past the officers creating a barricade.

'Miss, you can't go there,' one tries to tell me but Samira blocks his path, causing just enough of a distraction so that I can get to Suzie's side.

Up close, she looks so fragile. Thick black soot clings around her mouth and nose, as she slips in and out of consciousness. I don't know what to say to her, I just stare as they continue to push her to the back of the ambulance. As she is about to pass me, she grabs at my hand, trying to speak, but the mask is muffling her already weak voice. 'Please, she's trying to say something,' I beg, grabbing at one of the paramedics' coats.

'We have to get her to hospital – now!'

I walk alongside her as she tries to tug at her mask, slipping it to the side of her face.

'I – want – wanted – to – take – care of you.'

That's all she manages to say before the paramedic replaces her mask, pushing me aside as they lift her stretcher into the back of the ambulance. She wanted to take care of me? I stand stoically as they drive her away. The notes. The presents. Could it have been her all along?

She wanted to take care of me. Could it be that all those break-ins were meant to be genuinely caring, not sinister? Even the horrific haircut? Surely not.

'Miss Summers,' I hear a familiar voice behind me. I turn to see Officer Larson, her face etched with concern. 'Perhaps we should get you out of here?'

Samira and Officer Kerr appear next to her, and the four of us walk soberly to her house.

Inside, if it weren't for the blue lights reflecting off of Samira's living room walls, it would be easy to ignore that just a few doors down, my home is slowly being destroyed by flames. I sit there as the officers ask me question after question about the fire, about Suzie, but I have no answers. I want to know how she got into my house and why it caught fire even more than they do.

'OK, thank you Victoria. If there is anything else you can think of, we'll be right outside.'

I listen as Samira leads them out of the house, standing to watch the melee from her front window – the crowd still enthralled by watching my home burn. Before Samira can close the door, I go back outside and watch from her front gate. The fire seems under control – grey smoke now mixed among the black.

Looking at the shell of my house, wet and blackened, the newspaper images of Serena's death and her burnt home come to mind. Two mysterious house fires, each with someone trapped inside. The pain rippling across my body is stopping me from piecing this all together. What am I not understanding?

This is Michael's doing. He must have thought I would be home by now. Maybe he saw Suzie in the house and thought it was me. I don't have time to think this all through. If Michael is repeating his previous crimes, then Gwen is in danger. I have to get to her.

'Where are you going?' Samira stops me as I reach for the gate.

'I have to see Gwen.'

'Are you crazy? After everything–'

'Look Samira, I'm sorry. I can't explain but she is in danger.'

Samira looks intently at me. For the first time she doesn't try and distract me or lighten the mood. 'I don't know what's going on, but first the car accident and now the fire… All that stuff you said about Michael's life... What is it you aren't telling me?'

I can't expect her to understand but I don't have time to say more. 'Please, can you text Gwen and tell her you're popping by… for a cuppa or something, to make sure she's home?'

Without question Samira complies. Within seconds she gets a text back. She looks at me and I can tell she's unhappy. 'She says she's home.'

I hug her tentatively, my shoulder hurting from the pressure of her grasp. 'Thank you. I'm sorry, I'll explain everything later. Love you.' Before she can respond I move through her house and out of the back door, taking the alleyway to further down the street so the police don't see me leave. I move as fast as I can to get to Gwen's.

When I knock on her door I can see her through the glass, hiding in the living room doorway. I knock again. I have to get inside.

'Go away, I don't want to see you,' she shouts, her voice shaking.

'Please Gwen, I need to apologise. I was totally out of order last night. I've been so stressed. Let me explain.'

I can see her silhouette move closer to the door, so I knock again.

'Please Gwen, I'm sorry.'

The click of the lock is all I've wanted to hear all day, and she opens the door to me. Her eyes are serious and red from crying. There is no smile, no warm hug. Nothing. She just stands back to let me in. 'I wish you hadn't come here, Vic.'

I nod, ignoring the fact that she doesn't take the immediate opportunity to check how I am since the crash.

'I had to.'

I follow her to the kitchen, sitting silently, waiting for her to face me. It isn't until she sits down that she can even bring herself to look at me.

'I'm sorry Gwen. I never meant to upset you.'

'You were a mess last night. Saying all sorts.'

'I know.' I fiddle with the glass of water she has placed in front of me.

'I'm really angry with you, but right now I just want to put this behind us. I'm getting married tomorrow!' The smile in her voice rings hollow. 'Do you want to see the dress? It's perfect.' She stands to lead me to it, but I resist the pull of her hand. 'Oh my goodness, I'm so sorry. Did I hurt you? I never even asked about the accident.' Sitting down, she keeps hold of my hand. 'Are you OK?'

I ignore her half smile of sympathy. 'Gwen, listen. Please. About Michael.' She moves her hand away instantly, her face changing as she shifts uncomfortably in her chair. I try to plough on. 'I–'

'Shut up Vic! I'm willing to let yesterday go, but you have to stop.'

I know I can't stop though. She's in danger.

Chapter Thirty-Eight

To Have And To Hold

'He's been married before Gwen, did you know that? Did you know she died?'

'STOP!' Her voice is raised as she slams her chair back to stand up, turning to rest her hands on the edge of the sink.

'Gwen, I'm not lying, I have proof… had proof… but someone took it when they broke in.' I slide back my chair and walk over to her. 'He's dangerous Gwen, he killed her, I know it. It was him that ran me off the road too.'

Spinning, she launches at me, pushing me back towards the table. 'Just SHUT UP!'

Her eyes are full of rage, her mouth pursed as she breathes heavily through her teeth. I can't believe she pushed me. The sudden pain of her shove radiates through my tender body. Straightening myself up, I walk back towards her.

'He was in love with her, then started cheating on her. Sound familiar? I'm worried the same thing is going on here. He killed her for her money, and I think you're next, Gwen.'

In a split second she has pushed me again, screaming in frustration. 'You don't know what you're talking about!' This time I fall backwards over my chair, the agony roaring through my back and shoulder as I land on the floor, my breath knocked from me.

Instead of helping me up, she stands over me. There is no affection at all in the way she is looking at me. Her face seems calmer though, and she offers me her hand to help me up. There is silence when we are stood face to face, until she turns away again. I can tell from the way her shoulders are heaving that she's crying.

'Please Vic.' Her voice barely a whisper. 'Please, you must stop this.'

I take a deep breath in. I'm not done yet. I step back to her, placing a hand on her shoulder to turn her to me. 'Gwen, I don't want to hurt you but I am scared for you. I don't care how long it takes me, I'm going to find proof that he killed his first wife and that he tried to kill me.'

Her crying slows as her eyes meet mine. 'You can't find proof for something he's never done Vic.' Her voice is cold. 'I really wish you'd left this alone.'

Without warning, she grabs a glass and smashes it across my head. I slam down onto the table, falling to my knees as the shards pierce my skin and liquid spreads across my face – is that water or blood? On my hands and knees I try to blink – to look up towards her.

'What the fuck are you doing, Gwen?'

'What I have to.'

She strikes me across the face again. I succumb to the pain, falling to the floor. I feel a hand grab my hair and yank me up to sitting, with such ferocity it winds me.

'Why couldn't you just leave this alone?'

I put my hands up for protection, my eyesight still blurry – I can't see what she is doing. I'm surprised when I feel Gwen drop down next to me on the floor, sobbing, leaning against the cabinets.

'Everything was going so well ... you've ruined everything.'

She pulls her knees up, resting her head on them as she continues to mutter that I've spoiled it all. Keeping my eyes firmly on her, I try to push myself up from the floor. What the hell has got into her? I want to lash out but I have to remain calm – I don't want to antagonise her. 'I'm just trying to protect you.' My words are barely a whisper. There's that all too familiar taste of blood in my mouth again as pain ripples across my face.

'Stop talking! STOP. TALKING!' Now she starts banging her own head with her hands. I cannot compute what is happening – the way she is reacting. She must be in shock but I have to get through to her.

'He killed his wife, Gwen. Her family think so too but he threatened them to keep them quiet. He did to his wife what he tried to do to me today. He burnt my fucking house down!'

Only my rage is fuelling me to continue now. Gwen finally sits still. There is only silence, before she calmly dries her eyes and looks straight at me.

'You won't find any proof.'

'I can try–'

'You won't find any proof because he's not guilty.'

'Gwen please–'

'You're not listening! You won't find proof that he did it, any of it, because he didn't. I did.'

The silence is deafening. What did she just say? I stare at her, looking for anything that can help me understand but she is staring back at me, blankly. No emotion.

'What do you mean?' I beg. 'Stop covering for him!'

'He never started the fire that killed Serena. I did.'

She stands, walking away from where I am slumped. Did I mention Serena's name? I don't think I did.

'She never deserved him, she never loved him like I do.' Gwen begins to smooth her hair, uncrumpling her clothes in her usual pristine manner. This feels like a nightmare. 'She got her claws into him before I could even have a chance. He never even noticed me back then.'

'What? You didn't know him back then. I was there when you met.'

She ignores me, carrying on. 'I went to uni with Serena, that's when I used to see him with her. He was her trophy, someone to hold her bag at her charity events. I met him again, before you did, a couple of years ago at an art exhibit out of town. That's when he finally saw me as the person he should be with.'

My ears are ringing and my whole body is throbbing. None of this is making sense.

'I-I don't see how–'

'Yes you do.' Gwen is towering over me again. 'Put it together. Fate brought me back to him and we fell in love.

We tried to keep the affair secret but Serena grew suspicious and would have left him with nothing. We pretended to meet in front of you so no one would ever know we were together when he was married. We just wanted a fresh start.'

The affair Anna told me about was with Gwen? I sit flabbergasted as finally she is joining all the dots for me. 'But he's been breaking into my house, Gwen, leaving threats–'

'I'm sorry Vic. I was just trying to scare you, stop you digging into things you shouldn't.'

'You? You've done it all?' I wipe my eyes on the back of my sleeve to look at her. If she is lying to cover for Michael she is doing a very convincing job.

'Well, Suzie helped at first. She was so desperate to have a friend and she is, or should I say *was*, so fixated on you. It didn't take much to convince her to do what she thought were nice things for you.'

I feel a pain in my chest as it all finally clicks. Gwen is the friend Suzie made. I was right earlier today: the cleaning and gifts weren't threats, just Suzie trying to take care of me. Repaying the one person who always had time to listen to her. Surely there's no way Suzie would believe stealing things from my study and cutting my hair is a way of showing care?

'But my hair? The theft?'

Sighing, tears begin to fall down my face. Gwen however remains shockingly calm.

'You were so focused on Michael, you never suspected me. I copied your key long ago. Suzie helped take it from your office and it was easy for me to drop it back off. Even when you changed the locks, it wasn't hard for me to get one of the spares from your kitchen drawer. I took the envelope from your bag and your pathetic notes from your study. I cut your hair. I thought if you looked awful you wouldn't show up to the rehearsal dinner. You have to believe me Vic, I just wanted you to stay out of it.'

I feel like my mind is being torn apart. Who is this callous person in front of me?

'I just want to marry him, have his children. Have our happily ever after. That's not too much to ask for, is it?' she continues.

All I can do is stare. How have I been so blind? Her selfishness. Her complete inability to grasp the consequences of her actions. Have I been in Gwen's shadow for so long that I completely missed what would have been so clear in one of my clients? In anyone else I would have clearly seen the personality disorder but instead, I idolised her.

'But it was you who told me Michael was having an affair,' I say. 'You started this.'

She inhales loudly, nodding her head. 'You're right. I did, I needed someone to talk to. Michael *had* been behaving suspiciously. Secret calls and meetings, so I *did* think he might have been cheating. Thanks to your little outburst after the engagement party, we had a long talk, cleared the air. He'd been keeping Anna's threats to expose his past to himself so as not to worry me. It's kind of sweet when you think about it.' She holds her left hand up to gaze at her engagement ring, clearly thinking of Michael. 'Please Vic, you're the only person I can talk to, I need to speak to someone about all of this. I just want everything to go back to normal.'

There is the tone that I am used to. The one that gets her everything she wants, when she wants. I have been taken in by it all this time. What an idiot I have been. I need to get out of here. 'Gwen, you need help. Let me–'

'I don't need help!'

I flinch at her anger, completely out of guesses as to what her next move will be.

'I'm sorry Vic. I was wrong to keep all this from you. You're my best friend. Anyway, I had thought with everything you've been through that you'd understand?'

'What?' She's totally lost me.

'Well, you knew that your only route to happiness was to let Dylan die. That's how I felt about Serena. If anything, seeing how you were able to cope and get stronger despite having someone's blood on your hands showed me I'd be able to cope too. We're the same you and I. We can work this out.' Her eyes are glassy and vacant.

My mouth drops. Just when I feel she cannot betray me anymore she brings Dylan's suicide into it. I feel nothing but rage coursing through my veins.

'You utter bitch! Dylan killed himself. I couldn't have stopped him. But you… you're a cold-blooded murderer. Was it you who ran me off the road too? Do you want me dead too?'

'Be reasonable Vic! I never would have actually killed you, I promise. I even tried to check when your car crashed that you were OK but let's face it, you were driving pretty erratically anyway. And I knew you weren't home when I started the fire. Suzie, well poor Suzie, she had to go. She started talking about wanting to come clean and tell you what she had been doing or some crap.'

I feel sick at this casual confession of what she is truly capable of. I start to slide myself backwards towards the door.

'Where are you going?' Her tone is suddenly vicious as she marches towards me.

'I'm hurt, I need help!'

'No, you can't go, not until I know I can trust you.'

'Trust me? TRUST *ME*! I trusted you. I've tried to protect you. I doubted him and the whole time… the whole time you were betraying me!' I push myself up the cabinets to meet her eye.

'Vic, you don't know what you're saying. I was just trying to get you to leave Michael alone.'

'You're sick Gwen, you need professional help. Even Michael needs to be protected from you!'

Her face contorts and her eyes burn with fury. I had taken it too far.

'Sick? Do you think you're better than me? Serena thought she was better than me.'

She hurtles towards me, pushing me so I'm flat on my back and sits on top of me. I can barely breathe under the weight on my chest. Before I can try to force her off I feel the immediate pain as she lands a hail of blows across my face, sending the back of my head banging onto the floor.

'You're ruining everything!' She pushes herself onto her hands and knees so she can look at me directly, inches from my battered face. 'Why couldn't you have just been the maid of honour that I wanted?'

Now's my chance. I grab her hair, pulling as hard as I can, using my knees to push her off balance. She tumbles into the table legs as I scramble to my feet. Before I can take a step I feel her grab at my ankle, sending me back to the floor. I try to push her away but she clambers onto me, reaching for my throat. The pain is unbearable as I struggle to take even the slightest breath in. I reach up, scratching at her hands in a feeble attempt to be freed. When that fails I reach for her eyes, clawing at them – I can feel the warmth of her blood under my fingernails, forcing her to loosen her grip on me as she recoils from the pain. I shuffle backwards away from her, gasping for air. Staring at her as she reaches for the deep scratches I've inflicted.

'Look what you have done to my face, you bitch! I'm getting married tomorrow!' she shrieks, holding a bloody hand out towards me. How is this woman, who I would've done anything for, filled with such hatred for me? How did I fall for all of this?

'Gwen, what the fuck are you doing. Please…'

Her lips are pulled back in a snarl, eyes like pin pricks, and she's taking such deep breaths I know another attack is coming. I have so little energy left, I know I won't survive if I don't get out of here.

I force my body to listen to my pleas to survive. She storms towards me but I kick out, hitting her in the stomach. She doubles over and I use the sideboard to help me get back to my feet. I bounce against the narrow hallway walls, leaving bloody handprints in my wake, my sights set on the front door.

I can hear her slamming the chair out of her way as she comes for me. I reach for the door handle but with my hand inches from it, it turns of its own accord. Just as Gwen's fingers reach me, the door opens. Standing outside, looking horrified at what he sees in front of him, is Michael.

Chapter Thirty-Nine

For Better Or Worse

The whole world seems to pause as the three of us stand there in near silence. Gwen's heavy breathing is the only sound I can hear. Michael is open mouthed, surveying the bloody scene in his hallway.

'What… What is going on?' His eyes dart in all directions, taking in each of my injuries before firmly fixing on Gwen. 'What have you done?'

Gwen lets me go of me and I fall towards his feet. 'Please Michael, she's lost it – help me!'

He bends down, helping me to stand. The tenderness of his grip makes me feel safe – not something I would have ever associated with him. I have blamed him for so much.

My throat, painful from Gwen's attack, is raspy as I continue to plead. 'She killed Serena, she's trying to kill me.'

I cough, my voice little more than a painful whisper. His eyes lock on mine. 'What did you say?'

I look to Gwen, her eyes wide and filling with tears.

'She's trying to kill me.'

He looks at me, then at her. She is shaking her head as the tears begin to flow. 'I'm sorry, I'm sorry,' she mutters over and over, wrapping her arms around herself for comfort.

'It's all going to be OK,' Michael mutters.

I turn back to look at him and realise he isn't talking to me. He is looking at her. His grasp is getting firmer. 'You know this has gone on for far too long though, darling? She knows too much now.'

I feel my legs give way under me. He's part of this. Of course he is. I can barely offer any resistance as he pushes me back into the hallway, closing my only escape route behind him.

'I'm sorry Victoria, really I am, but I did try to warn you.' His words barely register in my ringing ears. I try to scream but nothing comes out. I don't have the strength to walk, let alone fight. That doesn't stop Michael dragging me back to the kitchen. Gwen picks up the dining chairs so Michael can sit me down. I watch as he fetches me a glass of water, before they both sit in a chair on either side of me. They start talking amongst themselves, as if I am not even here.

'I thought we weren't going to hurt her – just stop her coming to the wedding. How did this happen?' he asks Gwen accusingly, tapping his finger on the table to convey his mild irritation at the situation.

'Do you think I wanted this?' She is far less calm.

'It's happened now. You know what to do.'

I'm not sure what is worse, the fact that they're speaking like I can't hear them or that they are clearly planning my demise. I eye the door desperately but I know I'll never get past Michael. I sip at the water, it feels like swallowing razor blades. I persevere – I want to clear my throat, speak for myself. Gwen slams her hands on the table, before cradling her head in them, gently rocking back and forth.

They stare at each other, still ignoring me – the living, breathing person who doesn't want to suffer the fate they are planning.

'How can you do this?' I croak. 'I would do anything for you, Gwen.' For a split second I see the smallest amount of what looks like remorse on her face, then she averts her gaze from the injuries she's inflicted on me. He calmly nods towards her, then leaves the room.

'Where are you going?' I ask, fearful of what she will do when he leaves.

'I'll be back in a moment,' he says, still looking at Gwen. 'Tell her the truth, she deserves it.'

I look at Gwen as the kitchen door clicks shut. She still can't look me in the eye. I take another sip of my water.

'I don't know where to begin.' Standing up, she moves to a drawer in the sideboard. Sliding it open, she pulls out a large envelope. The envelope that she stole from my house. 'I guess this is as good a place to start as any.'

Gwen tips the contents onto the table, the familiar pictures and articles spilling onto the table. She spreads out each item but I can't take my eyes off of her. Her demeanour eerily calm. I'm horrified at how quickly she is flicking from extremely distressed to appearing composed; as if right now she isn't holding evidence that she has been breaking into my house and terrorising me for weeks. I watch as she pushes each picture aside until she finds the one she is searching for. Holding the chosen photo closer to her face, her jaw clenches before she slides it over to me. It's the photo of Michael kissing Serena on her graduation day.

'This says it all really, she made that day all about her. Look.' I don't know how to respond. 'Look!' She persists. I peer at the picture. It was the one that struck me as oddly familiar when I first saw it, but I still can't explain why. Gwen almost chuckles. 'You don't see it, do you?'

I shake my head. She taps on the photo and I follow her finger. She's not pointing at Serena or Michael but at the jealous looking strangers in the background. 'That was before Jessica gave me a makeover. I was always in Serena's shadow back then.'

I grab the photo to take a closer look, really examining the woman in the background, then looking at Gwen. The hair is completely different, her signature blonde curls used to be straight and dark. I rarely see Gwen without her expertly applied make-up – in the photo I can see without the extra lashes how much smaller her eyes look, and her cheekbones are less defined. Even her lips look thinner without her usual layers of lipstick and whitened teeth. The change in fashion taste is huge: the baggy jumper and ill-fitting jeans make her seem heavier than she is, far removed from the branded wardrobe she loves to model now. If Gwen hadn't said so, I probably still wouldn't have recognised her in this photo but it's definitely her. My head is throbbing and I'm still struggling to take it in when Gwen snatches the photo back.

'Everyone loved her at uni. Especially Michael – but he didn't know that she didn't love him like I can.' Her mood seems to be shifting again, erratically trying to stuff everything back into the envelope – perhaps she's done with telling me about those days.

'Wait,' I grasp her hand to stop her. 'How did you get away with it?'

Gwen sits staring at me, clearly contemplating whether to tell me, before looking back at the pile of photos and newspaper clippings with what can only be described as pride.

'It was easy really. First I made sure Michael had an alibi. The police always suspect the husband, don't they?' She smiles, but then looks awkward when I don't return it. Coughing to clear her throat, she continues. 'She always had candles in her house. All sorts of expensive fragrances. I just had to wait until she went to sleep and light a few, making sure to tip them over as I left. Michael had already made sure the smoke alarms had empty batteries fitted. It was fairly easy to make it look accidental.'

Finally Anna's question is answered. That's why Serena never woke up when the fire started. I don't know how to take this in. Where is my sweet, bubbly Gwen who wouldn't even kill a spider? It's painfully obvious she will be just as uncaring when she kills me. If I am to die today, there is more I need to know first. 'Is that what you did at my house, try and make it look like an accident?'

She stops. 'I told you before, I knew you weren't home. As for Suzie, it's sad but I couldn't see any other way – she was going to tell you everything. About me, about what I've been asking her to do. I couldn't let her do that. She was busy cleaning your room when I started the fire in your kitchen. Such a shame. Anyway, now you know everything.' She shrugs.

Who announces they've tried to murder someone and just shrugs? My heart feels heavy at the thought of how far Suzie had come, how much more she could achieve, yet now she's lying in hospital, fighting for her life. Gwen leans back in her chair, twiddling with the envelope, totally unaware of the devastation she is still raining down on me. I daren't tell her Suzie is alive. 'How do you even know Suzie?'

'I saw her sitting outside your office, pathetic little thing. She was so lonely.'

My heart aches with the thought of how Gwen has manipulated her. How she had manipulated me before Suzie, making us both feel like we mattered. The irony of that is painfully obvious now.

The door opens again as Michael comes back to sit next to me. The atmosphere chills as they begin to communicate with nods and glances.

'What happens now?' I ask, nervous at their silence.

There is that look between them again. Michael moves to stand behind me, Gwen watching him intently, then back at me. 'I'm sorry Vic, but we need to do this.' Michael grabs my arms. I strain to move, but he is too strong and I'm in so much pain.

'Please Gwen, you were so angry when he hurt me before. Why are you letting him hurt me again?'

For a split second she pauses, looking to Michael and then me. 'You're right, he never should've done that, but you're giving us no choice now.'

Reaching into Michael's pocket she comes back to sit with me, holding a packet of prescription painkillers. No, I think. Not that. Anything but that.

'Don't fight it Vic. You'll just go to sleep. People will think you took an overdose.' Her tone is almost comforting as she starts to pop pill after pill from the silver blister pack onto the table in front of us.

'Gwen, please.' I try to keep the panic from my voice. 'No one will believe that.'

'Of course they will. Everyone's spotted you've been acting strange. You've been under a lot of pressure with work and the wedding, *and* the stress of the break-ins and house fire – which they'll know to blame Suzie for now. They'll believe me when I tell them that you'd finally had enough. Feeling guilty for ruining my rehearsal dinner, you came here having already taken the tablets. Just the way that Dylan took his own life, wasn't it? Quite poetic really. Anyway, we end up in a physical struggle as I try everything I can think of to help you, but it's no good – you die in my arms.'

I swallow hard. How did she manage to come up with that so quickly? Not only will she justify my death but all the injuries we've sustained too. And linking it back to Dylan like that is a cruel form of genius. I wonder, when he realised what he'd done, if he was as scared of dying as I am right now.

She will look like a doting best friend who tried her best to save me, and I will be the unstable mess who just couldn't cope with life any more.

'For what it's worth Vic, I'm sorry. We both are.'

Before I can tell her that her apology is worth nothing, Michael moves his arm, locking it around my neck to hold my head in place. Gwen starts trying to force tablets into my mouth but I refuse to open it. The doorbell rings and they freeze. I start to yell but Michael quickly covers my mouth. I bite at his hand until he rips it away. I scream for help before Gwen slaps me hard across the face again. I hate her. They seem to hold their breaths as whomever was knocking on the door goes away. My heart sinks, realising that that was probably my last hope of survival.

Chapter Forty

To Love And To Cherish

I watch as Gwen and Michael sigh with relief, smiling at one another when the silence returns. This woman has been my best friend for three years, and she is smiling because she is about to get away with my murder.

I'll be damned if I'm going to make this easy on them. I throw myself forward, catching Michael by surprise, I slip from his loosened grasp. I launch myself at Gwen, but just as my fingertips brush her face, Michael grabs me by my hair, pulling me back into the chair, his grip even tighter than before. Gwen steps forward, picking up the tablets again. 'None of this would be happening if you had just kept your nose out of our business. Now open up.'

'You bitch!' I spit. 'You won't get away with this.'

Her face twists with rage, as she launches more slaps and punches at my face.

'Stop! STOP! Stick to the plan!' Michael commands, holding her hand still, his other still firmly holding me.

My eyes are swollen but I can see Gwen's chest heaving with exertion. Catching her breath she nods at him, and brushes the hair from her face before retaking her stance over me. This time she pinches my nostrils together. Within seconds my lungs are burning but I don't want to open my mouth. I can see her anger building again, her grip painfully tight as she forces a pill between my lips, scraping my teeth.

For a split second I wonder if I should just give in. Is this karma for me ignoring Dylan's calls, when I didn't realise he was slipping away? Deep down maybe I knew, after all of his threats, that it was only a matter of time before he took his own life. I let him die. His last words, *I give up – there's nothing left to fight for*, seem sadly apt right now. I begin to relax my jaw, swallowing the first pill. Gwen is quick to react, putting one after the other into my mouth.

Just when I am about to swallow more a massive crash resounds through the house. I can't move my head to see where it has come from until Michael loosens his grip on me. I follow where he and Gwen are looking, sheer horror on their faces. Isaac is trying to knock the back door down. Furiously kicking and punching at the panel, each smash moving the frame just a little, then a little more. I look to Gwen, frozen with fear. Clearly this was not part of her plan. Murdering me probably seemed easy, but what will they do about Isaac? By the time Michael releases me to react, Isaac is nearly through the door, his face rigid with anger and determination.

Michael tries to run towards him but as Isaac bursts through the door, the flailing wooden panel knocks him to the ground. With Gwen distracted, I spit out the tablets and try to stand but my legs barely respond.

'You're not going anywhere.' Gwen grips my face, her nails digging into my skin. This time though I scratch at her hands, trying with all my might to push her backwards. She falls onto me, knocking us both to the floor. Her weight is pinning me down, and behind us I can hear the dull sounds of punches landing their target, but I can't tell who is overpowering whom. Looking up at Gwen's face, I know there is no reasoning with her – she won't stop until I am dead. I can't give in to the excruciating pain rippling across every inch of my body. With every last scrap of strength I have, I push her off me, wrestling until I roll on top of her. Both our hands are flying wildly, trying to grab, punch and slap the other. I pin her hands down by her sides and that's when I see Isaac. He has forced Michael against the wall. He looks down at me and it is as if all the noise fades away. We both know that if we don't get out of here, this is where we will die.

'Run!' I can see his lips moving but I'm frozen. 'Run Victoria! Run!' The clarity of his words pierce the silence. I look down at Gwen and back at Isaac. Pushing down on her to help me stand, I scramble for the open door. I have to get help. She tries to grab at me but I kick her away. I see Michael's eyes widen as I run past him.

'Don't let her get away!' I can hear Gwen shout but there is nothing he can do – I'm already outside.

I stumble along the path running down the side of their house, Gwen's footsteps right behind me. When I make it to the front garden, I know I'm only a few short steps from the street. If I can make it there, I can shout for help. I yank the front gate open but as I take my first step onto the pavement my hair is ripped backwards and I fall, Gwen standing above me, Michael not far behind. I panic: where's Isaac?

They both try and drag me back to the house, my arms and legs kicking and punching out at them. I shout until I'm hoarse but no one comes to my rescue. Every part of me is in agony but I'll do whatever I can to not go back in there. There is so much confusion and alarm. I hear the sound of my clothes tearing as I free myself from their grasp, falling forwards towards the road.

First on my hands and knees and then stumbling, I make it back to the gate, then the pavement, but Michael is right behind me again, so I keep running.

My lungs are screaming in pain as I gulp in the icy air. I can't risk slowing down to bang on any doors on this street. If no one answers he'll catch me, so I must keep going until I see someone, anyone. Nearing the main road, I wave at the passing cars but none stop. So I keep running, my eyes watering from fear and the bitter breeze. I try to focus on the other side of the road – there's a café full of people queueing and sitting inside.

I don't even stop to check for oncoming traffic before I cross, horns blaring as they barely miss me. That's when I hear it. The screech of brakes, the sound of a car skidding and the most sickening, dull thud. I stop and turn around to see what has happened. I'm shivering. Michael's body is sliding down the bonnet of the vehicle that has struck him. The windscreen shattered and sprayed with blood – his blood. Gushing from cuts across his face, his eyes are staring right through me, wide open.

As he collapses onto the cold tarmac, his limbs contorted, a pool of red forms around him. I freeze, powerless. The sound of my heart thudding grows louder and louder, until I cannot hear anything else. Even as Gwen comes running to his side, shouting his name, screaming when he doesn't respond, I can't hear a thing. I can see Isaac running towards me but I can't speak. My legs give way and I crumple to the cold ground, Isaac holding me as I fall.

I sit level with Gwen, Michael dying in her arms. Cars are stopping to assist, people are pouring out of the café to take in the scene, but all I can see is Gwen's face. Screaming at Michael's body, willing him to live. In this moment I see someone I truly loved losing the one thing that matters to her, and yet I feel nothing.

Chapter Forty-One

The Honeymoon

2 weeks later

'Flight 102 boarding at gate 5.'

The tannoy calling for my flight fills me with joy. I'm glad I came to the airport early. Nearby, children are playing restlessly around their parent's feet, and couples are sitting holding hands, deep in conversation. It's just what I need, a little bit of normalcy. I want to get lost amongst people who don't know me. No one asking if I'm OK. No one giving me sympathetic smiles or even worse, looks of suspicion.

I hear the whispers of people wondering how I didn't know what Gwen was really like. She had been my best friend, and I'm a therapist after all. I guess that's a question I shall spend a great deal of time asking myself as well. I look at my phone: Isaac has texted, reminding me to call him when I land, and Samira is asking for perfume and a giant Toblerone from duty free. I don't know how I would've survived any of this without them both. They've been so supportive during my recovery. Especially Samira, who's let me stay with her whilst I recuperated. When my insurance money comes through I'll rent somewhere, so I don't overstay my welcome at her place before my house is repaired.

Even after the renovations though, I can't see me going back to that house. I need a fresh start. But I'll worry about that when I get back.

I sit myself near my gate, ticket and passport in hand, watching the queue forming. Looking out of the floor-to-ceiling window over the runway, I finally feel a sense of calm. There is so much to think about at home but I am about to fly thousands of miles away, take the space I need to get myself better. I have to make sure I am strong enough for yet more police interviews and eventually the court cases. I know Samira doesn't fully understand why I've agreed to be a character reference for Suzie, but she doesn't deserve to go to prison. Gwen on the other hand? I hope they throw away the key.

I shake my head to free myself of the image from the last time I saw her, covered in Michael's blood and no doubt some of mine too. I wish I could remember her as the person I once loved, but I'm not sure she ever existed.

As for Isaac, he is someone who brings a smile to my face. I do wonder if I should've invited him, but he would only have spent the whole trip trying to make me feel better. I need to sit and think, perhaps cry, without him trying to calm me. Without him feeling guilty that he can't stop the pain I'm feeling. He cannot fix me – only I can do that.

My phone vibrates again in my hand – it's Anna. We have been in touch a lot since Michael died. There is so much she needed to understand, so much I could finally explain for her, so she could find some peace. Understandably there are still questions, and I know Anna's appetite for the truth about Serena's death has been reignited. She yearns to know even more: who committed what acts, how long the duo had been planning it. We all have our ways of coping with grief. My coping strategy however is soon to begin once I board the plane. I open her text.

> Not sure if you're already on the plane. Can you call me ASAP.x

I sigh. This will no doubt be yet another call full of emotional questions. I ponder whether to just turn my phone off, save myself the hassle, but what is one more call before I leave? She picks up immediately.

'Thank goodness I caught you.' Her voice is hurried and breathless.

'Are you OK?'

'I've figured it out,' she blurts, ignoring my question. 'The money, Serena's money, that's what it's all been about.'

We know this. I roll my eyes and feel a sense of relief that I'm near the front of the queue and can hang up without seeming heartless.

'Victoria, where's Serena's money gone?'

I pause. I'd never thought of what would happen to Michael's fortune now he's dead. Considering he only gained it by being part of his then-wife's murder.

'What do you mean? Surely your legal team can look into Michael's accounts?'

'They have – the money is gone.' I feel that familiar sense of dread. I don't know what she is getting at but it clearly isn't good. 'There's more, Vic. Look, we need to talk properly. When you get back, we can meet up?' There's no way I can go away for two weeks wondering what she has to tell me, I need to know now. Stepping out of the queue, I urge her to continue. 'All of Michael's accounts were cleared. Other than small properties, there is nothing left.'

'I know the money is important to you Anna, but he's dead. We can't exactly ask him about it can we?'

'I don't care about the money, I care about the truth.' She stops, apparently checking her impatient tone. 'Don't worry about it Vic, I can do this by myself.'

'Do what?' I wish I wasn't interested but I feel like I have been ignorant to so much Gwen has done these last three years, that the more I can understand, the safer I will feel.

'Do you remember when you first visited me? I didn't want to say it at the time but I felt like someone was watching us. I know people at the hotel and café, so I asked them to check their CCTV. We were being followed.'

My blood runs cold. I desperately want to hang up before she says something I can't unhear but I have to keep listening. 'By who?'

I dread to hear yet more evidence of how I completely missed clues to Gwen's crimes. 'A man. I don't know him but I think I saw him at the engagement party.' My stomach is churning. Why would someone at the engagement party just so happen to be following us? 'Vic. I'm going to send you some stills from the cameras. Will you let me know if you recognise him?'

I hang up, impatiently waiting for the text to arrive. I feel sick at the thought of what I will see. Sliding the messages open, I fall back against the tall windows. I know immediately who it is. Picture after picture of Isaac. My Isaac.

Sliding to the floor, I try to work backwards. Every phone call, every visit where I poured my heart out to him. Every time he'd shown up in the nick of time to help me, to defend me. Every secret I had trusted him with. I gasp: even the first night he approached me. He has been part of it all along. I clench my hands as I relive every hug, every kiss. Had it all been to gain my trust? Find out what I knew, or what I was planning on doing? He helped Gwen and Michael keep one step ahead of me the whole time. My heart aches at the knowledge that none of what we had together was real.

I scroll to Anna's number, ready to confirm Isaac's identity. As Michael's accounts manager, if the money is missing then he is the only person that could've made that happen. I clench at the memory of him complaining that Gwen had been too interested in Michael's fortune. Money he may now have taken for himself. I fight back the angry tears, frustrated that once again I failed to see someone's true nature. On an impulse, I scroll to his name and click on that instead.

'Hello beautiful,' he says, affectionate as ever. 'Shouldn't you be getting on the plane?'

My chest is heaving, trying to stem the sobbing. I so desperately want for him to deny what I am about to say. 'You followed me, when I went to find Anna. You told Michael everything I told you. Were you really part of it all along?' The longest silence follows. 'Fucking answer me!' I yell, much to the dismay of the final passengers getting ready to embark.

'Please,' he says, his voice breaking with emotion, 'let me explain. I never wanted you to be hurt. That's why I stopped them. But the money Vic, I needed it, to protect all of our investments.'

'You mean, *your* investment?' The money. I'm so sick and tired of hearing about the bloody money.'

'Victoria, please. I never meant to hurt you.'

'Was any of it real? You and me, I mean?'

His voice calms. 'Yes, all of it! And it still is! I swear I didn't know where the money came from. Not until you came to me. But I've invested too much in the business to see it fail. I never knew about Serena. You have to believe me. He promised me they wouldn't harm you, just scare you a little…'

I move the phone away from my ear. There's no point listening to anything he has to say. I don't know what he's done, I don't know why he saved me and I simply don't care. I don't need any more dishonesty in my life.

Hanging up, I dial the direct number I have to the police station. I have cried so many tears, lost so much sleep already, that I just feel numb recounting what I have learned in the last few minutes to my liaison officer.

'Last call for flight 102. Flight 102.'

I look at the dwindling queue. Sending one last text to Anna, I turn my phone off so I don't miss my flight. Within a matter of minutes I am in my seat ready for take-off. I don't know what chaos I have just created or what will be left of my life when I get back, but right now I don't care. All I want to do is get as far away from here as possible and surround myself with strangers. Other than Samira, I would trust the company of people I don't know over those that I thought I did.

On one hand I feel as if I am awful at my job, failing to understand these people's motives but on the other, people are far more complex than any book or university course can teach. I won't take responsibility for the choices of the sick individuals who have come into and *will* leave my life. All I can know for sure is that I am never going to allow anyone to take advantage of me again. From now on my head will be clear and my eyes open.

Acknowledgements

I spent so long keeping my writing a secret, a special project just for me, and I'm beyond amazed that I'm now in a position to write a list of acknowledgments! It goes without saying that this wouldn't be happening without my fantastic editor Daisy Watt, who has been so incredibly generous with her time and knowledge. Daisy helped build my confidence as a writer and played a massive part in turning the ramblings of a tired teacher into a novel I am incredibly proud of. A dream I never thought I'd realise. Daisy, I cannot express the importance your kind words had at the start of all of this – your expertise and warmth at every step of this journey have been nothing short of phenomenal.

I realise though that Daisy is part of a fantastic team at HarperNorth, full of talented people that have helped my debut come to life. Including Alice Murphy-Pyle, Lydia Bernard-Brooks, Heather Fitt, Katherine Stephen and brilliant cover art from Dom Forbes. I'm sure there are many others I have not named but please know that I think you're all truly amazing.

Yet of course none of this would have been possible without my support at home. My husband Craig, who over the last couple of decades has always offered me unwavering support in whatever I do. Providing me with words of encouragement, Craig, you always tell me to do what makes me happy and are right by my side. Together with my daughter Yasmin – we've spent so many road trips bouncing ideas around for this novel that I don't know how I would've done it without you. From plot holes to character arcs, you never shied away from telling me what you did and did not like. Every writer needs a cheerleader (and photographer) like you! You make me proud every day. I also appreciate the pair of you disappearing off so selflessly to watch many, many football matches together to give me time alone to write! I know how lucky I am to have you both supporting me – this novel is very much our achievement.